GUT CHECK

GUT
CHECK

ERIC KESTER

Farrar Straus Giroux • New York

Farrar Straus Giroux
An imprint of Macmillan Publishing Group, LLC
120 Broadway, New York, NY 10271

fiercereads.com

Library of Congress Cataloging-in-Publication Data
Names: Kester, Eric, author.
Title: Gut Check / Eric Kester.
Description: First edition. | New York : Farrar Straus Giroux, 2019. |
Summary: When star quarterback Brett suffers a terrible concussion, his
brother Wyatt must decide if keeping his brother's secret is worth the
risk to their relationship and their town's economic future.
Identifiers: LCCN 2018039308 (print) | LCCN 2018046725 (ebook) | ISBN
9780374307608 (ebook) | ISBN 9780374307622 (hardcover : alk. paper)
Subjects: | CYAC: Brothers—Fiction. | Football—Fiction. | High
schools—Fiction. | Schools—Fiction. | City and town life—Fiction. |
Humorous stories.
Classification: LCC PZ7.1.K51 (ebook) | LCC PZ7.1.K51 Gut 2019 (print) | DDC
[Fic]—dc23
LC record available at https://lccn.loc.gov/2018039308

Our books may be purchased for promotional, educational, or business use. Please
contact your local bookseller or the Macmillan Corporate and Premium Sales
Department at (800) 221-7945 ext. 5442 or by email at
MacmillanSpecialMarkets@macmillan.com.

For Leigh and Alden

GUT
CHECK

CHAPTER
ONE

I guess I'll start with how my parents came *this close* to naming me Thor. Seriously. And you know what? As ridiculous as the name sounds, I kind of wish it was mine. Thor is a beefy name and it would've fit me well since I'm a pretty beefy dude. Like, as a Thor, I'd proudly lumber down the hall and cute girls would stop and think, *There goes 260 pounds of twisted steel and sex appeal*, rather than what they think now, which is probably more like, *There goes 260 pounds of cheese cubes and man boobs.* I'm sure girls would still laugh when I accidentally broke a pencil in my big clumsy paws, but it would be a flirty laugh, like a giggle, and they'd say, "Oh, Thor, your giant hands are so strong . . ." and I'd reply, "Well, you know what they say about guys with big hands . . ." and they'd grin and be like, "What *do* they say about guys with big hands?" and I'd be like, "Greater risk for cancer" or something equally stupid because I'm so awkward around girls I blow it even in my fantasies.

Thor, God of Thunder. Has a gritty ring to it, right? Much better than my actual name, which is just Wyatt. Apparently it was a compromise between my parents, back when they actually agreed on stuff. My dad wanted me to have a tough-sounding name like most of the men who live here in Grayport. Practically every guy in my town is called Hunter or Gunner or Archer, like they were named after what job they'd have if we were surviving in a postapocalyptic shantytown. Frankly, Grayport isn't far from that. A postapocalyptic shantytown, I mean. Our local economy went to crap eight years ago, and half the stores in town are still boarded up. Our beaches, if you want to call them that, aren't filled with people, but are littered with debris brought in from the storms that constantly rock our coast. Hell, even our high school football stadium, the jewel of the town, is falling apart. The whole thing is made from lumber we've recycled from shipwrecks, and our long row of state championship flags flies atop poles that are actually old ship masts.

Grayport doesn't have much to be proud of besides our football team and our general aura of blue-collar toughness, so it's no surprise that my dad proudly claims that I'm named after Wyatt Earp. He was this legendary Old West gunslinger with a "don't F with me" attitude and an absolutely savage mustache (google the guy—he had so much testosterone I'm pretty sure even his mustache had a mustache). But my mom says I'm really named for her uncle Wyatt, who, if legends of *his* greatness are to be believed, was an assistant librarian with a moderate case of asthma. I'll let you figure out which Wyatt I take after.

But I also have another name—a secret identity, if you will:

Poncho Pete. Only three other people know about it, and frankly that's three people too many. It isn't exactly a privilege being Poncho Pete, so I'm relieved that so few people know I'm the loser hiding beneath that claustrophobic mascot costume. One person who knows is my best friend, Nate, a fellow freshman and my coworker. Nate helps me sell rain ponchos at our little wooden booth underneath the stands of Grayport High's football stadium. Since most everyone in Grayport already has a rain jacket to protect against the constant storms, our poncho sales were lagging big-time, so our boss, Mr. Cliff, created Poncho Pete, a giant caricature of a fisherman whose nose comprised like 75 percent of his face. For some reason Poncho Pete wore a cape. It was a poncho.

The third person who knows my secret identity is Dad, who made me take the job in the first place. My dad is *not* a guy you argue with, but I complained pretty hard since this job meant I'd be working during our home football games, and in Grayport you're a nobody if you aren't out there cheering on our boys to another state title. Plus there was the humiliation of being a mascot—what if somebody from school recognized me through the eyeholes cut into Poncho Pete's nostrils?

This argument seemed to really piss off my dad. A few days before the football season we were eating breakfast and I brought up the humiliation thing. He just sat in silence, stirring his whiskey and coffee. After a while he mumbled the word *humiliation* to himself, real bitter-like, and stormed off to his fishing boat in the harbor. I was still salty about the situation later that day when our landlord stopped by our apartment and handed me a letter addressed to my dad. I couldn't see much when I held the envelope up to a light, but I did make out a faint *final warning on late payments.*

I put the letter on Dad's dresser and then called old Mr. Cliff to say, *You got yourself a Poncho Pete.*

"You feel that, Wyatt?" Mr. Cliff held out a wrinkled palm and caught a raindrop that seeped through a crack in the wooden bleachers above us.

"I can't feel anything in here, Mr. Cliff," I shouted from the muted depths of my oversized fisherman head. It was actually the most comfortable part of my costume, since my bright yellow rain slacks were two sizes too small.

Nate sat coiled on a stool behind our booth, an empty cash box in his lap. He was pouting because I'd convinced him to be our cashier. A second raindrop plopped on his nest of curly blond hair, and he pulled up the hood of his complimentary poncho.

The rain must've been coming down hard. It was the opening night of football season—fourth quarter against our biggest rival, Blakemore High—and the electric excitement in the air seemed to have coalesced into an actual storm.

I tilted my head back so I could inspect the bleachers above through the eyeholes in Poncho's nostrils. Suddenly, as if responding to the mystical power of Poncho's giant schnoz, the bleachers began to shake. Raindrops shook loose from the wooden boards and sprinkled down on us, and the long row of glowing lanterns began to sway from their creaking ropes, throwing creepy shadows across our stadium's makeshift concourse. The rumble quickly crescendoed into a quake of cheering and clapping and foot stomping. You could literally feel the wooden boards of our shabby stadium rattling like a leaky ship in a storm.

Grayport touchdown. Must've been.

The dank underbelly of Grayport Stadium was suddenly abuzz with activity as dozens of vendors scrambled for their AM radios. Behind each booth a blur of hands frantically contorted antennas and twisted volume knobs to better hear Bobby Tingle deliver the play-by-play from the world above. Cliff, Nate, and I huddled around our radio, and I held my breath to better hear Tingle's call through my fisherman head.

". . . and Grayport retakes the lead on Brett Parker's thirty-three-yard QB keeper!"

Tingle's voice always trumpeted with pride, despite his moderate but passionate listenership. Since practically the entire town was packed into the five-thousand-seat stadium, the only radio listeners were us stadium vendors, the parking attendants outside, the lighthouse operator by the bay, and all those Grayport fishermen enduring another dark, wet night on boats bobbing somewhere in the Atlantic.

"I'll tell you what, folks: We just got our answer to whether the much-feared Blakemore linebacker, Derek Leopold, would be able to

bottle up Brett Parker. The league's reigning MVP just juked Leopold outta his socks on his way to his second score of the game. Parker's sensational play has really got this place jumping . . . and on cue, here comes the rain, thick and heavy!"

Mr. Cliff clapped his hands together. "Alright, boys, man your positions! Wyatt, this is your moment. Just like we rehearsed."

Mr. Cliff proudly referred to the rain dance as *Poncho Pete's Blood Rite of the Merciless Monsoon*, but really it was just me swaying awkwardly while Nate tooted out "Mary Had a Little Lamb" on his recorder. I reluctantly stepped in front of our booth and began hopping around with my arms extended like an airplane. I always *hate* dancing in any setting. When people look at a guy my size dancing, they don't see coordination or confidence or even comedy. They see jiggles.

As I danced, the guys working the Italian sausage stand next to us shook their heads and smirked before averting their eyes when the secondhand embarrassment got too strong.

Other than that, thank god, I didn't have an audience.

It really wasn't a surprise. Other vendors (like the guys selling food, game programs, Grayport football shirts, etc.) rake in tons of cash on game nights. Nate's right when he says that Grayport football is the life vest that keeps the town from drowning. But the poncho business was a real struggle-fest. It rains in Grayport like every freaking day, so you'd be certifiable if you didn't already own a waterproof outfit. Besides, there was *no way* anyone was going to leave their seat right now. This was what Grayport lived for: fourth quarter of a tight game against

Blakemore, our hated rivals who couldn't handle the sloppy, difficult conditions that our team and fans thrived in. This was our home-field advantage—and the only advantage, it seemed, to calling Grayport home.

But, man, was it a big advantage on Friday nights. It was like our pride in enduring storms gave us this magic ability to see through the thick coastal mist as Brett—*our* Brett, from just over there on 528 Pine Street—threaded passes that somehow got better the worse it rained.

Midway through the fourth quarter the rain was pounding the bleachers so hard that we could barely hear Bobby Tingle on the radio. Somehow Blakemore wasn't bothered by the torrential rain, and they were now beating us by five, causing the mood among the vendors to take on the same gloominess of our cavelike concourse. I took off my Poncho Pete head, confident that nobody I knew would come down and discover my secret identity. A few drenched scouts from USC (there to watch Brett, no doubt) slogged over to us, but otherwise it was quiet.

That is, until a pack of six girls materialized through the fog into the concourse. The sausage guys stopped flipping their meat so they could concentrate all their energy on the girls. Each was rocking a matching pink sports bra, and on their skinny tan stomachs were the letters *B-R-E-T-T* spelled out in red paint. They were dripping wet, and coming right toward us.

I noticed that one of the girls in the pack wasn't matching her friends. She sported a crop top Grayport High T-shirt, which to me seemed braver, and in a way hotter, than if she was matching her friends. I felt a weird pull toward her, and as she glided forward through the dim orange glow of the lanterns, her aura sharpened into something real. Her brown hair was clumped in a wet tangle, and she had a cute perky nose like a little hill in a meadow of freckles. Actually, now that the girl was closer, she looked more and more like—

Oh shit.

I quickly grabbed Poncho Pete's head and slammed it back on.

"Nate," I hissed. "We've got a problem. Haley. She's coming."

"So . . . ?"

"So, the other day I might've kinda definitely told her that I'm on varsity football."

It wasn't a planned lie, I swear. It just slipped out. A harmless little fib that was about to bite me in the butt. See, Haley sat in front of me in biology, and I had what you might describe as a debilitating crush on her. Every day throughout class I'd wonder about this cute girl in front of me, wonder who she was wondering about, wonder if she even knew my name, and wonder if my wondering would eventually have some sort of telepathic effect on her feelings for me. I also sometimes wondered why I was getting such a shitty grade in biology.

Then, after two weeks of wondering if Haley's world existed only in front of her, she turned around at the end of class and smiled at me.

"Hey," she said. "Did Mr. Benson say the test was next Monday or Tuesday?"

I said, "Monday for sure," which was a guess, and Haley smiled again and said thanks. Then, as she tossed her notebook into her bag, she asked if I was going to the game Friday. It was a simple yes-or-no question that vaporized my brain.

"Uh, well, yeah," I said. "'Cause I'm playing in it."

Nate listened to this news and looked at me like I had two heads, which I guess I technically did. "Why the hell did you tell her that?"

"Because I'm a complete moron."

But also because I *had* to know, if only for ten beautiful seconds, what it was like to be somebody different. To be respected, to be a guy who really *mattered*. Earlier that day I'd been cut from football tryouts, and even though I had known I had no shot and had been preparing myself for the bad news, I was really disappointed. Or more accurately, I was disappointed with how disappointed I felt, how much I desperately wanted to play. As I scanned the list that Coach posted outside the locker room, every name I read had been a new opportunity to see "Wyatt Parker," a new chance for my life to change. But in the end, each name had been just another mini disappointment until finally I reached the end of the list and was left looking at nothing. Just emptiness.

So when later that day Haley turned to me and hesitated a second because she clearly didn't know my name, it felt like some vague structure inside me, tall but flimsy, had toppled over. Buried in that rubble, I felt a sharp desperation and reached for anything that could pull me out, let me breathe.

So I looked at Haley and pretended that I had reached my goal, that I had made the team, and that on Friday I would finally be wearing a Grayport jersey with my number stamped front and back. A jersey that, once you put it on, transformed you from just another fat kid into a varsity lineman.

When the girls reached our booth, Mr. Cliff was bursting with excitement to finally have some customers. "Hey, Poncho Pete," he called to me. "Quit hiding back there and show these nice ladies how you called down the rain."

I was making a "please don't do this to me" face from underneath my mascot head. I was determined to stay in the shadows behind the booth.

Mr. Cliff frowned. "Come on, Poncho! Nate, start the tune!"

I slunk into position in front of the booth. Through Poncho Pete's nostrils I could see Madison Wheatley, Mia Torres, Dakota Babson, and Samantha Betts standing in a semicircle of terrifying poses, their arms folded across their pink sports bras as they traded obvious whispers and snickers. Haley was standing to the side, but her gaze was leveled right on me. I felt epically lame. Like, by comparison Nate looked totally badass next to me, and he was holding a recorder.

Nate brought the instrument to his lips, and I instinctively sucked in my stomach, as if that could actually squelch the unstoppable jiggle effect. I extended my arms into my pathetic airplane pose.

"You know, it's really okay," Haley suddenly interjected, her voice warm yet firm. "I'm sure Poncho is pretty exhausted from all this rain."

The other girls grumbled small complaints—*oh, come on, it'll be funny!*—but Haley just smiled and pulled a ten-dollar bill from her jeans pocket. Mr. Cliff shrugged and began stacking ponchos on the booth's counter.

Relief rushed through me, followed by a blast of gratitude. Haley, I realized, was one of those rare people who just get it, someone who can read social cues the same way Brett can read defenses and know exactly where to throw the ball. Then it struck me that maybe the other day Haley had known *exactly* when the biology test was, that maybe she just found a reason to brighten up the day of a kid who always trudged into the room, his shoulders a little slumped.

I grabbed the pile of ponchos to hand out to the girls. Then I had the terrible idea of saying something to them.

"So, are you guys, like, big Brett Parker fans or something?"

"Geez, what gave it away," snarked the girl with the *R* on her stomach. She snatched a poncho from me.

I handed one to Haley. Was I imagining things, or was she giving me an odd squint, like underneath my costume she could see the real me?

"Thanks," she said. "You're a lifesaver, Poncho. Really."

I was beaming under my mask. "Well, not all superheroes wear capes," I said, surprising myself with the clever line.

"But you *are* wearing a cape."

"Oh . . . right." It was time to quit while I was only slightly behind. "Well, stay dry out there!"

I spun around and *BLAM*, slammed Poncho's head directly into a lantern. I frantically reached up to grab the head as it tipped backward, but it was too late. It toppled to the ground with a crash.

I stood motionless, my back to Haley, trying to figure out a way to discreetly retrieve Poncho's head. I could feel her staring a hole into my back. A silent freak-out exploded in my soul as I realized there was no way around this.

I winced, took a deep breath, and slowly turned around.

Then, just before I faced Haley, a violent burst of clanging rang out from the sausage booth. Everyone in the concourse, including Haley, turned to check out the commotion.

The sausage guys were wildly banging pans with their tongs. This was their celebration for big plays.

"*. . . and Grayport is still alive!*" shouted a fevered Bobby Tingle through the radio. "*An unbelievable fourth-and-ten conversion by Brett Parker has brought the offense to the Blakemore fifteen-yard line. The clock has ticked down to the two-minute warning, Grayport trailing by five. Buckle in, folks!*"

The pack of girls, the vendors, Nate, Mr. Cliff—everybody—rushed toward the ramp leading up to the field. In the commotion I discreetly plunked Poncho's head back on.

At the mouth of the tunnel, one of Haley's friends yelled at her to hurry up.

"Coming!" she shouted back. Then, in a quick movement

that I might've subconsciously wished into existence, Haley pulled off her T-shirt.

Painted on her stomach was a big red 7.

Brett's number.

Haley unfolded her see-through poncho and slipped it on, then rushed to join her friends, disappearing up the ramp without looking back.

"Hey, Poncho, you coming or what?" Mr. Cliff shouted at me as he joined the mass of bodies funneling into the ramp toward the field. "We need your magical powers out there!"

Stepping into the open air of our stadium is like diving headfirst into the deep end of Grayport's soul. Perched delicately on a rocky bluff overlooking the ocean, the stadium pulses with a raw and invigorating danger. My favorite part is the sound of the waves crashing into the stone embankment and how you can hear the water crest then slam into rock with a steady *whhh-thunk whhh-thunk* that echoes through the stadium like our communal heartbeat, a reminder that we're still here, defiant and surviving despite it all.

At 6'2", I could easily see the field over the crowd of vendors huddled at the ramp opening, but I had to tilt my head back slightly to get a better viewing angle out of Poncho's nostrils. After two short runs and a quick slant pass that got stuffed for two yards, our offense was facing a fourth-and-one from the six-yard line. The crowd stood as one, but held a tense silence so the offense could hear Brett's play call over the whipping rain and wind.

Brett broke the huddle and strode to the line of scrimmage. I always found that watching him play football was mesmerizing, inspiring, and depressing all at once. It was mesmerizing to see how confidence and athleticism radiated from every one of his movements; inspiring to know there are actually people out there like this; depressing to know that this would never be me.

Still, I liked to imagine what it was like to *be* Brett, what it's like if you're at center stage, not some sideshow in a costume. I wanted to be down there on the field as the salty mists rolled in from the shore and enveloped the stadium in a thick cloud that gives the bulbs on the old light towers their fuzzy orange glow, like little halos floating in the dark sky. I wanted to take that exhilarating walk up to the ball as the booming waves spoke on behalf of the entire hushed town, who you can't even see through the fog, but who you can just *feel* all around you, rooting for you, getting soaked with you, practically *bleeding* with you because this moment right here, fourth-and-one in the rickety fishing town of Grayport, is all we really have.

"Hut, HUT!"

The shotgun snap was low but Brett easily plucked the ball off his shoelaces. He tucked it and took off on a QB keeper, off-tackle right. By stacking the line on the left, Blakemore was daring us to take it right, directly at their all-league outside linebacker, Derek Leopold.

Leopold easily threw aside his blocker and met Brett with an electrifying collision about one yard behind the line of scrimmage. He had Brett wrapped up and was driving him back. That was it, game over.

But just as the entire town groaned—a whole season lost on opening night—Brett somehow spun free from Leopold's claws. Now Brett stumbled backward a couple of yards and, regaining his balance, he rolled out in an angled sprint toward the sideline, right where the first-down marker was planted. The Blakemore cornerback on that side read Brett's trajectory and raced to meet him at the marker, while Derek Leopold also chased Brett from behind. At the marker, the cornerback crunched into Brett with a perfect form tackle, but Brett's momentum was too much as he bowled his opponent forward. When the two of them hit the ground, they were a few feet beyond the first-down pole.

The whistle blew and the crowd erupted in a deafening cheer that suddenly muffled into a silent panic as we watched Derek Leopold hurtle recklessly toward Brett. Everyone could see Leopold's target: Brett's left arm, which was planted firmly in the muddy turf as he pushed himself off the ground and out of the tackle. Leopold dove like a 250-pound missile aimed at the exposed limb.

My great-uncle Wyatt passed down his asthma to me, and I was wheezing by the time I ran my Poncho ass down to the ambulance zone outside the stadium. The snap of Brett's bone had made a deep, hollow *klok* sound, like a wooden bat connecting with a fastball, and it was still echoing through the stadium when my feet instinctively took off for this spot. Haley and her friends were among the dozens of others who had the same idea to wait for Brett at the ambulance. The outcome of the game didn't matter anymore.

The rain had stopped, and moonlight filtered through the fog and drenched us all in a weird, almost supernatural glow. After a couple minutes the group's concerned murmurs were cut off by medics shouting to clear the way. A gurney whirred toward the ambulance. Brett lay upright in the back, holding his arm. Incredibly, he didn't look to be in pain—he just lay there with a vacant stare, which was way worse.

A few onlookers screamed at the sight of blood spurting like a leaky hose from the spot where Brett's bone, so pristinely white, broke through the skin. The sight made me feel like puking. But that feeling, which was located high in my throat, wasn't nearly as bad as the wrench I felt twisting deep in my stomach. As they loaded Brett into the ambulance, I was leveled by the realization that this was going to change *everything*. What "everything" entailed, I couldn't yet say. And looking back now, there's no way I could've predicted the epic shit-storm that this event would bring to the town—and to me specifically. But I just had this feeling, this dread. Usually when the king goes down, the game is over for the pawns. For me, though, everything was about to begin.

Peering into the ambulance, I noticed that Brett's empty stare had shifted slightly, had taken on some life.

He was looking at me. Looking at Poncho Pete, that is.

Without thinking, I removed my head. I gently placed it on the ground, walked over to the back of the ambulance, and climbed in.

A paramedic planted a stiff-arm into my chest. "Whoa there, kid," he said. "Immediate family only."

"It's okay," Brett murmured from the stretcher. "That's my brother."

One year later.

CHAPTER
TWO

For the longest time I was a floater. I never committed to a major goal or quest. It's hard to be pumped about the future when, like most guys at Grayport, you're already destined for a lifetime of mopping decks on fishing boats. Sure, after a few decades of slopping up fish guts you might be named "first mate" or whatever, but the more realistic hope is that your mopping zone gets upgraded from the stern to the bow. With the view up front you can at least pretend you're sailing forward into an infinite horizon. Still, deep down you always know the truth: that you're drifting, and that every journey ends by anchoring back in Grayport.

But that changed after Brett's injury. I finally had a mission.

It all started in the ambulance, where the paramedics assigned me the job of distracting Brett while they jammed his bone back in place. This was pretty important, as far as side quests go, and I totally blew it. I just stood there like a fool, fumbling for words that never came. I couldn't think of *anything* to say to Brett. We'd shared bunk beds in our tiny attic room for my entire life, but somehow we'd never had a meaningful conversation.

It's not that Brett disliked me, necessarily. I think he always viewed me as a curious but mostly useless expansion, like when your iPhone requires a ridiculously large iOS update just to add a taco emoji. I swear some nights it felt like there was nothing more between us than a stale fart that had escaped my sheets and floated up to my big brother, who'd catch a whiff and not laugh at me, not yell at me, not do anything at all other than roll over and face the wall in a thick, awkward silence.

I thought we'd be tighter after sharing the traumatic ride to the hospital. Stuff got intensely real in the ambulance. It was a total frenzy of shouting and blood and shiny machines that beeped like crazy. But over all the chaos, over all the flashing lights and sterile needles and space-age devices, one item stands out the most in my memory: an ordinary stick of rubber. It was the size of a Snickers bar, and the paramedics placed it between Brett's clenched teeth so he wouldn't accidentally bite off his tongue in agony. When life is stripped of all its fluff, it can be pretty raw and brutal.

I guess that's a tough lesson everyone learns eventually. But I thought maybe a special bond forms when you learn it alongside someone else. Like it becomes a secret between the two of you. Granted, anyone visiting the poncho booth in the following weeks could see Brett's maroon bloodstains spattered across my mascot costume. But those people weren't there when the blood was bright red. Only Brett and I shared that.

Not that I expected us to suddenly become #bffs or #bros or hashtag anything at all. Brett was quiet around everyone, and I knew nothing would change that. I was just hoping we could reach a level of comfort that allowed conversations only long-time siblings could have. You know, the kind that start with "Hey, remember that time when . . ." and are answered by your brother with a nostalgic chuckle or, if it was a bad family memory, a quiet acknowledgment like "Yeah, man, I remember—that was pretty fucked up." And then just like that, neither of you is holding the weight of the past by yourself.

But we never got there. Not even close. For an entire year, Brett was focused solely on rehab and staying in shape. When he actually did talk to me it was nothing new, just typical blah questions like "What's for dinner?" and "Can I borrow your phone charger?" and "Did you know your shirt's inside out?"

The only—and I mean *only*—people Brett was close with were his teammates. So my mission for the following school year was clear: make varsity football. I'd been cut from the team the previous year, so this was my last chance to play with Brett before he graduated and disappeared to some big D-I college where he'd have a new roommate, a guy who'd probably be funny and cool and not a taco.

So my quest log was updated easy enough. Now all I had to do was make a nationally renowned football team that was essentially an army of highly trained athletic specimens. Easy as pie.

I spent the year preparing: I cut a little weight. I stopped eating pies and tacos and Snickers. It's no piece of cake going cold turkey on something you love, but that's how the cookie crumbles. I gained a little bit of strength, too, mostly doing body-weight exercises like push-ups and squats and pull-ups, because when you're a guy my size, those exercises are *plenty* difficult. In fact, I even went from being able to do zero pull-ups to being able to do two of them, which is technically an improvement of infinity percent.

So I actually went into my sophomore season feeling slightly optimistic. At the very least, I figured that the experience would be good for me. It would make me less soft, inside and out. After all, a football field is a lot like the inside of an ambulance. It's where life is distilled down to its most primal elements. Pain. Instinct. Survival. It's high-stakes chaos where you have no control over anything other than your response to the madness. You can discover a lot about yourself on the football field. You can learn what you're capable of. But what if you learn you're capable of terrible things? Now that's something I wasn't prepared for.

It happened about halfway through a preseason practice, though technically it was still tryouts for nonreturners like Nate and me. Actually, calling it "tryouts" is too generous. Preseason was more like a Hunger Games battle of survival where at any moment for any reason you could be mercilessly slaughtered or, even worse, cut from the team. Over the first few weeks the roster had been trimmed from eighty-five to forty-three, and somehow both Nate and I were still there. At first I was shocked we'd made it that far, but then again maybe this was proof that great rewards wait at the intersection of talent and determination.

"True, true," Nate agreed between squirts of water at our mid-practice break. "Though we can't discount the possibility that we haven't been cut because the coaches have forgotten we even exist."

That's why I hated being friends with a science nerd like Nate: He had a major hard-on for dumb things like facts and reason. But he did have a point. We likely weren't there because of football talent, but because of a skill we'd inadvertently demonstrated at every party and school dance: being invisible.

I snatched the water bottle from Nate and took a swig. "Well, I hope Trunk Greenhammer forgot I exist. I accidentally stepped on his foot at practice yesterday and he glared at me like I had just texted him a dick pic."

I nervously glanced over at Trunk at the far end of the water station. His massive chest heaved up and down as he ripped the cap off a bottle and poured water down his gullet.

"Did Trunk say anything to you?" Nate asked nervously.

"He said that if I ever stepped on his foot again, he'd go 'bitchcakes' on me. Whatever that means."

Nate furrowed his bushy eyebrows in deep thought. Even in his oversized shoulder pads, he always looked more like a professor than a football player.

"'Bitchcakes,' eh? Probably involves Trunk pounding you

into shapes once thought anatomically impossible. I gotta say, I'm pretty impressed that such a creative term escaped from the cobwebs of his skull."

We laughed quietly, but it soon fizzled into an uncomfortable silence.

"Are we stupid, Nate?" I said after the pause. "Thinking we could possibly compete with these guys? I mean, Trunk practically sweats creatine."

"Nothing is stupid," Nate said emphatically. "It all comes down to simple physics. Force equals mass times acceleration, right? So to hit with the same force as Trunk, you just need better acceleration to go with your mass."

That's why I loved being friends with a science nerd like Nate: To him, your weight is your mass and nothing more.

"Newton's third law for the win!" I said, extending a fist for what was definitely the dorkiest pound in the history of mankind.

Nate sighed and gently pushed down my fist. "Newton's second law, actually. The third law states that every action has an equal and opposite reaction. For example, in physics last week, when you should've been paying attention to this stuff, you were instead sitting behind Haley and creepily breathing on the back of her neck with a strong force that was equal and opposite to her feelings for you."

"See, that's where you're wrong," I said, grinning. "Because we can't discount the possibility that she forgot I even exist."

Nate started to respond but was interrupted by the shrill of a whistle. It came from Coach Crooks, our offensive line coach who was about infinity years old and who played Grayport football even before our granddads. Coach Crooks had only, like, seven teeth and even less patience, so Nate and I joined the herd of other linemen and ran over to him, buckling our chin straps on the way.

As we gathered around Crooks in a semicircle, I strategically positioned myself on the opposite end of Trunk. Nate slipped in behind me. A moment later I heard the usual *snap* as he unbuckled his chin strap. Nate had apocalyptic acne and the chafing of his chin strap must've been absolute torture. Every chance he got, Nate would unbuckle his chin strap, even if it was for just a few seconds of relief.

It tore me up inside, seeing Nate do this again and again. Trust me, I have always known what it was like to have a physical flaw on display for the whole world to see. But at least my weight problem was my own stupid fault. Nate's acne was bad luck, plain and simple. He was super sensitive about it, too. Like, Nate and I could joke about *anything*, but I'd never in a million years mention his acne.

Coach Crooks was standing next to a tackling dummy and staring down our group. His bony hands were on his hips and his thumbs were hooked under the waistband of his way-too-short gym shorts that I'll probably be describing to a therapist someday.

Crooks flicked his head toward the tackling dummy. "You all see this dummy?"

This was a rhetorical question, but Trunk said yes aloud.

"Well, it ain't a dummy anymore. From now until we play Blakemore, it's that son of a bitch Derek Leopold. We've cooked up a few tricks for that bush-league bastard, starting with a heavy dose of double-teams."

Trunk clapped his hands together in excitement and shouted something that was less English than it was gurgle.

I turned slightly toward Nate and whispered, "I think Trunk was bitten by a rabid animal as a child." This game of wise-cracks was dangerous, but Nate and I couldn't help it. Making fun of Grayport's macho football culture distracted us from how badly we wanted to be part of it. Nate responded with a snicker that was a little too loud.

Coach Crooks snapped his glare over to us. "Something funny over there?"

White-hot panic washed over Nate's face. "Oh . . . uh, no, Mr. Coach Crooks, sir."

Crooks leaned forward and spat brown tobacco juice between his front teeth. "Change of plans, fellas. No more dummy. Today we'll be using live bait. Let's go, Zitty Pimpleson—get your butt over here."

Nate glanced at me nervously.

"Told you the coaches know who you are," I said quietly. Not my best joke, but I don't think Nate heard anyway. He buckled his chin strap with a wince and ran to the front of the firing squad.

CHAPTER
THREE

The double-team drill was efficient, cold-blooded, and hard to watch. We formed two lines, and on Coach Crooks's whistle the two guys up front exploded into Nate with vicious smashes that easily crumpled him like an empty soda can.

At least Nate got a small break when it was my turn. On Coach Crooks's whistle, my blocking partner, a junior lineman named Justin, charged into Nate's chest, but I made sure my half of the double-team was nothing more than a whimper. It was a relief not to railroad Nate, but my weak hit was yet another example of what was quickly becoming one of my biggest shames. Over tryouts I was starting to realize that the real difference between me and Trunk (or Brett, or any guy on varsity) wasn't mass or acceleration. The difference was heart, grit, balls—whatever it is that gives you the ability to throw your body with reckless abandon, to hit with anger and without hesitation. I'm sure you've heard the saying that football is a game of inches. But I played football like I lived my life: a game of flinches.

As usual, Coach Crooks responded to my pathetic block with the worst reaction a coach can have, which is to say that he had no reaction at all. If I'd been a typical player, Crooks would've yelled, screamed, kicked dirt, said *Do it again*. With me, though, he just blew his whistle. Next.

Crooks's intensity started to pick up when Brett, flanked by his entourage of assistant coaches and backup quarterbacks, stopped by our drill on his way to the water station. Brett always had a royal air to him that made everyone stand a little straighter, hit a little harder, and dig a little deeper.

We continued our drill while Brett watched quietly, his piercing green eyes underlined in bold by smudges of eye black. Coiled around his right arm was a long scar. Bright pink and wormlike, it somehow seemed fresher now that Brett was back on the same field where the scar had been born.

Each time Crooks blew his whistle, Nate absorbed the full weight of revenge. Impressively, he kept scrambling back to his feet. Dude didn't say a word.

"Stop tiptoeing around and *hit*," Coach Crooks shouted at us between reps. "This is *Derek Leopold* here!"

As I got closer to the front of the line for my next turn, my heart began racing, keeping pace with the mantra that was now pulsing like a siren in my head:

Brett's watching. Brett's watching. Brett's watching.

I didn't even notice that Trunk was standing next to me in line—my next double-team partner—until he grabbed the side of my face mask and yanked me within inches of his seething red face.

"Enough of this crap," he hissed as Crooks cursed out two more linemen for not hitting Nate hard enough. "It's time to end this kid. I'll go low and tee him up for you."

In the span of ten seconds, about a hundred considerations ignited in my head. My first thought was, *That sounds a lot like an illegal chop block*. Next I thought, *But, man, would it be an impressive hit*. And my last thought was, *And Brett's watching. Brett's watching. Brett's watching.*

When it was our turn, I approached the line and looked up at Nate. A chunk of grass was wedged in the corner of his face mask and a dark splotch of brown blood began to ooze through his chin strap. He flashed me a goofy grin that said, *Don't worry, I'm alright*, followed by a subtle roll of the eyes that said, *The meatheads have really taken it to new heights, huh?*

I didn't know what I was going to do as I crouched into my three-point stance. I didn't even know what I was going to do when Crooks blew his whistle.

But it turns out that my body knew.

Trunk and I shot out of our stances, and Trunk immediately dove low. His shoulder swept out Nate's legs, leaving the live bait dangling in midair for me. It was just too easy. Everything was right there for me to take.

I threw all of my mass into Nate. Combined with the equal and opposite force of Trunk's low hit on the other side, my impact caused Nate to flip ass over teakettle. When his body finished cartwheeling, he landed on his chest with a spectacular *crunch*.

All the guys erupted in wild cheers. Nate, meanwhile, was curled up and wheezing.

I was gut-punched with instant regret for the personal foul. Even worse, the regret was coupled with guilt when I realized the hit—the surge of power, the raw immediacy of it—felt *good*. Really good.

The guys had surrounded me, cheering various forms of "fuck yeah" and "that's how we do it." They awarded me with enthusiastic butt slaps that in the football world are basically a form of social currency. But the dirty hit made it all feel counterfeit to me.

As crappy as I felt, though, it could've all been worth it. Life is about difficult trade-offs, and I'd made my choice. I spun around, looking for Brett, waiting for his pat on the shoulder, his *fuck yeah*, his *that-a-baby*.

Finally, I saw him. His back, actually. He was on the opposite sideline, getting a drink at the water table. He hadn't even been watching.

I turned back to Nate. He was still on the turf gasping like the wind had been knocked out of him. He motioned over Coach Crooks, and after a few failed attempts, he choked out one word: "Trainer."

This was unprecedented. Asking for the trainer was so frowned upon, so against everything Grayport stood for, that our team doctor stopped bothering coming out to the field. He just read magazines in the training room, the most deserted place in the entire town.

But Crooks seemed unusually sympathetic. He knelt by Nate's side and put a hand on his back. "Yeah, kid," he said quietly. "Let's get you up." He extended a hand to Nate, who got to his feet and started slinking toward the training room.

"Oh, and one more thing," Crooks called after him. "When you're done with the trainer, go ahead and pack up your locker."

Nate didn't respond. The rest of us stood in silence and watched the dead man walking.

I took a few steps forward. "Nate!" I yelled, unsure of what I was going to say if he turned around. I think I wanted him to yell at me, scream at me, kick dirt at me. Anything.

But all he did was slowly raise a hand up to the side of his helmet. For a second I thought he was going to flip me the bird.

Instead, he just unbuckled his chin strap.

CHAPTER
FOUR

The only argument Nate and I ever had took place behind the poncho booth our freshman year, the next home game after Brett got injured. The fight was over Haley. Like, we were literally *over* Haley, or rather her Facebook picture on Nate's phone, examining it like scientists at a petri dish. Nate said something like, "Wyatt, how can you be so obsessed with a girl who has such a bad case of sorority arm?," to which I calmly replied that I liked sorority arm—*loved* it, in fact—and that I'd explain why if he just quickly reminded me what sorority arm was. Nate grinned his black-and-orange Halloween braces and said, "Wyatt, my friend, you have a lot to learn about women," then explained that sorority arm happens when a girl in a group photo places one hand on her hip and juts out her elbow, forming a sideways triangle with her outer arm. It's a bit of optical wizardry that makes said arm appear skinnier in the picture than if it'd been hanging down flat like a dead fish. Sorority arm, Nate explained, is a technique every woman knows instinctively, like how birds are born with the ability to fly or how dudes are born with the ability to sit down without crushing our nuts.

Ultimately, sorority arm just made me want Haley more. I always saw her as a pristine picture of confidence, but it turned out that she might actually be insecure about her appearance, kind of like me. I wondered how and why a girl as pretty as Haley would feel such pressure to make her arm look skinnier, then I thought about what Nate and I were doing at that very moment—staring at her pictures and dissecting her appearance—and I knew who the real culprit was.

Anyway, now that I think about it, that wasn't really an argument at all. A disagreement, more like.

The roar of cheers and life-affirming butt slaps from my teammates did not echo into the next day. Just the opposite, actually—I was met with icy silence. The only person who spoke to me was Justin, who was standing next to me during team stretch.

"How's that kid?" he blurted all of a sudden. His eyes remained locked ahead on Brett, who faced the team as he led us through stretches. Practice was already buzzing with a tense urgency. Opening night against Blakemore was just four days away, and I overheard some of the guys speculating that today we'd be installing a much-rumored special play into the offense.

A big, big deal, this secret play. Our coaches had spent most of team stretch pacing the field, nervously looking over their shoulders for Blakemore spies.

It took me a moment to realize that Justin was addressing me, and that he was asking about Nate. "He's fine," I muttered, though I wasn't sure.

"Wasn't he your buddy?" Justin asked coldly. Clearly this was more of a statement than a question, so I didn't answer.

Nobody said another word to me until the end of practice, when Coach Crooks ordered me to stand in front of the first-string offense. "More live bait today, boys!" he announced. "But no double-teams. Today we're cooking up something special."

Crooks grinned, and I could sense everyone lean in, just slightly, toward him. Here, finally, after several days of rumors and speculation, was the unveiling of the secret new play.

"On Friday we're going to punch Blakemore right in the mouth, but we're also going to beat them with our brains." Crooks tapped his temple with a *thunk* of pruney fingertips. "And how are we gonna do that? Well, I got two words for you fellas: Tackle. Eligible. Pass."

Upon hearing that he'd be the target of a pass play, Trunk clapped his giant hands together and unleashed a "WOO!" that could be heard all the way in Blakemore.

Next came a walk-through of the play. Crooks had the offensive lineup on the ball, their backs to the oceanfront end zone. I remained facing them, arms outstretched in a T.

With Grayport's constant shroud of mist and with its rain

always going sideways into your eyes, it's common to think you've seen something and only later discover it was an illusion conjured by a few twirling wisps of fog. That's why I kept my mouth shut when, during Crooks's walk-through of the super top secret tackle-eligible pass, I thought I saw two dark figures lurking on the top row of bleachers behind the seaside end zone. One form was sitting while the other was standing. But after blinking away the moisture that had collected around my eyes, they had vanished. Maybe they disappeared behind a cloak of mist, but more likely they were just another vague illusion courtesy of the Grayport coast.

Meanwhile, Coach Crooks was walking Brett and the offense through a fake handoff that culminated in a rollout left, Brett's non-throwing side, a move that would require some fancy footwork and throwing mechanics that even some NFL QBs can't do, but which Brett could pull off no problem.

Next came the blocking assignments. "We'll go with standard zone blocking," Crooks explained. "'Cept for you, Trunk. Now everyone listen up here, 'cause this next part is the most important point you'll hear all season." Crooks was standing behind me now, and I jolted with surprise when he slammed a hand onto my right shoulder pad. "This here is the opposing outside backer, in other words that scumbag-piece-of-shit bastard Derek Leopold. Now Trunk, when you release off the line to run your pass route, you must, must, *must* first put a shoulder into Derek Leopold. You *gotta* at least slow him down, else he's gonna have a free run at Brett and rip his head off, and if that happens I'm gonna rip your nuts off, if you even got 'em. Understand?"

Trunk nodded firmly, like, *Murder Wyatt: check.*

"Alright, enough chitchat. Let's run the damn thing live!"

Crooks waddled his creaky frame over to the wall of backup players.

That's when I saw them again. The figures. The fog clouding the bleachers had lifted just enough for me to see a flash, or a glint, more like, from a shiny silver object (a knife?) dangling from the hand of the sitting figure. I squeezed my eyes shut and opened them. The two figures were still there.

Tackling dummies aren't supposed to speak, but this was probably a good time to open my mouth for the first time all preseason. "Um, Coach?"

Coach Crooks didn't hear me. His old-man ears were big enough to hold the mysteries of the universe within their labyrinths, but they were pretty rusty, hearing-wise.

The offense approached the line of scrimmage. Brett crouched down and put his hands under the center. Trunk stared at me like he was already debating where to hide my carcass.

"Coach!" I shouted again. "Coachcoachcoachcoach!"

Crooks blew his whistle and the offense rose from their three-point stances. "Christ, Wyatt! This better be good."

I pointed toward the bleachers. The entire team swiveled around.

An army of Russian battleships could've been in the harbor and Crooks would've reacted less dramatically than when he saw the two lurkers. His jaw dropped so far the entire wad of tobacco fell out of his mouth. He fumbled for the whistle hanging from his neck and in his panic yanked it clean off the chain, then began frantically blowing into it.

Clearly this was a matter for Coach Stetson, our head coach.

"Everyone back to individual position drills," Stetson shouted. "And in the meantime, someone's gotta check out what's going on with our visitors."

Stetson paused like he was considering which player he could most afford to lose via murder from knife-wielding spies.

"Hey, Wyatt," he said, addressing me for the first time ever. "Hustle over there and report back."

CHAPTER
FIVE

The dark figure with the knife didn't even look at me as I approached. He was perched on the edge of the wooden bleacher, completely absorbed with our practice. In his right hand he held the glistening blade, which even from a distance I could tell was a fishing knife. A fillet knife, to be exact, which any Grayport kid knows is about eight inches long, slightly curved, and sharp enough to gut a seven-hundred-pound tuna with a quick flick of the wrist. The man was leaning forward. He held the knife vertically so its point dug lightly into the wooden bench in front of him. As he observed practice he'd casually spin the knife, using the tip as its axis, then grab its handle just as the blade's rotation slowed to a wobble.

I looked at him from the bottom row of the bleachers and saw a thin face peppered with blades of black and gray stubble. The face was intense, focused. But you could sense a deep exhaustion in it, too. As I got a closer view, I realized that I knew this face well, better than I wanted to. I still wasn't sure about the second dark figure, who was a few rows above, but this man

here was no Blakemore spy. He was a Grayport legend responsible for three of the championship flags hanging on the ship
masts high above us.

I tentatively climbed up a few rows toward him.

"Hey, Dad."

My father nodded. His eyes remained locked on the field.
Locked on Brett. "Hey."

"Coast Guard shut down the harbor again?"

"Fog."

I winced. This meant there'd be no fresh fish for dinner.
Instead we'd fry up our small reserve of frozen mackerel, a fish
that tastes like, to put it politely, the ocean's grundle.

Back on the field, the team had started some generic passing drills to kill some time until they knew whether we had a
spy situation. From the stands I heard a loud cheer from the
field, and I turned around to see a receiver, about sixty yards
downfield from Brett, striding toward the end zone with the
ball. The row of assistant coaches behind Brett subtly extended
their hands to each other for low fives. Brett, meanwhile, was
already calling a new huddle like, *Come on, let's get to the next
rep already.* Dad didn't react one way or the other. He continued
to spin his knife.

There was also another sound mixed in with the cheers, a
sound that you *never* heard in Grayport: a man giggling. With
delight.

I knew of only one man in Grayport who laughed like that,
and sure enough, when I looked through the fog at the second

mysterious figure, there was Murray Miller. He was waddling down the bleachers toward me.

"Holy cannoli, did you *see* that pass? Must've traveled fifty yards *on a line*." Murray Miller giggled again, this time with childlike wonder.

I waved down to the coaches and gave a thumbs-up. No Blakemore spies here.

I turned back to Murray Miller. I liked talking to the guy, even though he never remembered my name. He was super short (the top of his head barely came to my chest) and shaped like a bowling ball. He was always fidgeting with a pair of thick glasses that rested snugly upon his round chipmunk cheeks. Basically, Murray Miller was the answer to what a Cabbage Patch Kid would look like if it were fifty years old, balding, and sporting a fuzzy mustache. I sometimes had to suppress a weird urge to tickle Murray Miller.

"Um, this isn't a big problem, Mr. Murray Miller, but I don't think you're supposed to be here. This is a closed practice."

"Whaddya mean? It's Media Day! Practice is open to the press. Or did the coaches forget again? Please don't tell me the coaches forgot again."

It was funny hearing Murray Miller refer to "the press" and "the media." As the lone reporter in all of Grayport, Murray Miller *was* the media. Like, all of it. And I have to say, he was pretty good at his job. People devoured his annual Football Preview in the *Grayport Gazette*. He was the oldest of the old school—dude wore a fedora on his head and kept a pencil behind his ear. He referred to news stories as "scoops," and I once heard that he still used a typewriter. I think if poor old Murray Miller discovered that most written communication these days was through something called "emojis," and that spitting a good emoji game could even get you *a date*, his head would explode into a confetti of a million little frowny faces.

"No, no, the coaches didn't forget," I lied. "It's just that, well, we've got this new secret play, right? And—"

Here I got distracted by Murray Miller's eyes, which had widened to three times their normal size. I'd made a big mistake letting it slip about our new play.

"It's just that our coaches want some privacy," I quickly added. "So maybe you can just, you know, quickly get the info you need and then, like . . . leave."

A frown nestled into Murray Miller's curved mustache. "I suppose I could skedaddle," he said. "But I can't leave without a quote or two."

"Yeah, okay. I mean, probably. I'll tell Coach. You know Brett doesn't do interviews, but maybe we can send over Trunk Greenhammer or someone."

Murray Miller shook his head. "Naw, I don't need to talk to Trunk. Heck, I don't even care about interviewing Brett. I'm here to talk to *you*, the newest member of the team!"

Murray Miller must've been confused. "Well, tryouts are still happening," I explained.

"Not according to this final roster, they're not." Murray Miller unfolded a single sheet of paper in his tiny hands. "Coach

Stetson gave me the roster this morning. Very official. Take a look."

My hands were trembling as I took the roster. I scanned down to the bottom. There, listed right below "Parker, Brett," was my very own name. Not "Brett's Little Brother." Not "Thor, God of Thunder." But "Parker, Wyatt." Sophomore. Right tackle. Number 67.

I felt so happy I could puke.

Murray Miller must've felt uncomfortable being a part of this little moment I was having with myself, because he softly cleared his throat before interrupting. "Gee, don't look so surprised, kid. Now, mind if I ask you a couple questions?"

Murray Miller reached into the pocket of his corduroys and pulled out a mini notepad. My pulse was jackhammering. I was still trying to process the news, and now I had to give an interview? Soon my thoughts would travel from my mouth to that notepad, then to Murray Miller's typewriter, then to the entire town, to my team, to my whole school.

With this blast of anxiety came a second kind of rush, one that I'd never really felt before. It was like adrenaline, but more than that. A part of me felt like: *You know what, Wyatt? You're on varsity now, and hell yeah people want to talk to you and hear your thoughts and your one-liners and your scoops. And you know what else? You deserve this attention. You worked your ass off this summer. You earned this.*

Man, that moment was energizing, standing there with Murray Miller, the town's megaphone, as he held pencil to notepad.

This was what it was like to experience pride. And not superficial pride like when you get a triple kill in *Call of Duty* but real, actual, in-your-heart pride, the kind that comes when, for a brief and surreal moment, your inner voice and the outside world synchronize to say in a single confident declaration: *You did good.*

"First question," Murray Miller said, angling his notepad to protect it from the slanting wind and rain. "How, in your opinion, is Brett feeling about the season?"

Oh.

I should've known. I really should've. Brett's a quiet guy, an impossible nut to crack, so people have always tried to get in his head through me, the guy who's shared a bunk with Brett for the last sixteen years.

"Brett and I have talked a lot about this upcoming season," I lied. "A *lot*. And he told me that he's excited."

"About . . . ?"

"The season."

"I see."

A row below us, my dad sighed and got to his feet. He took his knife and slowly made his way down the bleachers, one half step and one grimace at a time. He'd move by taking a regular stride with his left leg followed by a long, looping swing of his right leg, which was stiff as a board. Dad messed up his hip in the championship game of his senior season, and now twenty-five years later the doctor said all the cartilage in his right socket was gone. With each step bone was grinding on bone. He needed a hip replacement, but when Dad saw the surgery cost he said he could catch every fish in the sea and still not have enough dough to pay that type of goddam bill.

When Dad reached the bottom row of the bleachers he sat down and continued watching and knife-spinning.

"So far Brett's looking like he hasn't missed a beat," Murray Miller said. "Have you noticed any limitations from the . . . um, you know . . . from what happened last year?"

Both of us looked down at the field, where Brett roped another bullet to a streaking wideout.

"He seems good to me," I said.

"So Brett's fully recovered, right?" Murray Miller asked.

"I think so."

"And in good shape?"

Three days after the surgery to reset the bone, my dad got Brett a used stationary bike. We had no clue how Dad got it to our duplex, considering we didn't own a car. I joked that maybe Dad had ridden the bike home. That got a laugh outta Brett. And even though he was real high on painkillers at the time, I felt something like pride in my joke.

"Yes, Brett's in good shape."

"And it's fair to say that Derek Leopold and Blakemore have something major to worry about this coming Friday?"

I sensed what Murray Miller was trying to do here, and I was pretty impressed with myself for recognizing it. There was no way I was going to get suckered into insulting Blakemore and giving them "bulletin-board material" for inspiration. Luckily,

I've watched enough NFL interviews to know the art of giving non-answer answers.

"Well, we respect Blakemore as a team," I said. "We're going to come out and try to run the football early. We'll also try to pass the football early. We'll kick the football early, too, if we lose the coin toss."

"Yes," Murray Miller said with restrained frustration. "But we're going to get revenge on Friday, right?"

"I just want to thank God and my teammates for the opportunity to play Friday."

"Yes, yes," Murray said dully. He wasn't writing any of this down. "But it's fair to say we're looking good again, right? That Grayport's going to be back on top?"

And then something occurred to me. As I looked down at Murray Miller with his wide imploring eyes and his furry little mustache, as I took in his faded tweed jacket with holes so big you could see them through his cloudy plastic poncho (which also had holes), I realized that Murray the Reporter didn't need assurance of our dominance so much as Murray the Grayport Resident did. All of Grayport needed it. Every day the town opens the *Grayport Gazette* to see a blast of the usual headlines: Crime is up, jobs are down, and the rain will be sideways. But when the annual Football Preview hit the stands in three days, they'd also get to read some good news: Grayport football is back and ready to kick some effing ass.

"You know what, Murray Miller?" I said, suddenly emboldened. "Come kickoff Friday, we're going to punch Blakemore right in the mouth. In fact, you might even say we're going to go bitchcakes."

"Bitchcakes?"

"Bitchcakes."

"Alright, bitchcakes." Murray Miller giggled and wrote this down. I started feeling that adrenaline-type rush again, but now it was laced with a lust for revenge. I fueled the fire by thinking of Derek Leopold and how all he got was a personal foul for his hit on Brett. And while Brett spent the next year on a stationary bike with his arm in a cast, Leopold went on to lead the county in tackles and sacks, become the league MVP, and make a verbal commitment to play college ball at USC, where it never rains and where the water is too warm for mackerel.

"Not sure I can say 'bitchcakes' in the paper," said Murray Miller between giggles. "Got another way of putting it?"

Unlike Nate, I didn't have a big brother who kept me updated on the coolest new lingo. But I *did* remember Trunk bragging in the locker room about how that summer he took some kid named Tyler to Pound Town. That sounded decent enough.

"Let's just say we're pretty fired up to take Derek Leopold to Pound Town."

Alright, I'm going to pause a moment to share three important points with you. Maybe you already knew them, but I sure as hell didn't:

First, Tyler can sometimes be a girl's name. Second, "Pound Town," it turns out, is typically located in bed, on a couch, or in the back seat of a car. And, finally, to get to "Pound Town," you don't take the Pain Train, as I thought. You take the Boner Express to Penetration Station.

Of course Murray Miller knew none of this either. "'Pound Town'—I love it," he said, furiously scribbling on his notepad. "This really is good stuff. 'Pound Town,'" he repeated. "I mean, that's headline material right there!"

"We've been waiting all summer to take these guys to Pound Town," I added. "We know they're into being dirty. But you know what? We can get dirty, too. We're gonna stuff them. And as Coach Crooks said just today, we're gonna to keep coming and coming and coming."

"This is perfect. Just perfect," Murray Miller said, still scribbling. "And I can quote you on this?"

"Oh, definitely. The name's Wyatt. Don't you forget it. W-Y-A-T-T."

CHAPTER
SIX

"We're Taking Derek Leopold to Pound Town," Vows Brett Parker's Little Brother
Grayport Prepares to Get Dirty with Blakemore Friday Night

I wasn't too psyched about the "Brett's Little Brother" part, but overall, since I didn't yet know about my Pound Town gaffe, I was happy with the headline. I pounced on the paper when it hit our steps, then sprinted up to our attic bedroom so I could read my interview. I was so excited I didn't notice the Grayport sweatband looped around our outer doorknob. That was Brett's signal that he wanted privacy.

I had never in my life seen Brett flustered. But, for the half second as I flung the door open, I saw a brief yet vivid flicker of panic in him. I couldn't pick out many features of the object in his hand, other than that it was shiny and sharp. I did see where he quickly stashed it, though: under his top bunk, between his mattress and the piece of old plywood that supported it.

* * *

It'd been about six years since I last checked under Brett's mattress. He was in sixth grade at the time, and his class was away on a field trip to the Museum of Fine Arts, about forty-five minutes south in Boston. Only Brett wasn't allowed to go. Mom had moved in with our aunt Jackie by then, and Dad refused to sign Brett's permission slip because he said art was "some wussy bullcrap." Art was a gateway to becoming soft, he said, which made you a liability to your teammates, who were counting on you to go balls out every play. After Dad's lecture Brett nodded and said, "Yes, sir," as always.

The afternoon of the trip, while Brett worked on agility drills with Dad at the field, I took the opportunity to snoop around his stuff and peek under his mattress. That's where I found a secret folder brimming with watercolors painted on computer paper that Brett must've swiped from the printers at school. They were pretty good, actually. Each one depicted the same scene over and over: a sun rising over the ocean horizon that lies just beyond Grayport Field. The focus was on the sea, which was uncharacteristically calm and bursting with colors that danced on the waves, a mix of oranges and reds and purples all bleeding into a dark blue sea whose horizon seemed to stretch to infinity, or at the very least Boston, where Brett's class was now touring the Museum of Fine Arts without him.

I remember being surprised at how much those pictures made my heart hurt. My eyes got a little moist as I stood there holding those watercolors, each one painted so painstakingly, signed so proudly, folded up so carefully, and tucked so shamefully under the mattress. I didn't allow myself to cry, though. Wussy bullcrap and all that.

An inch of the mystery object was sticking out from beneath Brett's mattress. Yup, it was definitely metallic and pointy. It looked sharp.

Brett was only in his boxers. He continued his morning routine as if nothing had happened, slabbing on deodorant and throwing on a pair of old jeans.

I sat down on my bed and pretended to read the paper. I was scared and I wasn't sure why.

"Hey, Brett?" I said after a moment.

"Yeah?"

"I was wondering . . ." My voice trailed off as I figured out where to go next. "Well, I was wondering why Dad's making bacon downstairs."

"I think some guy is having breakfast with me and Dad," Brett said.

On cue we heard the buzzer go off on our apartment unit. Dad shouted at Brett to get his butt downstairs, so Brett slipped on a shirt and headed for the door. In one fluid movement he pulled it closed while he quietly slipped the Grayport sweatband off the knob and into his pocket.

Even after pulling it out from the mattress, the mystery object remained a mystery to me. I'd never really seen anything like it. It was a little like a pair of small metal tongs, only instead of the tips being flat and blunt, they were sharp and pointed. The two "legs" could be pulled about six inches apart, and there was a sliding ruler that measured the distance between them. It looked like some sort of medieval torture device. Next to the device was also a small notebook with dozens of tiny numbers in Brett's handwriting. Weird. I slipped both the mystery contraption and the notebook back under Brett's mattress and made my way to the stairs. On to the next mystery: the strange man below.

About halfway down the attic stairs there's a spot where you can sit down, lean your head against the left wall, and see most of our tiny kitchen table. It's dark in the stairway, and in my experience nobody notices you if you're real quiet.

I watched Dad open our kitchen door and let in a grave-looking man of about fifty. He was wearing crisp pleated pants, black sneakers, and a mesh polo shirt. This is the unofficial uniform of college football recruiters. They used to come by all the time, spinning dreams of scholarships and Heisman Trophies and NFL draft bonuses. But that was before the injury. Now we get this guy, the lone recruiter to come all year. And we had to impress him. Hence the bacon.

My dad forced a big fake smile and beckoned in the scout. "Sir, I'd like you to meet my son Brett."

The recruiter shook Brett's hand, then took a full step back to scan him from head to toe. Scouts have no hesitation sizing you up right there on the spot, like a farmer inspecting a prized steer for sale.

"Looking good there, Brett. Looking *real* good," the man said. "I can see that the famous Grayport fish diet is getting you nice and lean."

He reached into a duffel bag he'd brought with him and pulled out a scale. "Mind if we get the measurements out of the way?"

The man and my dad watched as Brett unbuckled his belt and jeans and slid them down to his ankles. He slipped off his shirt and moved toward the scale.

"Socks, too," mumbled the scout.

Brett followed orders, then stepped on the scale. The scout recorded the number. My dad craned his neck to see what he was writing. The scout pulled out a tape measure and took Brett's height, then after rummaging around his duffel for a moment, he pulled out the same strange contraption Brett had hidden under his mattress.

The scout got down on one knee and with his thumb and index finger pinched together the skin on Brett's stomach. With the other hand he brought the metal device and clamped the sharp points onto the skin. He turned his head sideways to read the number on the sliding ruler. Brett was stone-faced.

"Twenty-eight point six body mass index," he said, getting back to his feet. "Not bad, but generally we want our skill position players to be in the twenty-six range."

Up on the stairs, I was feeling funny. Watching Brett get poked and prodded like a piece of meat made me feel bad for him, but I was also annoyed. Almost angry. Clearly, Brett was hiding the body-fat measuring tool from me because he thought it'd make me feel bad. Like my fat self was too sensitive to watch him measure himself every day as he honed his perfect body by fractions of pounds. Who was he to decide that I needed protection from reality?

At the same time, though, I knew he was probably right. I *would* be rattled whenever I saw that fat-measurer thing. For me losing 2 percent body fat would be as unnoticeable, weight-wise, as tossing a deck chair off a steamship. I had lost ten pounds from training over the summer, and my body fat percentage was still probably way off the charts. I didn't need a constant reminder of that. I bet that stupid thing wouldn't even stretch wide enough to measure the rolls of my stomach.

I'd seen enough. I got up from my step, but the mass of my weight creaked the stairs loudly. Everyone downstairs glared up at me.

"Would you look at this big fella!" the scout exclaimed. "Why don't you come down here and have some breakfast with us." He held out a piece of bacon like he was beckoning a zoo animal.

I tentatively made my way down the stairs and sat at the table with the scout, my dad, and Brett, who was still in his underwear. I took the scout's bacon.

"This here is my other son, Wyatt." My dad awkwardly patted me on the shoulder. "As you can see," he added, chuckling uneasily, "Wyatt ate all of Brett's tartar sauce growing up."

The scout and my dad laughed, and I did, too, hating myself the whole time.

"They really are brothers, though," my dad confirmed, addressing the elephant (literally) in the room.

"Wyatt trained with me all summer," Brett interjected. He stared hard into the scout's eyes.

"The boys worked their butts off this spring," my dad said. "Brett got his forty time down from 4.48 to 4.42 seconds. Isn't that right, son?"

"That's right."

The scout looked pleased. "Well, we're monitoring your progress carefully at Boston College, Brett. Show what you had when you were fully healthy your sophomore year, and that you can stay healthy for a whole season"—here he glanced at the scar on Brett's elbow—"and we'd be thrilled to get you over to BC. You ever been to Boston, Brett?"

"No, sir," Brett said dryly. "Only time I ever leave Grayport is to take care of business on away games."

"Well, you'll see the city soon enough," said the scout. Then, darting his eyes between Brett and my dad, he added in a hushed voice, "And you know, we can make admission assurances for Walter, too, if that would help convince Brett to get on board with us."

I racked my brain trying to think of Walter, that lucky

bastard. When I realized "Walter" was "Wyatt," and Wyatt was *me*, the whole awkward conversation was suddenly worth it. I'd never imagined an alternative to my future on the fishing boat, sifting through tangled nets of mackerels and seaweed. This news was even more mind-blowing than making varsity. But I had to act cool. *Come on, Wyatt, act cool.*

"Boston College with your brother. What would you say to that, Wayne?" the scout asked.

I forced myself to look the scout in the eyes because that's what normal, confident people do. "That . . . that'd be pretty amazeballs."

Instant regret. *Amazeballs? Wyatt, WTF?!*

Now all four of us were staring at our plates of bacon, enduring the heavy silence needed to fully process and recover from my cringeworthy comment.

That's when my phone buzzed in my pocket—a miraculous life vest tossed into this sinking conversation. Even better, the text was from Nate. We hadn't spoken since my cheap hit, and it was gnawing at me. I couldn't wait to tell him about Boston College. I quickly tapped open the text.

Hey dumbass do yourself a favor and google "Pound Town+ Definition."

Uh-oh.

Meanwhile the scout had scooted out his chair and extended his hand for a goodbye shake.

"It was great meeting you boys, and good luck, Brett. Just show us you can stay on the field all season and I'm sure we can work something out for you and Watson here." He then turned to my dad. "And it was a real honor meeting you, Mr. Parker. You boys probably know this, but your old man quarterbacked one of the great teams in high school history. You're lucky to have a mentor like that."

My dad's mouth twisted into a genuine smile, such a rarity it almost seemed like it hurt him. Then he clasped his hands together and instinctively fiddled the gleaming 1972 championship ring that rested where his wedding ring used to be.

CHAPTER
SEVEN

I definitely wasn't *scared* of going into our locker room's communal shower, despite what you might've heard. Sure, the idea of a sophomore like me stripping down and showering among an army of hairy, towel-snapping upperclassmen would've been plenty of reason to be intimidated. And yes, I've got a little extra padding on my stomach that makes my body feel carved more from marshmallow than from marble. I'll even confirm allegations that I sometimes swim with my shirt on at the pool, but that's only under unique circumstances, like if I suspect a girl is within fifty miles of me.

But I swear the only reason I spent the entire preseason showering by myself, way after the last hairy butt or six-pack left the shower room, was because of my post-practice duty of dragging all the tackling dummies into the equipment shed. It was pure coincidence that the showers would be empty by the time I put away the dummies, trudged all the way to the locker room, trekked all the way *back* to the shed to double-check that

I'd locked it, then hiked back again to the locker room, taking detours as necessary if I saw a piece of trash in the distance that was, like, ruining Grayport's natural beauty or whatever. I wouldn't say I'm an environmentalist, but I do my part.

All new players on varsity were assigned a team chore, and I was pretty pumped that I got Dummy Duty. This was a real big responsibility since the dummies were pristine and beautiful and expensive, a much-celebrated donation from Trunk Greenhammer's dad. He owned the biggest fishing boat in town, making the Greenhammers one of the wealthiest families in Grayport, a point that Trunk liked to remind you about every now and again and again and again.

The dummies were probably the most expensive equipment we had, so you can imagine my stress when I got to the equipment shed before our first official "game week" practice and found the lock missing.

The door was cracked open, so I peeked in. Ten faces were staring back at me.

Whoever had broken into the shed to "decorate" the dummies must've done it in the dark. The "head" section of each dummy had newly acquired eyes and frowning mouths outlined in silver duct tape, but they were slapped on crookedly, like a Picasso portrait. They were clearly faces, though. Clear, too, was the number the silver tape had crudely sketched on each chest section. It was 67, a lineman's number.

My number.

Well, here was a good old-fashioned mindpretzel. This

situation could've meant two very different things. On the one hand, this seemed like an obvious and somewhat elaborate attempt to humiliate me. This wasn't exactly like looking into a mirror, but it definitely hit home seeing those bloated dummies staring back at me. They were blobbish, a little squishy, pathetic-looking.

67, 67, 67, 67.

There was also a threat-ish feeling to this. Tackling dummies are targets, and I imagined my teammates eagerly lining up to smash the Wyatt dummies, like in movies when guys take turns throwing darts at a picture of their enemy's face. So I did what you always do when you discover someone may hate you: I scanned through all my flaws/mistakes/annoying traits to figure out what I'd done wrong. A real good exercise for your self-esteem, let me tell you. An avalanche of potential evidence crashed down. My Pound Town gaffe was an obvious one. And in case you were wondering if I'm an asshole, I once used the term "cognitive dissonance" to complain about a plot hole in *Toy Story 2*.

But what bothered me most was a series of linked fears that I'd been trying to ignore since I'd made varsity a few days earlier. I was petrified that my teammates thought I only made the team because my brother was the star quarterback. Even worse was my fear that they might be right. Maybe I didn't earn my jersey, my #67. Maybe a name on a roster didn't automatically make you a true member of the Grayport brotherhood.

But but but! What if—and hear me out for a sec—what if

those dummies were actually my initiation into the brotherhood? When it came to ball-busting, guys on the team were *ruthless* to each other, and the insults they zinged at each other actually made their bonds tighter. Like the other day I'd overheard Trunk tell his best friend, Gunner, that his birth certificate should've been a written apology from the condom factory. Sometimes the guys would even give *Brett* shit, and he was easily the most respected dude on the team.

So maybe these Wyatt dummies were just some good-natured hazing? Maybe when I dragged them onto the field everyone would laugh, and I would, too, which my teammates would respect, and the prank's ringleader would throw a friendly arm around my shoulders and tussle my hair and be like, "Aw, we're just screwin' with you, kid," before adding, "Hey, tonight me and the guys are throwing back some beers with some girls, if you wanna join." And then on cue I'd be like, "Sorry, bro, I already got plans to give your mom a tour of the condom factory," which wouldn't even make total sense, but everyone including the ringleader would crack up at my sick burn, and it would be understood that yes, count me in on the beers with the pretty girls.

It's said that anonymous wrongs are the most cowardly sort, but I now know that they're not gutless—they're pure, diabolical genius. Because here's the thing: Since I didn't know who taped my number to the dummies, I couldn't help but be paranoid and suspect that *everyone* on the team was in on it.

Throughout warm-ups nobody said a word to me about the

dummies *or* Pound Town, and it was driving me insane. Like, was this over, or just beginning? Was it one guy, or many? Did Brett know about it? This was mental terrorism at its finest.

After stretches and individual drills, it was time to run through a few reps of the tackle-eligible pass. This would be a great chance for Brett to show off his skills to the Boston College scout, who was watching practice with my dad and Mr. Green-hammer. I was once again the live bait for the drill.

While I stood in my T-pose waiting for the play to start, I had a chance to scan most of the team, who were all facing me. Nobody was laughing at me or using their finger to mime a knife across their throat, the universal gesture for "I'm going to kill you for publicly announcing that we want to engage in homoerotic coitus with our archenemy." So I still had no idea what, if any, type of shit I was in. What I did know was that during Coach Crooks's review of the play, and then again while Brett called the pass in the huddle, Trunk stared at me unceasingly.

Brett, on the other hand, was distracted. I could tell. During practice his focus was usually laser sharp, but that afternoon I noticed he had that kink in his neck, that frequent yet subtle side glance to the bench where our dad stood with arms crossed and a sharp toothpick dangling from his thin lips.

Brett never said it, but I could tell he *hated* playing with Dad there. After each incomplete pass Brett's head would twitch, seemingly against his will, toward the sideline, where Dad would be motioning to him to get his elbow up, his front shoulder level, and his *head outta his butt*. Dad's presence made no difference to me—once it became clear my body type was more lineman than quarterback, he lost all interest in my development. Probably a good thing—I'm not sure fathers beam with pride when their sons are demoted to below a tackling dummy on the depth chart.

"Hut, HUT!" Brett took the next snap and glided back in his five-step drop. Trunk exploded out of his three-point stance and chugged at full steam toward me, the stand-in for that scumbag-piece-of-shit linebacker Derek Leopold. I stood there, loyal tackling dummy that I was, and braced for impact.

The past couple of practices Trunk had followed Crooks's orders by giving me a quick forearm shiver before proceeding downfield on his pass route. But something felt different this time. Something felt really wrong. Trunk's all-out sprint seemed fueled on a reckless rage. The Pain Train was coming my way, and I wasn't a pit stop but the final destination. I saw seething eyes, flaring nostrils, pulsing neck veins. I saw murderous intentions. I saw a flash of my gravestone: *Here Lies What's Left of Brett's Younger Brother, May He Rest in Peace and May His Internet History Never Be Checked.*

I saw Trunk lower his shoulder and launch every ounce of his armored frame at me, and then I watched my feet, acting on some primal instinct I never knew I had, quickly shuffle to the side. I watched Trunk hurtle past me like a bull whiffing on a matador, and I watched his feet try—and fail—to catch up to his stumbling momentum.

Trunk landed a full spread-eagle belly flop in the mud. Brett's pass whistled in the air to the spot where Trunk should've been. The ball landed in a puddle with a horrible *splat*.

Coach Crooks's fury echoed across the old wooden stadium.

"GREENHAMMER, YOU SON OF A BITCH!" I felt instant relief that Crooks seemed to blame Trunk, and not me, for committing Grayport football's cardinal sin: making Brett look bad. And in front of a scout, no less.

Crooks can move pretty quick for a guy who waddles like he's got a giant dump in his shorts. He dashed at Trunk, who was now getting to his feet.

The old man grabbed Trunk's face mask and effortlessly pulled Trunk down within an inch of his snarling, tobacco-filled mouth.

"What in the fuck was that?" he snarled.

"Coach, it was Wyatt! He moved when he wasn't sup—"

"No excuses, Greenhammer! Wyatt's got the mobility of a fire hydrant! Sit your butt on the bench. Go on—get outta my sight!"

Benching Trunk in front of his dad and the scout was bad, but Crooks wasn't done. For committing the cardinal sin, Trunk had to be punished with something truly and utterly humiliating.

"Wyatt!"

"Yes, Coach?"

"Take Trunk's place. Let's go, men! Run it again!"

Now *I* had that damn kink in my neck. I glanced at Dad on

the sideline as I ran to the huddle, and I peeked his way twice as Brett called the play. I don't know why I kept doing it. Back in sixth grade I'd decided that if Dad wasn't going to care about my football career, if he'd rather take the focus he would've wasted on me and repurpose it to double down on Brett, then I wasn't going to care about his opinion. He was kind of a bastard, and it's dumb to give a shit about what bastards think, right?

So then why did I keep looking over to the sideline at Dad like he'd actually meet my eyes, give me a nod of encouragement? Or even a small smile in recognition that I'd finally made it to the first team huddle (even if temporarily)? Looking through the fog at his cold, uncaring stare gave me a sharp pang in my gut. It intensified when I shifted my focus to the scout with his intimidating clipboard and then to Trunk standing in the human wall with the backups, mud caking his jersey and hatred sneering his face.

In the huddle I heard Brett growl out the play call. "E-2, 34 play-action, tackle-eligible pass."

I snapped my attention back inside the huddle and looked at Brett, who'd been watching me watching my dad.

"Hey, Wyatt," he said, quiet but stern. "Let's do this."

Just five words, but I swear it felt like I'd just heard the Gettysburg Address.

"Alright, boys, on two, on two. Ready, BREAK."

I hustled to the line and quickly got into my three-point stance so I could still my shaking hand against the cool ground.

I always loved getting into my three-point stance. I don't care if you're in Pop Warner or the pros, there's always something so electrifying about putting your hand in the dirt and coiling your body into a compact ball of potential energy. That's gotta be up there with the world's most satisfying feelings of antici-pation. I may not be able to tell you what it's like to ask a girl out, or what it's like to crack open a fresh beer on the beach with friends by your side, stars above your head, and a whole Satur-day night of laughter ahead of you, but I *can* tell you about the exhilaration of crouching into a three-point stance with ten teammates at your side, ready to go to war with each other.

Brett strode up to the center slowly, confidently. I looked ahead. So much open field in front of me.

"Ready, set! Hut, HUT!"

Do you ever have nightmares where you're desperately trying to run away from a zombie or a Trunk or a zombie Trunk, and your legs refuse to move fast enough, like you're in quicksand? That's how it feels for us fat kids every time we run. I didn't so much burst out of my stance as ooze out of it, like the last glob of tartar in a glass bottle. As I slogged downfield, churning my feet and pumping my arms forward, my stomach bounced back and forth in large heaves, cutting against my momentum like a fierce crosswind. Take it from me: The one thing worse than feeling embarrassed by your body is feeling betrayed by it.

When I made it fifteen yards downfield, I glanced over my shoulder to gauge how the play was developing and to see if practice had ended in the time it took me to run that far. Even as I looked back I made sure to keep sprinting ahead, remembering how with Brett you just need to keep running your route and trust that he'll deliver the ball into your lap. I saw him bouncing lightly on the balls of his feet, his arm cocked by his right ear and his eyes locked on me downfield. Then in an instant his back shoulder dipped and his arm morphed into a blur as it whipped forward. The ball soared into the sky, slicing through the shelf of fog that hung resolutely above us, and disappeared.

I snapped my head forward and kept running my route.

Alright, I retold this next part to Murray Miller and his notepad so many times that I'm kind of sick of it. But here's a quick version of what went down:

Basically, I'm hauling butt downfield, right? And just as I'm about to reach the end zone I look into the gray sky. Sure enough, there's the football magically rematerializing through the fog like an old lost promise from Brett to me. Tight spiral, on time, on target.

I extend my arms to haul it in, but then, outta the corner of my eye, I see a *second object* falling from the sky. It's about the size of a football, but wobbling like crazy as it missiles to the earth. I keep my focus locked on Brett's pass. Gotta catch it. *Gotta* catch it. The ball floats down onto my fingertips, and I'm about to wrap it in my warm embrace when *WHAM*, I feel the impact of that second falling object slam hard into my collarbone.

I stumble. I fall. I groan. Brett's pass falls with a *thud* and skitters out the back of the end zone.

I'm lying face-first in the mud, enjoying a good wallow, when I hear shouts of confusion as my teammates and coaches rush toward me. I sit up and look at my unidentified flying assailant.

Lying next to me, its neck grotesquely twisted, is a dead seagull.

Two senior wide receivers, Ranger Waxman and Maddox Ownsby, were the first to get to me.

"Jesus, Wyatt, what happened?" Ranger said, taking a knee next to me.

Dazed, I unbuckled my chin strap and took off my helmet. "The seagull. It's dead."

"Yeah, no shit. Did the pass hit it?"

"No, it, like . . . it just fell from the sky. Onto me. I think it died in midair."

My collarbone was starting to sting. I rubbed it, but that hurt more. I felt something gooey on my hand. The seagull's beak or talons or whatever must've cut me, because blood was smeared on my fingertips.

"Dude," Ranger said.

"*Dude*," Maddox added.

"Back away, back *away!*" Coach Crooks urgently brushed past Maddox and Ranger and me, then crouched down to inspect the bird, probably to check if it was dinner material.

The rest of the offense followed behind him, some surrounding me, others studying the bird. Its beady yellow eyes and half-open beak were frozen in an expression of shock. Maybe it had seen me trying to run.

"Wyatt, man, you should probably go to the trainer or something," Ranger said. "That thing's probably got nasty bird diseases. Like bird herpes or whatever."

"There's no such thing as bird herpes," I said more hopefully than confidently.

"Why not? There's such a thing as cat herpes."

Ranger had me there. I specifically remembered how my freshman year this girl named Elizabeth Pope held a bake sale to raise funds for cat herpes research. I bought six brownies in the name of feline philanthropy.

"Wyatt, get your ass up," Coach Crooks said, waddling over to me. "No one sits on my field."

I scrambled to my feet, and a team manager handed me a water bottle. I squirted it onto my cut because it seemed like a badass thing to do. It stung like a mofo, but I held back a wince. Showing pain was expressly not allowed on the Grayport football field.

"I don't think you can just *wash off* bird herpes," Ranger said.

This was all getting very overwhelming. "I'm fine. Really."

Coach Stetson had arrived now and he crouched next to the seagull with my dad. He called for Coach Crooks, who hobbled over and squatted his stiff body down next to the two crouching men. My dad had taken out his fishing knife and used its point to gently lift up one of the bird's wings.

"Coach, you ever seen anything like this?"

Coach Crooks looked at the seagull's underwing and froze. Thin, bright red lines, like veins, spider-webbed across its pink flesh. A thin film of red goop covered the skin.

Crooks rose slowly to his feet and, without saying a word, limped over to the stands in the back end zone.

My dad watched him warily. "You alright, Coach?"

But Crooks said nothing as he climbed the wooden planks of the stands. When he reached the top, about twenty rows up, he looked out onto the ocean. The wind howled. The rain was picking up. A tingle shot down my spine when I saw the expression on Crooks's face, an expression I *never* thought I'd see from him: fear.

Coach Stetson looked nervous, another emotion you just never saw on the Grayport football field. "We're calling it a day, boys," he said quietly, still looking at Crooks.

We all stood there confused. This was unprecedented. In Grayport, calling off football practice was like the Church calling off Christmas.

Stetson sensed us all standing around. "Did I stutter?" he snapped. "Let's go! Hit the showers. Especially you, Wyatt. I don't know what killed that bird, but you should wash off quick as you can."

"But, uh, but . . . I got Dummy Duty."

"Forget it today. Shower up with your teammates."

Trunk has the type of presence you can feel even when he's standing behind you, and I instinctively flinched a split second before I felt his giant hand clomp down onto my shoulder.

"Come on, Wyatt," he growled. "Let's hit the showers."

CHAPTER
EIGHT

I know you'll hardly believe this, but I should confess that I was, in fact, a little scared of the communal shower. And by "a little" I mean I'd rather die of bird herpes than set foot in there with Trunk & Co.

When I got to my locker I pulled off my shoulder pads, dabbed my bird wound with a towel, plopped down on the chair, and pretended to have trouble untying my cleats. I waited until the majority of guys had disappeared into the shower room before getting naked myself. First I peeled off my wet T-shirt. Then in a single, carefully planned motion I pulled down my girdle, snatched up the towel I had positioned by my feet, and quickly wrapped it around my lower half.

A picture of my dad from his Grayport football days hung alongside a dozen other grim faces on our locker room's Wall of Fame, and he watched me as I walked the plank to the block of heavy steam that marked the entrance to the shower room.

The air wafting from the showers was hot and sticky and smelled like Axe body wash—you know, that sickly-sweet soap that comes in scents called "Alpha Downpour" or "Midnight Pulse for Badass Dudes with Extra Sensitive Skin" and whose glowing colors are so neon that a single drop on your skin will ensure all your future children will have nineteen toes and three very jacked arms.

My towel came a few inches short of wrapping all the way around my waist, so I had to use both hands to hold it together. I was squeezing the life out of it as I stood at the threshold of the steam listening to the guys inside chat and blurt out their fucks and faggots and cunts over the hot hiss of the showers. I was waiting for an ideal time to enter, as if the group would suddenly break into a conversation about how chicks love dudes with chest hair that sprouted only around their nipples, and then I'd roll in all arrogant, like here comes Mr. Steal Yo' Girl.

Spoiler alert: That's not how it went down. I did overhear the conversation turn to me, though.

"No but seriously, how crazy was that bird hitting Wyatt?"

Ranger's voice. I had to really concentrate to make it out over the loud patter of the showers. Man, I was really choking the hell out of my towel.

"The thing kamikazed right into him!" someone added.

"Like it was aiming for him."

"Naw"—this was Trunk, no mistaking his gravelly rasp— "it was sucked outta the sky. Wyatt's gut is so big it's got its own gravitational pull."

In my alternate timeline as Thor, God of Thunder, Taker of No Shit, this is when I stroll into the shower room and say,

"Trunk, you sure know a lot about physics for a guy who's failed it twice." But I'm just Wyatt, God of Stalling, Needer of Wider Towels. I kept idling by the shower entrance, out of sight.

"Hey, have you guys considered"—here was Ranger's voice again—"that maybe—and I'm just throwing it out there—that maybe, judging from Crooks's reaction and all, that the gull died from, like, you know, that what killed it wasn't bird herpes or whatever, but maybe, if you think about it—"

"Range, what the fuck are you blathering about?"

"Yeah, man, you're rambling like Crooks on a bender."

Ranger's voice took a sudden sharp edge. "Oh, come on, do I really have to say it? Fine. That bird died from red tide, and all you assholes know it."

No retorts, no jokes, no vocal response at all—just the heavy patter of shower water hitting ceramic tile. Ranger's words wafted through the air and were inhaled like poison deep into our cores, where long buried memories of red tide waited to erupt at the slightest disturbance.

It'd been eight years since red tide last hit our shores, eight years since rumors that the ocean had magically changed colors spread through the halls of Grayport Elementary, prompting us all to sprint eagerly from school to Grayport Field, where we climbed the bleachers so we could see in the far distance the enormous blob of bloodred water oozing toward the beach. The girls made faces and said "gross" but we guys said "awesome" and awaited the red blob's landfall eagerly, naively, stupidly.

I remember using my street hockey stick to poke the first dead seal that washed in with red tide. I was so excited I practically needed my inhaler. I poked the second dead seal, too. But then came the third, the fourth, the fifth. That's when I realized the red algae that had colored the bay bright crimson wasn't amazeballs or awesomesauce or even the tits—it was an outbreak. The poisonous microorganisms were unstoppable, ruthlessly killing everything that swam in them. At night Brett and I had to sleep with our window closed because the rotting flesh of the seal carcasses, now numbering in the hundreds, smelled worse than death. Our shore was littered with thousands and thousands of fish decaying in red slime.

Grayport Harbor shut down, and our town, poor even before red tide, had to survive three months without fishing earnings, which would be like asking you to survive three months without oxygen. A few of the businesses that closed then have since reopened, but most of them, like my mom's old shop, called Fudge by Anna, are still boarded up now, eight years later. During red tide the only store with a line at the register was Hal's Liquor Emporium. And I'd need a whole 'nother book to describe the devastating rise of drug use. Heroin became a big effing problem because apparently it was dirt cheap compared to other drugs. Heroin was red tide's tentacles reaching from sea to land, snatching up the unemployed, the broken, and the hopeless.

Ranger, taking the room's tense hush as tacit agreement that the dead gull probably meant the return of red tide, was the first to break the silence. "If red tide is really back, do you think they'll cancel Friday's game?"

This was an absurd idea—the only disaster that could devastate the town enough to cancel Grayport football would be, well, the cancellation of Grayport football, which is to say it's invincible. But the somber mood of the room held the guys back from giving him shit. Plus there was definitely some communal sympathy for what red tide had done to Ranger's big brother, a former Grayport football player who's currently living at a heroin rehab facility that his family can't really afford.

Every guy in the shower room had his own never-discussed story about what red tide did to his family. Brett's is the same as mine, obviously, but he and I have never talked about those months so I wonder if he'd tell it the same way as I would. To me our red tide story starts two weeks after Dad's fishing boat had to shut down operations. This left Mom and her Fudge by Anna store as our only means of income. Things were a little tight (my parents' favorite phrase), so one afternoon Dad went out to sell our shabby car to a scrap metal business a couple of towns over. He returned after dark, and with no explanation he unplugged the TV in our living room and carried it up to the attic bedroom that Brett and I shared. Almost every night for the next six weeks my parents would come into our room, turn the volume way, way up on SpongeBob and his square pants, then head back downstairs to argue about money in the kitchen, always forgetting in half a second that they were trying to whisper.

The accusations came fast, furious, and loud: Mom telling Dad that there must be work *somewhere* if only you'd *look* a little harder; Dad saying I may not have a job but goddammit at least I'm not *losing* us money, which is the case with you and your goddam fudge shop, a real drain, that thing, your most expensive decision since Wyatt; Mom saying speaking of *drains*, that's where your stash of whiskey—there seems to be plenty enough money for *that*, by the way—is headed if you don't shape up and start acting like a man; Dad saying it's not whiskey I'm drinking but actually a magical antidote to your constant nagging, which, by the way, sounds just like *THIS*:

And he'd smash a plate or glass against the wall.

Then there'd be silence if we were lucky, Mom crying if we weren't, followed by the sound I began to dread most, the one I still fear, the slow *creak . . . creak . . . creak* of Dad limping his damaged hip up the squeaky stairs to our attic room, where, even if we quickly turned off SpongeBob and pretended to be asleep, he'd aggressively shake Brett's shoulder. Then, in a whiskey breath I could smell from my bottom bunk, he'd order Brett to get outta bed so they could review some Pop Warner game film. They'd sit in front of our little TV for hours rewinding and rewatching all of Brett's incompletions. With each errant throw Dad would curse and take a long swig of whiskey until finally the remote slipped out of his hand and he passed out snoring on our cold hard floor with nothing but a pillow that Brett would tuck under his head.

The day Mom moved out was the same day that her fudge shop closed for good. That was week ten of red tide. I would've been sadder if I'd known that she'd never live with us again, that the divorce papers were already filed, but I believed the "it's only temporary" bullshit separated parents say. Dad never talked about Mom or asked how she was doing whenever Brett and I got back from visiting her at Aunt Jackie's house. In fact, Dad didn't mention her once in five years. If it weren't for the ghost of Mom's shop still haunting Main Street—everything boarded up other than the FUDGE BY ANNA sign eroding in the salt air—it would've felt like she had never lived with us in Grayport at all.

Then, the day after my thirteenth birthday, we got a phone call from Sheriff Murphy, an old football teammate of Dad's. It was snowing like crazy that night, I remember. It must've been like two or three A.M., so Brett and I crept downstairs to listen to Dad through his bedroom door.

"Okay . . . yes . . . alright. Thanks for the heads-up, Murph. I'll take care of it."

Dad hung up without saying goodbye, then flung open his door. He didn't even flinch to find us standing right there, staring back at him.

"Get dressed, both of you. We're going to Mom's shop."

"Now?"

"Now."

Vandalism is common in Grayport, especially since red tide left a shit ton of frustrated and bitter people with too much time on their hands. Still, it was pretty jarring when we trudged two miles in the dark to Mom's shop and saw her sign covered in spray paint. Everyone in town (except Dad) *loved* Mom and her little fudge store. Grayport needed all the sweetness it could get. I saw nothing but hate, though, as I looked through the night snow at the crude black letters sprayed onto Mom's FUDGE BY ANNA sign. The vandal had crossed out the BY and added a few letters. The sign now read: I FUDGE**D** ANNA.

Dad, Brett, and I didn't say anything the entire night—didn't want to, didn't need to. We just got to work setting up the two ladders we had lugged with us. We had a bucket of paint and about four hours until sunrise. Nobody was going to know about I FUDGED ANNA except us, Sheriff Murphy, and the asshole who did it.

The funny thing is, as I write it now, I'm realizing that this is a weirdly happy memory. Well, maybe not *happy*—but reassuring, in a way. I dunno, there was something kind of nice about the atmosphere. Like, the air was so cold that not only Grayport but also time itself seemed frozen still. Brett and Dad sat perched atop each ladder with their paintbrushes while I stood watch on the ground and supported each ladder with outstretched arms, the tips of my fingers numb 'cause Mom wasn't home to tell me to wear mittens. All three of us were working together and freezing our balls off until dawn, when the sun finally rose up to warm our red faces and melt the black ice that had crusted over Main Street. It was an act of love, what we did that night, maybe the last one our family's ever had.

If you asked Brett, I bet he'd say it was an act of duty. But I'm starting to think that a deep sense of duty toward someone is about the most raw and sincere form of love there is. You gotta believe that, anyway, or else you'll spend your whole life wondering if certain guys love anything at all.

Here in Grayport we're not so hot on things like love and the touchy-feelies. But if there was one scrap of positivity that rolled in with red tide, it was a general uptick in empathy. At least, that's the mood I was hoping for in the shower room when I took the red tide conversation as a (relatively) safe opportunity to creep in.

Of course, a guy my size creeps like a crack of thunder whis-pers. Amazingly, though, no one seemed to notice me when I first shuffled in, head down and both hands clutching my towel like it was the edge of a cliff. On muddy days (which in Gray-port means most days) the two drains in the middle of the room get clogged with muck and grass clippings. The water on the floor was already an inch deep, which wasn't so bad since normally by the time I finished Dummy Duty I'd be slushing through a soup of dirty water and soap suds up to my cankles.

The wall immediately to the right of the entrance was

covered in green tiles and lined with towel hooks. I lingered by the hooks for a moment as my eyes adjusted to the sting of the hot, soapy-sweet steam. Then I scanned the room, praying that one of the corner showers was free so I could implement my "shower and cower" technique that I had just invented in my head.

No dice. In fact, all the showers were taken.

Wait, never mind: I had overlooked a free showerhead right over ther—

Oh crap.

Crapcrapcrap.

Next to the lone open shower was Trunk's hulking frame. Huge, thick, and firm in all the places where mine sagged, Trunk's body faced the showerhead, revealing a massive back smeared with a collage of bruises, gashes, and seething red zits.

At least Brett was on the other side of the open showerhead. I'd be safe with him there.

Trunk spun around to rinse off his back. He was facing me now so I stood perfectly still. Predators have movement-based vision.

But I forgot they also can smell pheromones of fear. Trunk immediately locked eyes onto me.

"Well, well, well," he boomed. "Look who graced us with his presence. The man of the hour: Wyatt Porker! Shit, sorry—I mean Wyatt *Parker.*"

Trunk let loose a deep, loud chortle. But as he laughed I saw him subtly glance sideways at Brett. It wasn't a nervous glance,

I don't think. It was more of an investigative one, like he was gauging whether Brett would be bothered by the shot at me. The entire room was also looking at Brett for a cue on how to react. Permission to laugh, really.

Brett was expressionless. He casually reached for the soap dispenser. A cream-colored liquid shot into his hand and he began working it into a lather.

Permission granted.

Trunk's lips curled into a sneer as he looked back to me. "There's an open shower right here, Wyatt baby. Whaddya waiting for?"

There was nothing I could do now except hang up my towel and walk the longest ten yards of my life.

CHAPTER
NINE

You know how some people, usually stoners smoking pot or preppy kids eating red velvet cupcakes, talk about having an out-of-body experience? This was the exact opposite. I'd never been so *in* my body. As I sloshed naked through the inch-deep water to the showerhead, I felt every crevice, hair, stretch mark, and appendage being scanned by a small army of devastating-joke makers. The problem wasn't that I was the only player on the team who carried extra weight; the problem was *how* I carried it. Gravity was everything. See, while other linemen on my team also had big stomachs, love handles, and even stretch marks, their extra padding was solid and sturdy. Mine was soft and droopy. Theirs fought back against gravity, holding firm, bolstered by underlying muscle. Mine gave in to gravity, surrendering to its whims with each bounce and jiggle. Their weight was strength. Mine was weakness. *That* was the difference.

Take it from me: It's possible to be in a room with twenty-five guys who aren't wearing clothes, yet still be the only one who's naked. Worst of all, this was my fault because I didn't go into the shower room the first day of preseason with everyone else. Yeah, there might've been a couple wisecracks slung at me, but it would've ended there. Instead I avoided the shower room to the point where my daily absence became notable, which in turn made my entrance right now an *event*.

No one said anything during my walk. They knew this would be Trunk's show. When I got to my shower I didn't even wait for the water to warm up. I plunged right into it like it was a curtain I could hide in.

"Dude, you can stop sucking in your stomach now," Trunk said loudly. "We're all friends here."

How'd he know I was sucking in? Now I couldn't unfurl my stomach for my entire shower, a problem considering I was getting short on air.

"Actually, Wyatt, now that you're finally here, you can help us settle a little debate we've been having the last few weeks."

I was resolutely facing the wall, and in my periphery I noticed Trunk take a few steps to the center of the room. I glanced back and saw him, hands on hips, pissing into the drain, which was the center of the rapidly deepening stew of water, mud, soap suds, and now urine. Trunk looked over his shoulder at me as he pissed.

"We've been wondering," he went on, "when you're naked, right, and you look down, can you even see your dick over your gut?"

I can't. I'll admit that to you because you seem pretty alright.

I mean, you've now had to picture me naked in your head (sorry about that, btw) and you haven't chucked my book across the room. But Trunk's about as sensitive as a walrus, so I decided no answer was the best answer. I kept facing the wall. To my right Brett casually scrubbed out a stubborn patch of dirt on his left elbow.

My shower's water was warm now, and the cut from the seagull pelting was starting to sting. The heat of the room's steam suddenly hit me all at once. Beads of sweat joined shower water and poured down my forehead. It was so, so hot in there. I felt dizzy.

But Trunk was just starting to roll. "Holy shit, guys," I heard him shout from the center drain. "Wyatt, face me for a sec. I think I just realized something."

I slowly pivoted to the center of the room. My stomach had never felt so fucking huge, like it was inches from touching the floor.

Trunk had finished pissing, and now he was making a rectangular frame with his thumbs and index fingers. He held it up to his face and squinted one eye as he looked through the frame at me.

"With the two brothers standing side by side, it looks like one of those Weight Watchers 'Before and After' pictures!"

This got a big laugh from the group, and finally a response from Brett. He smirked, shook his head, then went back to scrubbing mud off his arms.

Trunk sloshed over to me and stuck his bright red face inches from mine. I noticed his right hand was clenched into a fist. He looked down at my stomach.

"Jesus, I gotta say, Wyatt, you really put the 'offensive' in 'offensive lineman.' I mean, look at that thing. Probably scares away girls big-time. No wonder you want to fuck Derek Leopold so bad—he's your only shot at ever getting laid."

Then Trunk did something that was infinity times worse than a punch to the gut. He loaded a curled index finger into his thumb, forming an OK sign, slowly placed it an inch from my belly button, and uncorked a single flick into my stomach.

THWOP.

I was pretty disappointed by my stomach's endurance, jiggle-wise. The whole room watched my flab ripple like the waves of the Grayport shore. This was humiliation on a scale I'd never thought possible.

My expression must've reflected my mortification because suddenly Trunk seemed to ease up. "Shit, Wyatt, I'm just fuckin' with you, man."

He stepped beside me and slapped a beefy arm around my shoulders. "You gotta loosen up, bro. Kinda like you were out there on the field today."

My neck rested in between the crook of Trunk's bicep and his forearm. I felt his muscles start to tighten like a vise.

"You were just so *smooth* with your footwork when you dodged me! Really showed off that famous *varsity* skill of yours." Trunk was smiling big and wide, but his arm coiled itself tighter around my neck. He pulled my head down a few inches into a semi headlock. I tried to subtly wriggle free, but his grip clenched even harder. I could hardly suck in any air.

"Yup, you made the Trunkster look like a real asshole out there. In front of the coaches . . ."

More pressure.

". . . in front of the scout . . ."

More pressure. Now I couldn't breathe. I felt faint. I was going to faint.

". . . and in front of my *FATHER*." Trunk's arm crunched down with ferocity. My windpipe was being crushed. I frantically wriggled my torso in attempt to break free but the death grip around my neck was permanent.

My next move was instinct. I barely even remember doing it at all. I lifted my right foot, and with 250 pounds of force, I slammed my heel down into the bony flat of Trunk's foot.

Trunk yelped and released me in one instant, then slammed a fist into my stomach the next.

"FIIIIIGHT!"

I wouldn't have called this a fight, but the declaration sprang from someone's mouth and made it so.

I was doubled over from the punch and gasping for air, but still managed to sense Trunk charging at me. I took a quick sideways step, so Trunk only managed to get one arm wrapped around me. His momentum carried both of us toward the wall. Brett dodged out of our path and my spine slammed hard into a protruding shower handle. Trunk's forehead hit the wall, opening a small gash that leaked blood down his face.

Trunk threw a hard punch into my stomach, and for a second I felt like I was going to puke up internal organs. He went for a third, but this time I managed to grab his meaty forearm with both hands. We were stuck in a kind of tug-of-war, and as I desperately clung to Trunk's arm I shot a quick look to Brett, like "help me, dude, please." Come on Brett please help me I'm scared. Please Brett you have to do something. Come on man please you're my After picture.

Brett watched intently. But that was all he did. He watched.

Trunk wrenched his arm free from my grip, and with both hands he grabbed on to the skin on the side of my ribs. His fingernails tore through my skin as he flung me to the floor at the center drain.

My knees and elbows smashed down at the same time. The soup of dirty water was a few inches deep now and it spattered in a small arch as I landed.

Suddenly it felt like there wasn't any air in the room for me to breathe. The physical exertion of the fight coupled with the room's wet heat had triggered a familiar suffocating feeling in my lungs, like I was trying to breathe through a straw. The asthma attack was here, a bigger threat than even Trunk. My lungs felt like they were shrinking into nothing. I opened my mouth to scream for help, to beg someone to get my inhaler from my locker, but the only thing that escaped my mouth was a desperate heaving as I gasped for air.

Trunk sauntered up to me. His face was drenched in blood. I frantically tried to get up. I even made it onto my hands and knees. Then Trunk unleashed a wicked kick into my stomach. A mist of bloody vapor sprayed from my mouth like spume from a whale's blowhole.

I crumpled back to the floor. The dirty lukewarm soup was continuing to rise so I used what little strength I had left to tilt my head sideways and upward so I wouldn't swallow too much of it. I wheezed and heaved and heaved and wheezed, and as I lay coughing and choking on blood and water I watched my brother, who just stood there watching me back. In a room full of twenty-five dudes I felt the deepest, blackest loneliness of my entire life.

Trunk stood over me and I coughed and gagged and thought, *Why, Brett, WHY? I'd do anything for you. ANYTHING. A single word from you could've stopped this but you did NOTHING. What have I done to you other than exist?*

And as I lay there with one ear pressed into the disgusting soup, as I choked for air and wondered if Brett hated me, Trunk took a step toward my head and leaned down.

The sneer had left his face. An eerie calm seemed to take hold of him. He tilted his head slightly and considered me with an expression of almost innocent curiosity, like a little kid inspecting a wriggling ant. Then he slowly put his giant hand on the side of my head. I tried to resist but he pushed down as the soup came up.

"Listen to you wheeze," I heard him say as he pressed my face into the water. He spoke evenly and softly, but still loud enough for the room to hear. "You really are a fucking embarrassment to this team. Maybe you shouldn't have spent so much time stuffing your face at 'I Fudged Anna.'"

Then darkness.

I snapped back to consciousness when a blast of compressed air shot down my throat. The bitter taste was instantly recognizable—it's kind of like a freezing cold spray of black licorice. The air whooshed down into my chest, instantly unlocking it. My lungs filled with rich, beautiful, life-giving oxygen.

I opened an eye and saw a set of bloody knuckles wrapped around my plastic inhaler. The hand belonged to Brett, who was naked and crouching over me. He held the inhaler to my mouth in one hand and cradled the back of my head with the other.

Brett knew to shake my inhaler's tiny canister between puffs, which surprised me. He must've seen me do it before. He must've noticed, remembered. After he shook the inhaler, he gently placed the mouthpiece back on my lips. Blood trickled from a gash in his knuckle and dripped onto my cheek like a splotch of red watercolor falling onto his Before picture.

With another blast of spray from the inhaler and another few gulps of oxygen to power my brain, the rest of the shower room began to assemble around me. To our left the guys were crowded around a heap on the floor, staring in shock. Trunk lay faceup in the soup, writhing in agony. The gash in his forehead was still leaking everywhere, and now it was joined by syrupy red blood bubbling up from a grotesque broken nose that looked like a crumpled piece of origami. With one hand, Trunk, our all-league starting right tackle, our invincible protector of Brett's blind side, clutched his right shoulder, which was jutting out of its socket.

"Come on," Brett said to me. "Let's get you home. You've got two days to learn the playbook."

CHAPTER
TEN

The rectangular brick of fudge on my lap weighed exactly two pounds, as always, but today it felt heavier than that. I traced my finger lightly along the hard edges of its wax paper wrapping, then did the same to the twine crisscrossed tightly around the package. I was always fascinated by how the rock-hard fudge could also contain such delicacy, dissolving the instant it touched your tongue in a gush of sweetness as simple and pure as its ingredients: salted sweet cream butter, Tahitian vanilla bean extract, and 63 percent cacao dark chocolate, all precisely measured and mixed to create this heavenly compound with a melting point of 98.6 degrees. Each bite would leave a lingering sweetness as perfect as it was fleeting, and next thing you knew, your hand would know a solution to a problem your brain hadn't yet recognized, reaching for the next piece—and the next and the next—in an uncontrolled urgency that would alarm you anew no matter how many times you'd recklessly housed a whole brick of Fudge by Anna. The guilt and shame would come later, but the next piece was coming now.

The key is to not even get started, so as my mom stepped on the accelerator and shot us out of the driveway, I transferred the fudge from my lap to the car mat. With my feet I nudged it under my seat so it was out of sight. I noticed Mom glance over, but she knew better than to ask if something was wrong. The internal struggle over whether to eat the fudge would be a war I'd endure on my own.

"Thanks for the chocolate," I mumbled, officially completing the fudge transaction that was a certainty of every visit from Mom. "And thanks for coming out here to help. But you didn't have to borrow Aunt Jackie's car and everything just for this appointment. It's not a big deal."

Mom turned toward me and smiled. She looked so small, even a little frail, behind the wheel of Aunt Jackie's SUV. But she also looked healthy, less exhausted. It was like every day away from Grayport had reversed a day of aging.

"Well, it's a big deal to me," she explained. "You'll understand one day when you're a mom." She glanced at me again and fought back a little smile. I found myself grinning wide in spite of—or maybe because of—the lame mom joke.

"So how's school? How's Nate been doing?" she asked cheerfully. "He invented a time machine yet?"

"I wish," I muttered, thinking back to my cheap shot at practice.

We drove a little farther in silence. I was tense the whole time, knowing that the line of Mom questions had been opened and a deluge was sure to pour down any second.

"I heard the boat got docked." Mom mentioned this casually, though she was clearly pretending that the thought had just randomly popped into her head. "You getting enough to eat?"

"What does it look like?" I glanced down at the bulges of fat ballooning out around the straps of my seat belt. But the truth was that meals were getting light. We probably qualified for food stamps, but I knew Dad would NEVER go to the food bank to fill out the required paperwork. Imagine if someone saw the great former QB Henry Parker, Grayport legend of the past, father of the present, shuffling in line at the food bank, hands pathetically stuffed in pockets, his shoulders stooped.

"And how is everything at the apartment?"

"You mean at *home*?" I snapped back, surprising both Mom and myself.

She took a long breath in through her nose and adjusted her grip on the steering wheel. "Yes. At home."

"It's good," I lied. "We're good."

"You sure?"

"Yes, I'm sure."

Mom only nodded in response. We reached a red light and idled there in silence. Mom flicked on the blinker, and we listened to it click on and off, on and off.

"What?" I said finally.

"Nothing."

I shook my head in frustration. "This is stupid."

"What's stupid?"

"Even when I tell you things are good at home, you get upset. It's like you *want* me to tell you that things suck here."

"You know that's not true." The light turned green and we lurched forward again. "It's just . . . I'm worried. You come out of the apartment with a big welt under your eye and you say it's from football, but I'm not an idiot, Wyatt. I know fists don't fit through face masks. And then there's Dad's boat getting docked, and then there's red tide and how the last time it came . . ."

. . . *it ruined everything.* She didn't say the words aloud but we both knew. The last red tide was when Dad's occasional whiskey and Coke turned into his nightly whiskey and generic cola, and then eventually his morning whiskey and coffee. It was when Brett got lice and my parents rinsed his hair with paint thinner because it was cheaper than the medicinal shampoo at the pharmacy. It was when Dad started blaming Mom for his own mistakes, and when Mom stopped forgiving Dad for making them. It was when Fudge by Anna closed for good because nobody in Grayport could afford the luxury of a little sweetness.

Mom was clutching the steering wheel almost as tightly as she was clenching her jaw. Finally she said, "You know that if things get bad at the hou—at *home*, you can always stay with me at Aunt Jackie's."

I laughed bitterly at the idea. "And sleep where? On the pullout couch with you? Or how about the bathtub? Maybe curled up at the foot of Aunt Jackie's bed like a dog?"

"What's gotten into you?" Mom snapped. I was looking out

my window, forehead to glass, but I could feel her glaring at me. "Is it this appointment?"

I felt a sudden urge to lower my window, grab the brick of fudge, and chuck it into the street. This goddam fudge. So much like my mom, so strong and so sweet, the cause and solution all at once.

But I could never do that to Mom. For all the pain Mom's fudge had brought me over the years, it also symbolized a connection to her that I couldn't afford to lose. See, in third grade Dad stopped inviting me to come along with him and Brett to practice football, so to help me feel better Mom let me make fudge with her at the shop. While Brett was spiraling footballs, I was swirling gooey chocolate with an oversized spatula in big stainless steel bowls. Mom taught me everything she knew about her craft, and soon she started referring to her fudge as "our fudge." I almost forgot about Brett and Dad and football entirely when I was with Mom in the shop's back kitchen. Making our fudge together was *that* fulfilling.

Problem was, it was filling, too, on a very literal level, and as I taste-tested batch after batch of fudge, the pounds started piling on. I had always been kind of pudgy, and frankly it hadn't ever really bothered me. But then Halloween of third grade happened. The day after trick-or-treating, I noticed that my candy bag was significantly lighter than it had been the night before. Clearly someone had stolen some of my hard-earned treats, and that someone had to be my traitorous roommate of a brother, Brett. So I approached him all calm and mature, and gently inquired into the whereabouts of my candy. Then, before he could answer, I kicked him square in the shin. It was one of the only times I *ever* hit Brett, but my candy bag was sacred and he had desecrated it.

When he was done howling in pain, Brett told me that he was innocent and that he had seen Dad sneak into our room, take my bag, and dump half of it in the trash. I was confused and asked if Dad had done the same to Brett's bag, and Brett got awkward and mumbled no. I looked at Brett, so lean and athletic, and I looked down at my stomach that used to be my tummy but was now suddenly my gut, and all at once I knew Brett was telling the truth. And I knew another truth that's stuck with me ever since: that I was fat and it was not okay.

Mom and I were closer back then, so I went to her and asked if she thought I was fat. She said of course not, she'd always love me and my body the way that it was. Then I asked her if Dad thought I was fat. The hesitation before she said no was long enough even for an eight-year-old to understand.

"The appointment is *not* bothering me," I told Mom resolutely. "It's casual. Probably, like, a million guys get fitted for a suit every day. A couple quick measurements and you're done, right? Boom, boom, and you're outta there. But if you keep making it a big deal then it's going to feel like a big deal and I don't want to feel that right now, okay?"

"Okay," Mom answered quietly. She loosened her grip on the steering wheel and softened her grimace into something of a smile. "I'm just excited, that's all. Your first suit! There aren't many Grayport traditions I'm fond of, but it's pretty neat that all the varsity players wear the same suit to the opening pep rally."

I picked up the fudge from the floor, untied its twine halfway, then changed my mind and tied it up again and placed it back by my feet. Even out of sight, I could feel it calling to me. Mom had made it in Aunt Jackie's kitchen instead of her old shop, but it still tasted like the best parts of my childhood. I hated that Mom brought it for me on each monthly visit, and I hated that I loved it too much to tell her to stop. Mom must've known how much it tormented me, but she also knew she couldn't *not* bring it. To suddenly stop making me fudge would be a statement as powerful as Dad tossing my candy in the trash.

The tailor's shop was located on a side street off of Main, wedged between Primo's Pizza and a vacant storefront. The lot was empty and Mom pulled into a spot right up front. She turned off the engine.

"Ready?" she asked.

"Yeah."

"Just a couple of quick measurements and we're out."

"I know."

"You're going to look so handsome."

"Come on, Mom."

"Your first suit."

"Come *on*."

"My little guy is growing up."

I unbuckled my seat belt, opened the door, and stepped out of the car, careful not to step on the fudge. I looked at the tailor's front window and saw my blob of a reflection staring back.

My little guy.

CHAPTER
ELEVEN

An automated *ding-dong* announced my arrival as I pushed open the door to the tailor shop, and stepping in I immediately found myself surrounded by a gang of sharply dressed mannequins, all with waists smaller than one of my thighs. The shop's worn brown carpet and beige walls flecked with peeling paint made the room feel pretty dingy, but the bright fluorescent lights overpowered the shabbiness with an aggressively clinical glare. Mirrors were everywhere. In the back corner was a chest-high counter. On it was, among other things, an old cash register, a calculator, and a tangled mess of paper receipts, pincushions, and measuring tapes. So many measuring tapes.

Behind the counter a curtained-off doorway led to a back room, and scurrying out of it came a frazzled red-faced man with wispy straw hair.

"Hello there," he said.

"Hi."

"Can I help you?"

I glanced at Mom, who gave me an encouraging nod. At

some point in the past couple of years she'd stopped talking to strangers on my behalf. It drove me crazy.

"I have an appointment for a fitting."

"Ah, of course. Let me just check our calendar." The man pushed aside a stack of loose papers on the counter and picked up a notebook buried underneath. He flipped to what seemed like a random page. He held the notebook angled toward his chest but I could see that nothing was written on the page.

"Name?"

"Wyatt Parker."

"Hmm, let's see what we've got." He ran his index finger up and down the page. "Ah, here we are. 'Wyatt Parker.' One thirty P.M. Right on time. Very punctual." He motioned toward a small wooden platform in front of a mirror. "Take off your shoes and step onto the fitting platform and we'll get started."

When I crouched down to untie my shoes, a phone rang on the counter. The tailor reached for it but it was tangled in a knot of measuring tapes. He angrily clawed at them until the phone was free, then held the receiver up to his ear.

"Grayport Tailoring."

I could hear a man's voice frantically yammering into the tailor's ear.

"Okay, calm down, sir. We can handle this. What kind of stain did you say it was?"

More breathless yammering.

"Sir, I'm a tailor and not a priest, so as far as I'm concerned, how you got that stain is best left between you and God. But I won't lie to you, it's gonna be a tough son of a gun to get out, especially from wool. I got some ideas, though. Just hold on a second while I get my assistant to help with a customer I have here."

With one hand the tailor held the speaker end of the phone against his chest and with his other hand he rang a small bell on the counter. He paused a moment, then rang the bell three more times rapidly.

An annoyed voice came from the room behind the curtained doorway. "I heard you the first time, Dad."

The curtains fluttered and a girl stepped through. As she walked she was tying her hair back in a loose topknot, and stopped suddenly when she saw me.

"Oh," she said in surprise. "Hi."

I felt like I had been kicked in the gut. Standing before me was Haley Waters, a tape measure draped over her shoulders.

"Hi," I squeaked out.

"Physics, right?"

"Right."

"You here to get fitted for a suit?"

If the universe were truly balanced, as Hinduism (and physicists) say, then this moment of absurdly terrible luck would be counteracted by an equal and opposite force of impossibly good luck. But unfortunately as I stood there trying to think of a way out of the situation, I didn't spontaneously combust into a ball of flames.

"Yeah, I have an appointment."

"Okay, cool. Just step up on that platform and I'll get your measurements." Haley was clearly uncomfortable—her voice seemed higher-pitched than usual and she was talking way faster than she ever did in physics class, where she answered questions in a poised, steady cadence.

My legs felt numb and I watched them in a daze as they shuffled me over to the wooden platform. It creaked loudly when I stepped up onto it. In front of me was a full-length mirror. Haley's dad was talking on the phone again, and she slid past him to grab a clipboard next to the cash register. She was wearing a white button-down top untucked over a pair of dark jeans. As she walked over to me on the platform, she reached into her front pocket and pulled out a pencil.

"Okay, I just gotta fill out a few things first." Haley rested the clipboard on the inside of her forearm as she scribbled the date and *Wyatt Parker* on top of the form.

She knows my name.

"Of course I know your name. You sit right behind me in class."

Great. Apparently I couldn't even trust that my inner monologue was remaining inner.

"So, Wyatt, first thing: You looking to rent or buy?"

Mom and I briefly caught eyes in the mirror. My throat felt so dry I could barely croak anything out. "Rent."

"Right, okay. And what kind of lapel do you want for the jacket?"

I felt sweat start to gather on the back of my neck. "Lapel?"

"Notch, peak, or shawl?"

"Um, can you repeat the question?"

Haley smiled gently at me. "Notch looks best with broad shoulders, so I'm going to put you down for that."

"Notch was my first choice, too."

"Cool, so we're set on notch." Haley hesitated a moment. "Alright, so I guess we'll just do these measurements now." She put the clipboard on the floor. Then she used both hands to pull one end of the tape measure that was looped over her shoulder, effortlessly sliding the slack through the palm of her top hand until she was left holding the very tip, with the rest coiled on the floor. She took a step closer to me. "Just stand straight and relaxed."

Suddenly it felt like earth's gravity doubled in strength as it relentlessly pulled, tugged, stretched, and drooped down every ounce of flab on my body. Haley started by reaching up to my neck, a doughy mass that swallowed my chin so much that it was merely a rumor of a chin. She wrapped the tape measure around where she probably thought my Adam's apple would be if it were actually visible. When she was done with the measurement, she reached for the clipboard and recorded a number on the form. I peeked down to see what she was writing in the neck measurement box, half expecting her to write an exclamation point after the number. She did this all in a silence that could've meant nothing or everything.

Haley put the clipboard back down. "Okay, now for the . . ." She trailed off, then looked to the ground and cleared her throat. "For the waist. Can you face me?"

I slowly spun around. I could feel my pulse pounding all the way up into my temples. Holding the end of the tape measure in one hand, Haley reached around my waist with both arms. But they couldn't extend all the way around to pass the end of the tape measure from one hand to the other. She quickly jerked her arms back to her sides. I started to say sorry but stopped and just stood there as sweat trickled down the back of my neck. Haley was blushing, I was pretty sure, because the little constellation of freckles peppering her nose had mostly vanished into a rosy flush. She tried reaching the tape measure around me again, but it just wasn't happening.

"Haley," hissed her dad in a half whisper that I could easily hear. He had finished his phone call and was watching from the counter. She turned to him and he mouthed the words "use the jump-rope technique." I pretended not to be looking while he mimed the rotation your wrists make while jumping rope.

"*Dad,*" she snapped. "*Stop.*"

Haley turned back toward me and adjusted her grip on the tape measure so she held several feet of slack between two hands, kind of like a jump rope. While still gripping the two ends in each hand, she flicked her wrists and looped the tape measure over my head and tugged it toward her as it caught around the back of my waist. She then drew the two ends together just above my belt buckle, pulling them until the tape measure was snug around my waist. She looked at the number and picked up the clipboard again.

"My dad is *so* embarrassing," she mumbled, maybe more to herself than to me. She really looked pretty upset about it.

"Don't get me started on embarrassing dads." I didn't expect that response from myself. The words spilled from my lips. It felt pretty good, to be honest.

Haley's eyebrows flickered upward just slightly. She looked up from the clipboard. "Try me."

No way was I going to dive into Dad's drinking or general assholery, but I was eager to keep the topic off the measuring. "Well, for one thing, instead of saying 'you guys,' my dad says 'youse guys.'"

"Oh, come on. That's not bad at all!" Haley put down the clipboard again and took up the tape measure. "My dad plays the banjo. Stand straight."

She gently pressed the end of the tape measure into the side of my hip and crouched as she ran the tape down the length of my leg to my ankle.

"Banjo can be kind of cool," I said.

"Not when you're, like, fifty years old and play horribly emo country songs on your very own YouTube channel."

"Bad, but still not terrible. Some emo country songs are decent."

"What if I told you his YouTube name is 'Tailor Miffed'?"

A chuckle blurted out of me. "Okay, yeah. That's terrible."

Haley was now smiling full on, and let me tell you, it was the sweetest thing in the world.

"So it's settled. I win 'Most Embarrassing Dad,'" she declared in mock pride.

"Hey, I'm not out of the running yet. Like, my dad tucks his shirts into his underwear."

"Yeah? Well, my dad doesn't even *wear* underwear."

I glanced over at Haley's dad behind the counter. He was using his pinky to pick something out of his ear.

"Really?"

Haley giggled. "No, not really. Come on, Wyatt, you can't be *that* gullible. Arm straight by your side, please."

She took my sleeve length, recorded it, and reviewed the measurement form. "Alright, I got the basic measurements here. Let me check our suit inventory in the back to see if—" She cut herself off. "I mean, to see what we've got for you."

When Haley returned from the back room, she handed me a hanger with an enormous navy-blue jacket and a matching pair of dress pants.

"This looks like a parachute on a hanger," I mumbled. I'm not sure why I'm always so quick to joke about my weight, but I think it's a defense I developed as a kid, an attempt to get in front of the teasing. It never seemed to make me feel that much better, though, and I felt even worse when Haley didn't laugh. Instead, she just looked at me kind of funny. I felt embarrassed for the cheap shot at myself.

There was a small changing room connected to the inventory

room, and Haley, her dad, and Mom waited in the main room while I tried on the suit. The jacket fit over my shoulders easily enough, and the pants' waist seemed about right. As I walked back into the main room, I was surprised by how comfortable I felt with the fit. Part of me desperately wanted to look at Haley's face to see her reaction, but I was too nervous to look at anyone but Mom, who was beaming. Then I looked into the full-length mirror.

I was devastated. I looked objectively terrible. The jacket was just so damn big and rectangular; it fit across my shoulders okay but from there it fell straight down my sides like it was a tablecloth or an enormous square cape. The pants were even worse. Yes, they fit my waist, but the width of each thigh stayed uniform down throughout the entire pant leg, all the way to my ankles. The legs were so baggy I looked like a clown attending a funeral. I guess that's how it goes with a guy my size. As a whole, the suit looked like a giant tarp that you toss over a wheelbarrow in the winter.

"Very handsome, Wyatt," Mom gushed.

I opened my mouth to say something, but I felt a burning in the back of my throat. I was *this* close to crying.

"No," Haley interjected suddenly. "No, no, no. The suit is all wrong. I mean, it's fine—you look fine, Wyatt. But this isn't the right suit for you. It doesn't do you justice."

"Justice?" I asked weakly. I was confused.

"Just give me a couple minutes."

Haley dashed off to the back inventory room. She returned

with another navy suit that, on the hanger at least, looked identical to the one I was wearing. I really didn't want to try it on, but I also didn't have it in me to deny Haley, so I reluctantly took the suit and plodded back to the changing room.

As I put on the new one, I noticed that it *was* different from the other suit. Not so much in its color or design, but in its texture. The fabric was so much softer and smoother.

When I returned to the mirror, I was stunned by what I saw. The suit wasn't baggy, but it wasn't tight, either. The jacket tapered down from my shoulders toward my waist at a slight angle, so my shoulders appeared broad and powerful. It even made my waist look smaller in comparison. My legs were proportionate, too, sturdy rather than billowy. I didn't suddenly transform into a model or anything, but I think I looked—

"Pretty great, right?" Haley said, looking at me looking at myself. "You're *wearing* that suit, know what I mean? That other suit was wearing you."

I glanced at Mom. I don't think I'd ever seen her smile so big. She reached into her purse and took out a tissue and dabbed at tears glistening in the corner of each eye.

"*Mom*," I said. "It's just a suit."

I turned back to the mirror and scanned myself again, fighting and failing to suppress the giant, dopey smile that stretched across my face. "Why does this look so much better than the other one?" I asked Haley.

"It's all about the fabric," she said excitedly. "See, the other suit is made from a mix of synthetic materials. Sixty-five percent polyester and thirty-five percent rayon, to be exact, and that particular ratio yields a very stiff material. And between you and me, I'm almost certain the manufacturer didn't do enough crimping after the polymerization, which is why it looked so boxy on you. Almost crusty, you know? The suit you're wearing now, though, is made from long-staple pasture wool, which is from the Teeswater breed of sheep found in Northern England. The fabrics they produce are crazy soft, and they tend to melt into your body shape and bring out its strengths in a very natural way."

Not gonna lie: Hearing Haley nerd out on fabric was sexy as hell.

"So basically this fabric is magic."

Haley giggled. "It's not creating an illusion, if that's what you're saying. It's just drawing attention to the best qualities of your natural shape."

A thought suddenly popped into my head. "If this fabric is so much better, why didn't we try it first?"

Haley hesitated. "It's just that, well, it's . . ."

". . . much more expensive." Haley's dad approached us holding a calculator.

"How much more expensive?" Mom asked softly.

Haley's dad showed her the number on the calculator. Mom stared at it for a long time. "Even to rent?" she asked.

"We don't rent out that type of fabric. Too high quality."

Mom squeezed her eyes shut very briefly. "Do you take payments in installments?"

I couldn't watch this. I'd seen Mom in a lot of shitty situations. I'd seen her nervous and furious and heartbroken. But I'd never seen her look desperate. It tore me up.

"I suppose, but I'd want to take a look at your credit score first."

Now an expression of utter helplessness replaced Mom's look of despair.

Haley tugged at her dad's sleeve and together they turned to the corner. "Dad," I heard her whisper. "Stop this. Please."

"We're running a business here, not a charity."

"Just give them a break. Come on. Please."

"You think red tide will give us a break when the economy goes down? I'm thinking of the future. Let the adults handle this."

I decided to wait in the car while Mom paid for the polyester suit rental. I couldn't stay in there any longer. When she was done, she climbed back into the driver's seat and turned to look at the suit, half on the back seat, half on the floor, dangling limply where I had flung it down. A smattering of fat raindrops began to splat and trickle down the windshield. Mom turned and looked at me, then at the piece of untied twine on the car mat at my feet, then finally at the brick of half-eaten fudge in my lap. I tore off another piece from the brick and stuffed it into my mouth.

"Wyatt," she said softly.

I kept eating, breaking off the next piece before I swallowed the last one.

"*Wyatt!*" she shouted. Then she ripped the brick of fudge out of my hands. Without hesitation, she tore off a giant piece of chocolate and stuffed it in her mouth. I watched, stunned, as she tore off a second piece and jammed it in with the first. She handed the remaining fudge back to me. We looked at each other and tried not to cry but we knew we were going to cry and we listened to the smacking of the raindrops and the smacking of our lips as we worked through our mouthfuls of chocolate. Then she twisted in her seat and leaned over the center console and pulled me in for a long hug.

"I'm sorry," she whispered. "I'm so sorry."

Her cheeks were wet and her breath smelled like her fudge. Like *our* fudge.

CHAPTER
TWELVE

"It's really pretty straightforward. Don't be intimidated by its size."

"Brett, if you sat on a seesaw and I dropped this ginormous playbook on the other end, you'd literally catapult into a new dimension."

Our playbook (man, I'll never get tired of writing that: *our* playbook) lay between each of our paper plates in the cafeteria. Brett looked down at it with furrowed brows, like he was seeing it for the first time.

"I guess it is kind of big."

"Yes. It is."

"But we can power through it together. What's your biggest worry with it?"

I leaned back in my flimsy orange cafeteria chair. I was thrown off by Brett's question, and I wasn't sure why. Then it occurred to me that this entire situation felt so weird, almost dreamlike. Here were me and Brett chatting it up during lunch, in public, with Brett asking me how I was feeling, what I was worried about. I had to fight back a smile. Things were trending upward since the brawl in the shower. Since Trunk had dislocated his shoulder—the result of "slipping in the shower," according to all witnesses, including Trunk, who knew better than to admit that he'd gotten in a tussle with the town's quarterback—I'd been elevated to starting right tackle. The coaches were none too pleased about this development, but since the other backup tackle was out for the year with a torn ACL, and since Brett shot down Coach Crooks's first idea of playing with no right tackle at all (in hopes of bewildering Blakemore into paralysis), I was reluctantly penciled in at the top of the depth chart. This was easily the most we'd ever talked over a two-day span, and even though I was still deciding whether I should be pissed at him for not coming to my defense faster in the shower fight, I couldn't help but feel lucky, even, dare I say, hashtag blessed to be talking football with *the* Brett Parker—the man, the myth, the legend. We never discussed the fight, and instead strategized together with hushed urgency about off-tackles and zone blocks and bubble screens— the language that only the few and the chosen could understand.

"I have the fundamental blocking schemes down," I said. "But the audibles make less than zero sense to me."

"They're not bad once you get the hang of them," he explained.

"Brett, this audible system is disguised so that not even elite Russian hackers could decode it."

He laughed and looked at me, grinning, like he was seeing me for the first time.

"Naw, it's more intuitive than you think. So to start off, if you hear me shout 'Austin' at the line of scrimmage, then the play is flipped to the reverse side. Got it?"

"Got it."

"Of course, if I shout 'Austin' a second time, then the first 'Austin' is a decoy, and you should wait to hear if I shout *another* state capital."

"Okay, so you shout Montpelier or whatever—what does that mean?"

Brett opened the small bottle of chocolate milk that we'd bought at the 7-Eleven on our walk to school, then poured half of it in a cup for me. Lately we bought stuff for lunch at 7-Eleven because it was slightly cheaper than the cafeteria food, and every dime counted since red tide came. No fishing money would come until the water was clear, and that could take months.

"Well, it depends," he said. "You're waiting to hear a second state capital, right? But only *below* the Mason-Dixon Line, because a city *above* the line would mean that we're actually running a third-down pooch punt."

"Okay . . ."

"Or a fake third-down pooch punt, if the number of letters in the city name equaled a prime number. But ultimately if the city is below the Mason-Dixon, then the original play has been switched to a play-action pass or, conversely, a half-back draw, depending on the current phase of the moon."

I stared at Brett, my mouth hanging open. "Please tell me you're kidding."

Brett laughed. "Yeah, man. Relax. I'm kidding."

"Thank god."

"But only about the moon part."

"Great . . ."

"Hey, you got any money left over from 7-Eleven? They're selling bananas half-price up there because they're kind of brown and mushy."

I dug into my pocket and pulled out a one-dollar bill and three dimes. Most days I didn't have a huge appetite in the cafeteria because it reeked of leftover microwaved fish that kids brought from home. That's what Brett and I did for most lunches, but of course fish lunches were gone now.

"A dollar thirty," I said, handing him the money.

"Thanks. Also, did Mom bring you any of her fudge the other day?"

Brett must've been *really* hungry, because typically fudge was way out of bounds for his meticulously healthy diet. Of course, I didn't have any of it to share since Mom and I downed the entire brick outside the tailor's shop.

"Naw," I lied. "But did you see that someone left a baked-ziti casserole at our door the other day?"

"Ms. Smolinkski, you think?" She was our landlord, who

lived in the two floors below our apartment. She was a nice old lady who mostly kept to herself.

"Could've been. Doesn't matter either way. Dad tossed it. Said he'd die before the Parkers would be viewed as a charity case."

Brett shook his head, smiling bitterly. "What an asshole."

Such a simple, profoundly true statement, and hearing it from Brett sent a rush of unadulterated relief through my entire body.

"What an asshole," I echoed.

"Alright, I'm gonna go grab a couple of bananas."

As Brett waited in the food line, I flipped to a new page in the playbook and reviewed the secret tackle-eligible pass play. Without taking my eyes off the diagram, I reached for the 7-Eleven hot dog on my tray. I didn't get a good handle on it, though, and the hot dog slipped out of its bun. It landed on the top of the page and rolled all the way down, smearing the page with nauseating light green grease. The ink became fuzzy, then started to run in the slime.

"Crap," I said aloud, frantically grabbing napkins from the dispenser in front of me.

"Sodium bicarbonate." Nate had appeared seemingly out of nowhere. He reached for napkins and helped me dab the stained page.

"Sodium what?"

"Bicarbonate. It's baking soda. Sprinkle some on this page tonight, and it will make the page readable again."

"Thanks," I said. "But I thought you were mad at me."

"I am."

"Don't blame you," I said. I waited to see if Nate had something to add, but he just stood there, arms crossed. I had to try another avenue in. "So how does it work?" I asked. "Chemically, I mean."

Nate took the bait. He couldn't help himself. "Sodium bicarbonate is a base, which neutralizes the oil stain, which is acidic. It raises the pH level of the liquid to make it more basic."

"So it's like a grease eraser."

"Basically." His pun made the corners of his frown rise just slightly.

"Nice one," I said, extending my fist for a pound.

"I'm still mad at you, but I'm going to accept your pound because frankly I deserve it. This is *not* a full pound I'm giving you. It's, like, an ounce."

"Okay, I'm not sure that last pun worked," I said, testing to see how Nate would respond to the playful jibe.

Nate smiled. "Yeah, you're right."

"So are we good?"

Nate rolled his eyes.

"I'm sorry about the hit. Really. It's just in the moment, all these things . . . I don't know. Coach Crooks. Trunk. Brett. I wanted to turn some heads."

"By practically knocking mine right off?"

"I was desperate. I wanted those guys to respect me so badly."

"At the cost of my respect for you."

"I know," I said. "It was stupid and idiotic and dumb. I can't stop thinking about it."

"Well, neither can I."

"Please, Nate," I said. "I don't want a five-second thing to erase thirteen years of us being friends."

Nate didn't say anything.

"Nate, I wish I could explain better how desperate I was. It's just, like, my whole life I've been trying to get Brett to—"

Nate held his hand up, motioning me to stop. "I get it," he said. "I understand."

Those two sentences summed up Nate perfectly. *I get it. I understand.* He's an amazing student because he can read books and instantly "get it." With me, though, he's a great friend not because he "gets it," but because he understands.

"Thanks, Nate. Really."

"Just promise me you won't become a d-bag just because you're on varsity now."

"I promise."

"Alright, good," Nate said. "Now I'm guessing you need some more help with that playbook, so let's see what we've got here."

He pulled up a chair next to where Brett had been sitting. I loaded the 7-Eleven hot dog back into its bun and took a bite, thinking about how much easier these next few weeks would be with Nate and Brett by my side.

CHAPTER

THIRTEEN

I can read body language as easily as you can read this very sentence. It's what happens when you live with a dad and brother who only say about ten total sentences a day. You develop a sixth sense, pick up meaning from even the most subtle movements. Take the way Brett closes the bathroom door. If he just casually flings it shut, then that means he's going to take a leak. But if he closes the door softly and lets the doorknob twist back into place with a gentle *click*, then he's going to take a dump. I have no idea why he does this, and I bet he doesn't even *know* he does it. But I notice it. And yes, I realize that devoting brain space to the intricacies of pre-deuce kinetic rituals seems weird at best. But when you live in a cramped two-bedroom apartment with limited air circulation, you need to know when it's time to clear out.

Then there's Dad: His entire mood is communicated through the way he holds his beer. If in between gulps he thumbs the tab of the can by pushing it down then releasing it so it vibrates, *poing-g-g-g-g* like a tiny springboard, then I know Dad is restless. And when he's restless, watch out.

Two nights before the Blakemore game, I was sitting at the kitchen table battling math homework when I heard the familiar *poing-g-g-g-g* come from the adjacent living room. Dad was on the couch watching *Wheel of Fortune*, from the sounds of it. The iconic clicking noise from the spinning roulette wheel drifted into the kitchen, followed by a muffled groan from the audience. The contestant must've landed on the "Bankrupt" slice. The host, Pat Sajak, said, *"Oh, shucks."* There was no reaction from my dad. Just another *poing-g-g-g-g*.

I squinted down at my homework, trying to direct my focus back onto my math problem. This one question about factoring binomials was kicking my ass:

$$(3x^2 + 2y) \, (x^3 - 12y)$$

My brain felt wobbly, like a roulette wheel spinning around a question and landing on everything but the answer. I was so distracted I couldn't remember stuff I knew well just the day before. In what order was I supposed to multiply all the variables in the parentheses? And when combining exponents, do you add them together or multiply them? Do they need a common base? Could I just smash x's and y's all up on each other, like $2xy$ or something? Do they need to stay separated or do they just throw their hands up and say let's get nasty together?

Poing-g-g-g-g.

Muffled audience applause came from the living room as a

contestant spun the wheel, then guessed a few correct letters to the hangman puzzle. From my chair I could see into part of the living room—one of the armrests of the couch and part of the TV. The screen flickered light onto the walls and ceiling of the dark living room in staccato flashes, like a silent lightning storm through your window in the dead of night. On the floor next to the couch was a toppled stack of empty beer cans. I counted seven. Number eight must've been in Dad's hand. *Poing-g-g-g-g.* My stomach churned.

Concentrate, Wyatt. I looked back down at the question. On the line beneath the problem, I tentatively started to work through the binomial, writing down 4×6. As soon as I crossed the *x*, though, my brain skittered into the depths of my football play-book: all of those *X*'s and *O*'s that I'd crammed into my head the past forty-eight hours; all of those blocking schemes and audibles, the 43-34 off-tackles and 24-25 halfback crosses and wedge blocks on the two-technique sliding into a second level double *X*.

. . . ThreeXSquaredPlusTwoYTimesX . . .

Poing-g-g-g-g.

I noticed my right leg was bouncing anxiously. I stuck my pencil eraser-first through the thickest part of my hair and let it chill up there for a little while. I do that when I'm antsy for some reason. From the bedroom directly upstairs, there was a low grinding sound as Brett sharpened his pencil. He was doing his homework at our desk, which was essentially his desk, since he was the only one who used it. The kitchen table was where

I always did my homework. It had a small square surface and was a little chipped, and it got wobbly whenever the piece of cardboard became unwedged from underneath its back right leg. One side of the table was pushed up against the wall opposite the entry to our apartment, and if you want to hear about one of the worst thoughts I ever had, I'll tell you how it got positioned in that spot. See, the table used to sit in the middle of our kitchen, a chair on each side for Mom, Dad, me, and Brett. It was a pain in the ass, that table, because it took up most of the space in our little kitchen, and everyone, even Brett, who as you know is agile as hell, would bump into its corners. The door to our apartment led directly into the kitchen, so as soon as you walked in you were practically on top of the table. We all complained, but what choice did we have? No table? Then Mom left to live with Aunt Jackie temporarily. "Just a few days" became just a few weeks became just a few months became just drop it, Wyatt, and stop asking when Mom is coming back.

One day I came home from school and stubbed my toe on the corner of the table. I'd jammed my foot on the table a billion times before, but for whatever reason this one got me *really* mad. I hopped around on one foot cursing the worst curses my eight-year-old brain could muster, and during that outburst I had the sudden thought, or more like the vision, of Mom's chair and her whole side of the table pushed against the kitchen wall, a logical move that would've opened up all that wonderful space in the middle of the room for the people who still lived here. I immediately took back the thought, deeply ashamed that for a moment I wanted to trade Mom's spot at the table for a few more square feet. I remember storming into the bathroom and staring at myself in the mirror. I felt like screaming but instead I made a fist and punched the wall. I probably cracked a knuckle, to be honest, because it swelled up and hurt for, like, six months. Anyway, the table stayed in the center of the kitchen for a few more weeks until one day I came down for breakfast and boom, there was the table in its new spot, Mom's edge pushed up against the wall. Her chair was against the wall, too, its seat and legs tucked under the table and half of its rounded back poking up from the table's surface like a gravestone. Brett, Dad, me—nobody ever acknowledged the move, like who did it or how the opening of the extra space meant the closing of something much larger. Instead we just ate our cornflakes at the table like nothing had changed at all. Pass me that OJ. Did you see the Patriots traded for a new defensive end?

Poing-g-g-g-g.

I took the pencil out of my hair, erased what I'd written down, and stared at the problem some more. I thought about asking Brett for help—he'd taken the class a couple of years ago—but I'd never asked him for advice on anything other than football, and I was nervous to start now. Besides, usually I was pretty decent at math. Like when Dad would send me to the general store for toilet paper, I could calculate in my head that twelve rolls at $6.70 was a better deal than ten rolls at $5.90. I can even calculate how many more oddly specific bathroom references I can make in a single chapter before you start to wonder if I had some kind of permanent Freudian disaster when I was potty trained as a toddler.

But I just couldn't figure out how to multiply this binomial. I started plugging away at a few new approaches to it but got lost each time. *Poing-g-g-g-g. Poing-g-g-g-g.* I erased, started over, erased again. I stared at the problem real hard. No luck. I even narrowed my eyes at it, like the problem would be intimidated into complying with my furrowed brow.

Then suddenly—*magically*—I was struck by that incredible feeling you get when, after wrestling with a problem forever, everything just clicks into place and your brain somersaults into the euphoric realization that—aha!—the answer is in the back of the book.

I flipped to the back and copied the answer down on my paper, but my victory was short-lived when I remembered that my math teacher, Mr. Kenner, made you show your work instead of just writing the final answer.

He said it's so you can get partial credit on incorrect answers. Partial credit—what a stupid concept. Though I should admit in the past I used to actually like the idea. I definitely benefited from it on occasional math tests, but I think more than anything I liked the general concept of partial credit because it's so rare in Grayport. Everything feels so damn *consequential* here, so binary, so black or white. People here only care if you win or lose—doesn't matter how you played. You either had a good day catching fish or a shit day. For a town named after the color of its perpetual overcast skies, there were very few shades of gray.

But I've since turned on partial credit, and now I think it's BS. All partial credit means is that you started out right, but then you took a wrong turn. Who cares if you *were* good if you don't *stay* good? Your final answer on a problem shows where you stand on it now, in the present, and your "work" on it is merely the past. You can't just throw out some garbage answer and expect your past good work to make up for everything.

In the living room, my dad let out a thick, wet burp. A contestant on *Wheel of Fortune* announced that he'd like to try to solve the word puzzle. I glanced up at the TV and saw the board the contestant was working with:

SP_ _ _ _ CLEA_ _ _ _

"SPIDER CLEAVAGE!" my dad shouted at the TV. "Gotta be spider cleavage!"

The contestant told Pat Sajak his answer. I couldn't quite hear it, but whatever his answer, it was wrong.

"Sorry," Sajak said. "The answer we were looking for is SPRING CLEANING."

"Christ, Sajak," my dad groaned at the TV. "You're a real prick, you know that?"

For a guy who wasn't religious, Dad sure said *Christ* a lot. When I was a kid I once asked him why he didn't go to church with us on Sundays, and he said the only time I'd ever see him in a church would be at his funeral. I wonder if when your time comes, God takes a look at your entire life and gives partial credit.

A few minutes later I heard the familiar noise of Dad crumpling his empty beer can—a sign that he'd finished the last one he had brought with him to the couch. Dad lumbered into the kitchen. He didn't even look at me—just went straight for the fridge.

"Where's the food?" he snapped after a moment. The white light from inside the fridge illuminated the newest wrinkles on Dad's angular face. He looked so old and drunk.

"What do you mean?" I replied weakly.

"There used to be food in here. What happened to it?"

Oh, it went out for its Tuesday night art class at the rec center. Where the hell did he think it went? We'd eaten it. Brett and I didn't have money to buy groceries, and with the boat being docked, I don't think Dad did either. There were a few condiments, a jar of dill pickles, and a six-pack of beer. That was it.

Instead of closing the fridge door, Dad just stood there awhile, staring into the nothingness. The fridge hummed softly, so content and unaware of the danger it was in. In the living room someone bought a vowel. I kept watching Dad stand there, hand on the fridge door, frozen as a statue. It always amazed me how slowly he inhaled and exhaled when he was drunk. At times I'd swear he wasn't breathing at all. Then suddenly, as if someone flicked a switch in Dad's head, he burst back to life and slammed the door shut with such violence you could hear the glass condiment bottles shatter inside. He turned to the counter and yanked the toaster from the counter and slammed it into the floor so hard it literally bounced like a spiked football. With wild, seething eyes he swung open the fridge again and desperately groped for a can of beer like it was a grenade that'd save him from some invisible approaching army. He cracked it open, then, rearmed, limped back into the TV room and continued watching contestants spin the Wheel of Fortune.

Poing-g-g-g-g. Poing-g-g-g-g. Poing-g-g-g-g.

I got a roll of paper towels out from under the sink. The splattered ketchup bottle made the inside of the fridge look like a murder scene. I started by wiping the remaining beer cans clear of ketchup and shards of glass. Otherwise, Dad was going to cut his hand when he grabbed the next one.

I was about halfway through the mess when I heard the creaking from the top of the stairs.

When Brett got to the bottom, he looked at me by the fridge, then looked down at my notebook on the kitchen table.

He didn't say anything, so I did. "Do we have any more paper towels?" I held the cardboard roll up to him. "Ran out."

No answer, and if he shrugged I didn't see it. He walked to the coat rack next to the bathroom door, stepping over the toaster without even looking down at it, without even acknowledging it, like it was just another piece of furniture, like it'd been there broken on the floor all these years.

I don't know where Brett was headed, and I knew if I asked him, he would give his typical answer: "Out." From what people say around town, I think "Out" usually just means he's going with a couple of teammates to grab some pizza at Primo's—they gave him free slices there during football season.

"Foil."

I looked up at Brett as he slid an arm through his jacket.

"What?" I was confused. Foil wouldn't help with this mess at all.

"F-O-I-L," he spelled out. "First-outside-inside-last. That's the order you multiply the parts in that binomial."

I wanted to say thanks but instead I said, "Oh, cool."

And then Brett darted across the kitchen and left the apartment. That was the nice thing about the table being off to the side—made for an easier escape out the door.

CHAPTER
FOURTEEN

The next evening at the pep rally I was standing on our auditorium stage in my crusty polyester suit with the rest of the starters, and I could see Haley sitting in the audience staring *right at* me. Okay, maybe not *right* at me, but she was most definitely looking in my general direction. Okay, maybe she wasn't looking in my general direction as much as she was looking down at her phone, but she was certainly *facing* in my general direction, and it was easy to telepathically feel her passionate longing for me.

My job during the pep rally was simply to stand there and not be awkward, and I was doing an absolutely fantastic job of screwing that up. I had no freaking clue what to do with my arms. Under the scrutiny of about two thousand fans and all the face-melting stage lights, my arms suddenly felt like doughy, dangling appendages that should've been naturally selected out of the human anatomy a couple millennia ago. I noticed that Brett and the other guys on the team solved this dilemma by standing resolutely with their arms folded across their chests, their impressive biceps and forearms flexed menacingly underneath their suit jackets. I couldn't do this, though, because crossing my arms at my chest meant resting them atop the shelf of my gut, which, of course, I didn't want to draw attention to, since Haley was staring *right at* me.

I had to think of something for my arms to do, so I decided to casually (and repeatedly) reach behind my head and scratch the back of my neck. I did this at a rate of once every way-too-often, as if on the list of top female turn-ons, just behind "confidence" and "big biceps," is "a vague but terrible neck rash." Ultimately, I settled on shoving both my hands in my pockets.

I surveyed the chaotic spectacle before me. A dozen marching band drummers thumped the auditorium into a frenzy with their rhythmic beat while a small army of cheerleaders— all with bouncing ponytails, perfect white teeth, and Brett's #7 painted on each cheek—took turns catapulting each other high into the air. They'd practically scrape the ceiling and then plummet back down with a thrilling *whoosh* of reckless abandon and controlled elegance into a bed of their teammates' arms.

Ever since I was a little guy I'd dreamed of standing with the starters at a Grayport pep rally. But now that I was up here, something felt very off. For one thing, the location of the rally was all wrong. One of Grayport's oldest, most random, and most beloved game-week traditions is for the cheerleaders to post signs around town saying that the pregame pep rally is scheduled for eight P.M. on Thursday evening in the Grayport High auditorium. But then, still following tradition, the cheerleaders would spend Thursday mornings covering up these posters with a bright yellow addendum stating, DUE TO INCLEMENT WEATHER, TONIGHT'S PEP RALLY HAS BEEN MOVED OUTSIDE. So like clockwork the entire town would gather each Thursday night at the beach and huddle around a roaring bonfire, its orange flames proudly defying the rain. I always loved how its plumes of gray smoke poured upward into the black sky. How the marching band drums didn't compete with, but rather complemented, the crashing waves. How when a cheerleader was launched into the sky and disappeared momentarily into the mist, the whole town would gasp despite being absolutely certain—just as certain as we were that the bonfire would keep burning and that Grayport would win tomorrow's game—that the cheerleader would come back to us, landing softly in the bed of her teammates' arms.

It'd been like that every Thursday night of football season for as long as anyone could remember. But it was different this Thursday night. This time, the rain—the inclement weather— never arrived. Instead, a strangely serene climate floated in from the ocean and hovered eerily above our little town. The sky was bold and cloudless, and just before the pep rally, the setting sun illuminated the sky in brilliant streaks of purple, orange, and red. The bay was so quiet and still it looked like a painting. You could almost trick yourself into believing that the deep crimson color of the ocean was a reflection of the dazzling red sky, and not, as we all knew in our hearts, the red tide stalking toward us, choking our bay slowly and mercilessly.

So for the first time maybe ever, the inclement weather addendum wasn't posted. The town packed uncomfortably into the auditorium, where we didn't have to face the eerie, deathly calm outside. But you could still feel the suffocating unease inside the auditorium. At this pep rally, Grayport's common enemy wasn't Blakemore, but red tide—and that was one opponent where victory was far from certain. In the *Grayport Gazette*, Murray Miller devoted the entire front section to red tide, reporting the devastating news that the US Coast Guard had confirmed our bay was swarming with the poisonous red amoeba that would kill all the fish and, most likely, the little town whose economy depended on them. Murray Miller's headline read simply: IT'S COMING.

This all made for a super uncomfortable vibe during the pep rally. On the one hand, the music and the cheering felt kind of silly when we knew that in just a week or two many Grayport families wouldn't be able to afford meals. The importance of football is *never* questioned in Grayport, but in these circumstances we were forced to consider a horrible reality: that football is just a game. You could notice just the faintest restraint in the cheers. The drums were a little bit softer. The cheerleaders were tossed just a little bit lower into the air.

But then again there was also a sense of urgency connected to this game, this team. It's like football became *extra* important because it's nice—no, *essential*—that we have something that's just a game.

It's times like these when towns rely on their anchors, and that's why Coach Crooks was the first scheduled speaker of the rally. A bodiless voice from the overhead speakers called him to the podium, and the old man crept to the front of the stage. He was our town's ultimate symbol of survival: A veteran of three wars and dozens of state championship games, Crooks had seen it all. His body oozed (sometimes literally, which I won't get into) with age and experience; his spine was as curved as a fishing hook, and he was missing most of his right pinky finger, which he'd lost in various moments of badassery that seemed to change with each retelling.

When he reached the podium, Coach Crooks slowly held up that mangled hand to silence the crowd. He then snatched a canteen dangling around his neck and took a loud, swishy gulp. From my view on the side of the stage, I could see his white whiskers glistening around his crackly lips. He slowly reached into the front pocket of his tattered denim shirt and pulled out a toothpick. He tucked it between what was left of his side molars.

There was a long pause. Then Crooks cleared his throat.

"You all know I'm not exactly one for long speeches," he said, his gravelly voice echoing throughout the auditorium. "So, goodbye."

Then he slowly turned around and shuffled back to his spot among the other coaches.

There was a confused silence in the audience, then an eruption of cheering and laughter. This "speech," if you want to call it that, was so Coach Crooks, and the town loved it.

"Thank you, Coach Crooks!" the bodiless voice announced through the overhead speakers. "And now, ladies and gentlemen, we have a very special treat. Please welcome Brett Parker to the podium!"

The auditorium was suddenly abuzz with shocked murmuring as *everyone*—even the players and coaches onstage—turned to the person next to them and whispered similar words of disbelief: Was this really about to happen? Was Brett Parker, the quietest, most inaccessible guy in town, about to address two thousand people?

I felt a wave of nausea hit me like a Trunk punch to the gut, and I could tell by the way the audience murmured and squirmed in their seats that they felt the same discomfort. I mean, who *possibly* thought this would be a good idea? Brett was *not* a public speaker. Sure, with all the shit going down, the town needed Brett more than ever, but we needed the Brett who we knew and loved, the guy who glided instead of ran, the guy who was always in control, the guy whose passes got better the worse it rained. We needed to keep our idealized version of Brett intact, the version of Brett that strode up to the line of scrimmage with a contagious confidence. The last thing we needed was *this* version of Brett, the version that was now timidly stepping to the podium with his head down.

At the podium, Brett reached into his pocket and pulled out

a neatly folded piece of paper. He opened it up, and from my vantage I could see the paper trembling in his hands.

The auditorium fell so deathly quiet you could've heard the toothpick drop from Crooks's mouth.

I cringed. *God, get me out of here.*

"I've been thinking a lot lately," Brett began. His voice was low and quiet, but it was also as sharp and clear as his piercing green eyes. I think the entire auditorium was holding its breath. "And," he continued, "I keep coming back to book six of *The Iliad*."

Wait—what? *The Iliad*? The epic poem by Homer? Back when we were in elementary school and back when our parents were still together, my mom would read to me before bed while Dad and Brett reviewed his playbook on the other side of our attic room. At first Mom tried reading me *Charlotte's Web*, but Dad was having none of that shit. So he had Mom read me *The Iliad*, the two-thousand-year-old story about the Trojan War. It was pretty awesome learning about all those badass warriors like Achilles and Hector, but man, some of those battle scenes were pretty brutal for an eight-year-old to hear: *"The metal point of the spear,"* my mom would read to me, *"penetrated under his brain and smashed his white jawbones. His teeth were knocked out, his eyes filled with blood and, gasping, he blew blood through his mouth and nostrils.* Okay, Wyatt—sweet dreams!"

Brett had never read *The Iliad*, as far as I knew. Maybe all those nights he wasn't listening to Dad, but to Mom as she read to me.

"In book six," Brett went on, "the Greek army is advancing on the shores of Troy like an unstoppable force. Actually"—Brett suddenly corrected himself—"the Greeks weren't *like* an unstoppable force. They *were* an unstoppable force, and everyone in Troy knew it. They looked out at the ocean and knew their city was doomed. There was no question."

I'd been staring hard at my sneakers, wishing for all this to be over. But I couldn't help peeking up at the audience. No one was snickering. Some were still fidgeting in their seats. But the majority was rapt with attention. The unstoppable force, the advancement on the shores—clearly Brett was alluding to an opponent even more powerful—and relevant—than Blakemore High.

"So Troy is panicking. They're preparing for the worst." Brett's voice was starting to crescendo. "And Hector, their best warrior, he's not foolish enough to tell his people that everything's going to be okay. That would be a blatant lie. It would be unfair to them." Brett paused and looked down at his notes, as if he was considering his next words carefully. The paper was still trembling.

"But what he does tell them is that true honor, the kind that defines you, doesn't mean fighting to win. It means fighting when you know you've already lost. It means going down with a spear in the chest, and not a spear in the back as you run away." Brett's pace had picked up considerably. He had stopped looking at his notes and instead stared hard into the audience, his green eyes fierce and challenging. He was getting *into it*.

And so was the audience. You could feel the energy in the room building.

"'Cause Hector knew that what matters most is not how many times you get knocked down"—and here Brett glanced at me—"but how many times you pick yourself—"

"YEAAAH, number seven! Tell 'em, boy!"

Two thousand heads swiveled at once to the back of the auditorium to the source of the shout. There, in the last row, was the last person to wear #7 for Grayport football. He was slouched way back in his chair. His head was tilted up, his legs were splayed wide apart, and his left hand gripped what appeared to be a glass bottle in a brown paper bag.

No, god. Please no, I thought to myself.

Brett glanced up nervously at Dad, then back down to his notes. "Um, because, what Hector . . . well, Hector—"

"You tell 'em, boy!" Dad shouted again. The outline of his body in the back of the dark auditorium looked like a silhouette so sharp it was cut from metal. He took a swig from the bottle and wiped his mouth clumsily with his sleeve.

"Hector knows there are things you can't control," Brett went on. But now Dad started to cough violently. Again, the entire auditorium craned their necks to see the commotion. People giggled. People whispered, passing on to their neighbor the information about the identity of that jackass in the back.

Brett had that kink in his neck again, the same that he had whenever Dad was at practice and Brett couldn't stop glancing at him on the sideline.

He paused to wipe away a streak of sweat that had tumbled down the side of his temple. "And while it's true that you can't control everything, you can at least control your reaction to it."

"Hell yeah!" came a shout from the back. "That's how youse do it, slev—seven!" Dad took another swig, but this time the bottle slipped from his hand and clanged to the floor. It rolled down the aisle and he hobbled after it, grabbing underneath his left thigh to help his leg pivot faster in the socket of his bum hip. The bottle rolled to a stop a few seats away from where Haley was sitting. I looked at Brett. He didn't seem to know whether to keep speaking or let the moment pass. He wiped more sweat from his brow.

Suddenly, it hit me. I had to do what nobody else would: I had to get Dad outta here. It was my duty. My responsibility. I was going to walk right up the aisle, grab the bastard by the arm, and walk him right out of the goddam auditorium. I was going to step up and do for Brett what he didn't do for me when Trunk was pummeling me in the shower. I was going to do it. I swear it.

Later that night, I was lying in the bottom bunk, staring up at the plywood under Brett's mattress. He wasn't moving, but I could tell from the cadence of his breath that he wasn't asleep. After I realized that I wasn't going to muster the courage to apologize to Brett—to tell him that I should've stepped in to stop Dad, that I was going to, but was paralyzed—I started to think about the past, started to think about Mom. Dad's drinking had always been an issue, but red tide brought out the worst in him. With the fishing boat docked there was just way too little money and way too much time for him to think about all the things he could've been but wasn't. I thought about how the saddest part of *The Iliad* is when Hector prays that his son grows up to be a better man than his father. I wondered if Brett had read that part.

Anyway, I was lying in bed thinking about last red tide and how Mom was here for it, and I started to remember how whenever Dad grabbed his coat and started to stumble out our door—headed to the bar, the football game, wherever—my mom would call him back in. *Where are you going?* she'd ask. *I can smell the liquor on you from here,* she'd say. Then they'd get in a huge fight, and Dad would smash things and say things that he couldn't take back. Mom would usually end her night in tears, but she always accomplished her goal, because Dad would end his night passed out on the floor and not cruising around town, making his sons feel ashamed.

Tonight, Mom would've been brave enough to stop Dad. She would've blocked him from even leaving the apartment. She would've protected Brett, would've succeeded where I failed.

But I promised myself that tomorrow night would be different. Tomorrow, it would be my turn to block for Brett, and I wasn't going to let him down again.

CHAPTER
FIFTEEN

The blank white envelope taped to my locker was from Trunk. I was sure of it. It wasn't there when I got dressed before the game, but now as I returned to the locker room at halftime wet and muddy and bloody, I immediately noticed the envelope. It hung from the top shelf of my locker ominously, waiting for me.

From the moment I saw the envelope, I knew I wasn't going to open it. Even though this note could've settled the quandary, long debated by scientists, of whether Trunk could actually read and write, I wasn't going to give him the satisfaction of twisting the knife of humiliation that had already been jabbed in me, again and again, during the first half. I also knew that no matter how acidic and biting his words were about me and my putrid first-half performance, he would've been right. And I couldn't face that.

We were still in the game, at least, down 10–7 to Blakemore. I sat on the chair in front of my locker and watched Brett and our offensive coordinator in the far corner of the locker room huddle over the playbook and make adjustments to it. They spoke in quiet but adamant tones and made hurried scribbles in red pencil, slashing up a game plan that just couldn't work when your right tackle can't block for shit. As they revised the game plan, Brett didn't even seem to notice the two trainers frantically repairing his tattered body. One washed a gash in Brett's forearm and stopped the bleeding by plugging it with what looked like a clump of sawdust. The other trainer took off Brett's left cleat and sock before unfurling an entire roll of athletic tape to wrap and stabilize his swollen ankle. At one point Brett pointed to something in the playbook with his left index finger and noticed that his fingernail, raw and bleeding, had been ripped halfway off. With the pointer and thumb of his good hand, Brett pinched the remainder of the torn fingernail and slowly pried it off. He flicked away the fingernail and returned his focus to the playbook.

The locker room was dim, quiet, and intense. Coaches and players were focused on preparing for the second half, but it was impossible to ignore the air of communal resentment toward me. Crooks called together a group of linemen to go over some adjustments, but left me sitting at my locker in the corner and didn't say a word to me. Nobody even so much as looked my way—other than that goddam portrait of Dad on the Wall of Fame. He was seventeen years old when the picture was taken, but his scowl in the photo was identical to the one he wore all first half as he watched the game from the stands with the Boston College scout. Even in black and white, the photograph captured Dad's hard, penetrating eyes, which now glared at me as I hunched on my chair and took discreet puffs from my inhaler. I thought about my great-uncle Wyatt and how nice it would be to punt my life in Grayport and move out to Arizona, like he did, to open up his asthmatic lungs and feast on the region's oxygen-rich air. I'd never met the guy—never even *spoken* to him—yet sometimes I felt more connected to him than to anyone else in my family.

I had fifteen minutes of halftime to somehow reconcile the horror of the past two quarters with the future of the next two. I don't know how else to describe what I was feeling other than that I was scared. Growing up, Dad always reminded us that playing scared gets you hurt because when you're scared you start to hesitate, and when you hesitate your opponent becomes the hammer and you become the nail. But what he never mentioned is that for a lineman, playing scared doesn't just get *you* hurt—it gets your quarterback hurt, too. It leaves him bloody, beaten, and swollen, with pieces of him literally on the locker room floor.

Leading up to the game, I'd anticipated—even had come to terms with—playing nervous. But nerves are also a source of adrenaline, and I'd been hoping that this rush, coupled with my hate for Derek Leopold for the cheap shot he laid on Brett last year, would magically combine into some mildly effective play.

But I hadn't anticipated something: I couldn't hate Derek Leopold. To hate someone, you needed to be at odds with his values and have friction with the core of his humanity. From the moment I lined up across from Leopold, though, I realized that this guy—this *thing*—had no humanity. His eyes were huge, black, and depthless, and they stared ahead with a terrifying . . . I don't know, *absence*. His body wasn't flesh and bone but an indestructible mass that made your very soul feel tiny and pointless. Play after play, he hunted Brett with the ferocious single-mindedness of a creature that wasn't doing this for fun, or survival, or for any reason at all other than that he was *made* to pursue, to hurt, to kill. There was no rivalry between him and me. I was merely a small obstacle in his hunt, and he discarded me over and over with ruthless efficiency: a shoulder slammed into my jaw; a quick step toward me followed by an impossibly graceful spin move, leaving me grasping at the air where he'd just been; a bull rush straight into my chest, driving me backward into Brett like I was a rag doll. Whenever the whistle blew and Leopold stood over Brett, he didn't celebrate. He didn't acknowledge his teammates. I swear he didn't even *breathe*. So no, you couldn't hate Derek Leopold any more than you could hate a wild animal. All you could do was fear him.

It wasn't raining but the fog was the thickest I'd ever seen it. At the end of halftime we all lined up two by two and made the short walk back into the stadium and onto the sidelines. Following tradition, Brett led us out with a lantern, and following instinct, the crowd erupted in a deafening cheer when they caught sight of the warm, orange glow pulsing like a beating heart through the curtain of fog. But unlike the raw burst of joy that thundered from the stands in the first quarter when Brett connected with Ranger for our lone touchdown, this cheer felt strained, maybe a little desperate, like the entire town was *imploring* us to win. With red tide we needed the lift, but games against Blakemore always carried extra weight. It wasn't just that they were our toughest competition and that the winner of this game typically went to an undefeated season and league title. It was also that Blakemore, despite being just ten miles down shore from us, was everything that Grayport wasn't.

I don't know anything about geology or whatever, but for some reason Blakemore's shores weren't narrow and craggy and menacing like ours, but wide and sandy and welcoming. A meteorological wind channel along this section of Massachusetts blew all rainstorms out toward Grayport, so Blakemore enjoyed as many rays of sun as they had grains of sand. They didn't have to rely on fishing because they had tourism, beach house rentals, and rich visitors from New York paying $50 for halibut that Grayport fishermen had caught and sold to Blakemore restaurants for a mere $10. Blakemore had rows and rows of large Victorian houses cluttered with expensive antique chairs, so you're welcome to come inside but don't you even *think* of sitting there or there or there or anywhere at all. They also had an endless supply of little blond kids so perfect and "cute" it was downright creepy. These little angels were constantly reminded by their teachers that they were as unique and special as a snowflake. And it was true that these kids were like snowflakes: They were extremely cold, and when you saw one you wanted to stick your tongue out at it.

Aside from Derek Leopold, who didn't come from Blakemore

but rather was spawned from a demonic alternate reality, the guys on their football team were mostly stuck-up pricks—dudes named River and Cricket and Bentley who rocked a million sweatbands as random and superfluous as their names.

So like I said: I wasn't just letting down Dad and Brett with my putrid play, but the entire town.

At the start of the second half, the coaches tried moving me to the opposite side of the line, and for a few plays the deception worked: Through the fog the Blakemore coaches didn't pick up on the switch, and for a few glorious minutes I got to block an opponent who wasn't a demonic hell-spawn. But like a serial killer in a horror movie, Leopold eventually found me again, now lining up on my new side and staring ahead with his cold black eyes.

The game of counterpunches intensified as our coaches began exclusively calling plays in which Brett rolled out to the opposite side of Leopold and me. Blakemore responded by stacking that side with nine guys, leaving us no choice but to take our chances with plays toward Leopold. Essentially, it was me and Brett versus Leopold, but since I added nothing to the equation, the game was distilled down to a one-on-one bout between the two all-Americans.

Brett was well on his way for career lows in passing and rushing yards, but everyone in the entire stadium would agree that this was the greatest game he had ever played. Leopold was as inescapable as Death itself, but Brett never once flinched from the onslaught, defiantly waiting to throw until the last possible moment—even until Leopold had just planted his shoulder square into Brett's chest—so his receivers could have those extra milliseconds to get open. Brett's passes were short and quick and so were his runs, which never ended with him scampering safely out of bounds, but with a mangled pileup of bodies as Brett fought for those extra inches. Our running backs, meanwhile, had been getting stuffed again and again for short losses, so Brett began calling audibles for QB keepers. These runs were, essentially, nonrefundable appointments to meet Leopold three yards downfield in a cataclysmic collision that you couldn't always see through the mist, but that you could always hear and feel.

Three or four yards a play was enough to get us a few first downs, but we couldn't string together enough of them to get in the end zone. Good thing Blakemore was having just as much trouble offensively. Over and over their quarterback unleashed blind passes through the fog to receivers who had no chance of getting their hands on the errant throws. Unlike Brett, who almost seemed to *feel* receivers in the mist rather than see them, the Blakemore quarterback didn't have a prayer. Soon they abandoned their aerial attack altogether. This allowed our defense to key on their running backs and swarm them like sharks on a wounded seal. But Blakemore was playing with a three-point lead, and as the clock ticked down into the fourth quarter, the Blakemore end zone, now completely invisible through the fog, felt like it wasn't even there at all.

With just under five minutes remaining in the game, I

committed an inexcusable penalty. It's pretty damn hard to jump offside when the ball is meant to be snapped on the quarterback's first "hut," but I was so desperate to compensate for my lack of speed that I started my block on Leopold about a half second too early. Multiple referees whistled the play dead, and the crowd let out an immediate groan. At least with the heavy mist they probably couldn't tell that I was the one who—

"FALSE START, OFFENSE, NUMBER SIXTY-SEVEN," announced the head referee through the stadium speaker system.

As a ref picked up the ball and paced five yards backward, the crowd's groans transformed into throaty, resentful boos. Then chiming in clear as a church bell over the low growl of the fans came a punctuating "YOU SUCK!" from high up on the bleachers. Whoever shouted this was right. The crowd had had enough of me, and now the boos rained down from all 360 degrees of the surrounding stands. Crooks called me off the field, put his mangled claw hand on my shoulder, and politely invited me to "sit my fat ass on the damn bench." The penalty had been the last straw, and in my place they substituted a backup guard who'd never played tackle before.

The boos hurt. Not gonna lie. But what I was most ashamed about was how I was actually *happy* that I'd been pulled from the game. Some guys want to be on the big stage. Some guys want the ball in their hands, the team on their shoulders, the mental welfare of the entire town on their conscience. I'd hoped that would be me, but at that exact moment I learned that it wasn't me. With every ounce of my body I wanted to be back on the sideline. I even wanted to be back inside the Poncho Pete costume, watching the world pass me by through nothing but little cutouts for eyes. I was disgusted with myself.

My penalty turned a third-and-one into a third-and-six, and we failed to convert after Leopold batted down and almost intercepted Brett's pass attempt. We punted to Blakemore's twenty-one-yard line, and they swiftly bled out the clock with a steady onslaught of short but effective runs. We finally forced a punt after allowing two first downs, but there were only forty-five seconds remaining when Brett and the offense jogged back onto the field for one final shot to tie or win the game.

With no timeouts remaining and sixty yards to reach the end zone, we had to gain some big chunks of yards through the air. On the first play of the drive Leopold broke through the line, but Brett got the behemoth to bite on a pump fake. He must've known Leopold's near-interception minutes earlier had made him overeager to go for another. Leopold jumped at the pump fake, buying Brett enough time to shuffle laterally and connect with our tight end twenty-five yards downfield.

For a moment there was pandemonium as the crowd erupted and the offense sprinted downfield to quickly begin the next play. But before Brett could finish calling his audibles at Blakemore's thirty-five-yard line, the referees whistled a stoppage in play. There was a moment of confusion as five thousand people tried to figure out the reason for the stoppage, but we soon learned the reason: A crumpled body lay moaning on the ground back at our forty-yard line.

A trainer ran out to the field, followed by Crooks. The two of them disappeared into the fog, and when Crooks got close enough to the injured player to see his identity, he shook his head and put his hands on his hips.

"Wyatt!" he shouted toward our bench. "Get your ass back in there!"

Oh jeez. Oh god. Oh jeez.

One of my legs had fallen asleep sitting on the bench, so I did this weird hobble run to the huddle. Behind us, the trainer was still treating the injured lineman—a victim, no doubt, of Leopold.

When I took my place in the huddle, Brett looked at me intently. "Dude," he said. "Where's your helmet?"

I hobble-ran back to the sideline. Where *was* my helmet?

I checked on the bench. Not there.

I looked by the water table. Nada.

Back on the field, the trainer had gotten the injured player to his feet and was helping him limp off. Panicked, I spun around when—*there!*—I saw a stray helmet in the mud under the bench; I went to grab it, then froze.

Taped across the face mask was a blank white envelope.

You gotta be shitting me, I thought. I quickly glanced around for Trunk, who must've been slinking around somewhere, waiting for me to open the envelope. The thought of the lengths he went to to torture me was enraging, and for some reason that anger felt kind of powerful—maybe something I could use on the field. So I decided to double down on the anger. I tore open the envelope and pulled out the note.

Only it wasn't a note. It was a page from a textbook. I squinted at the small print. It looked like some science book. Biology maybe? I saw dozens of careful notes written in the margins, and that's when it hit me: This was Nate's handwriting. This was from Nate's textbook. But why? I skimmed over the page, then saw a note scrawled in all capital letters: *RIGHT HERE, DUMMY.* A hand-drawn arrow pointed to a single line in the text. It was under a section titled "Genetics." The beginning of the sentence was filled with some gobbledygook about alleles and diploid organisms, but it reached this conclusion, which Nate had underlined:

. . . *siblings share 50% of their DNA.*

"Christ, Wyatt, hurry your ass up!" Crooks screamed. My leg was awake now and I sprinted back to the huddle and buckled on my helmet en route.

I didn't have time to fully translate Nate's cryptic message. But as I looked at Brett, his entire body caked in mud and the gash in his forearm oozing blood, I thought about how *I—me— Wyatt*—was 50 percent Brett. Coursing through me at that moment was a surreal surge of power. It wasn't that I suddenly thought I could be as athletic as Brett, but I now knew the scientific truth: Buried somewhere inside me was at least some of

Brett's talent. This wasn't a guess or a desperate hope. It was science.

"Alright, fellas," the head ref shouted to us once the injured player was off the field. "Fifteen seconds on the clock, starting on my whistle."

"You heard 'em," said Brett, crouched in the center of our huddle. "It's do-or-die time. I want everything you have left. Too far for a field goal, so we're going with a 33-44 waggle right. Let's go—we're winning this thing."

Brett broke the huddle and we jogged up to the line. The ref blew his whistle, and the clock started counting down.

I crouched into my stance and looked up into Leopold's black eyes. In my peripheral vision, I could see Brett crouch under center. But something was off. I could see it in his eyes.

Suddenly, Brett took a step back from the center. "Austin, Austin, 47-Chicago!" he shouted.

A second passed as our offense deciphered Brett's audible.

"What the hell?" the guard next to me wondered aloud. And I was thinking the same thing: Was Brett seriously changing the play to the tackle-eligible pass?

I was the tackle eligible.

It had to have been a mistake. But then again, Brett didn't make mistakes. Not when the game was on the line.

The clock ticked down to five . . . four . . . three . . .

"Hut-HUT!"

Our center snapped the ball to Brett and I shot out of my stance. Crooks's repeated instructions to Trunk about the tackle-eligible pass echoed in my head: *Before you run your pass route you MUST chip block Leopold so he doesn't get a clean run at Brett. You MUST slow down his rush.*

I took two steps forward and in an instant I was upon Leopold. I lowered my shoulder, went square for his enormous chest—and completely whiffed.

I stumbled forward a bit as Leopold dodged me like a matador dodges a bull, but all I could do at this point was keep running my route. I'd made it about ten yards downfield when I glanced back at Brett. I saw Leopold fully outstretched and flying helmet-first into Brett's jaw. Then I noticed Brett's throwing hand. It was empty. The ball was already in the air.

I looked skyward and there it was, a foot away. Out of the corner of my eye I saw Blakemore's safety charging at me. The pass was high and slightly behind me, so I swiveled my shoulders around and reached back to the ball with one hand, which was all I could get on it. Using some instinct I never knew I had, I flicked my wrist and batted the ball up, popping it back into the air. It sailed forward in a small arc over the oncoming safety's head, and I continued my full-body swivel into a complete 360-degree spin. My forward momentum was still carrying me ahead, and when I completed the spin, the ball finished its parabola and fell into my hands.

I scampered the final ten yards into the end zone. Touchdown.

* * *

What happened next was mostly a blur.

I remember the stadium fog horn blaring in celebration. I remember getting absolutely leveled by about a dozen teammates jumping on top of me. But what I remember most was an image that haunts me to this day. Back on the thirty-yard line, through the mist, was a motionless body sprawled out in the mud. Hovering above it was the silhouette of a giant. He stared down at the body. Then he nudged the body with a prod of his foot. Brett didn't move. The giant unbuckled his chin strap and walked off the field.

More guys pig piled on top of me. They screamed exuberant nonsense. They told me they fucking loved me.

Panicked, I wriggled free from the bottom of the pile and looked back at the thirty-yard line. Brett's limp body was gone—vanished into the fog.

"Hey!" a voice suddenly rang out behind me.

I spun around.

"You did it," Brett said. "You did it."

Then we hugged.

CHAPTER
SIXTEEN

There was no question who got to ride shotgun to the postgame party. Maddox had been sitting in the passenger seat of Archer's pickup truck as it idled in the parking lot outside the locker room, but when Brett and I approached, Archer quickly hopped out, smiled wide at me, and said, "It's all yours, big man." I wanted to ride in the bed of the truck, though, so Brett took shotgun while I stood in the back with my hands laid flat on the roof for balance. Behind me in the truck bed a few of my teammates sat and cracked open beers, but I stayed standing when Maddox revved the engine and peeled out of the parking lot. I stood facing forward the entire way, taking in the exhilarating rush of wind and speed. Through the soles of my shoes I could feel the powerful torque of the truck's tires biting into the gravelly and twisting seaside road as we climbed up and up through the salty fog to the highest point in Grayport. Until that night, I'd never actually been to the town lighthouse, knowing it only as a distant and probably haunted pillar of solitude standing eerily atop a tall and jagged cliff. The

Grayport football team knew it well, though, because they always held their victory parties on the field of crabgrass between the lighthouse and the ocean cliff.

Maddox parked the truck alongside the dozen or so cars that had arrived before us. The guys who didn't see much game action leapt nimbly over the wall of the truck bed, but the rest of us were so battered we waited for Brett to let down the tailgate so we could gingerly slide our butts off the back until our feet softly touched the ground. From the other side of the lighthouse you could hear beers cracking, bonfires crackling, and people laughing. My teammates shuffled slowly toward the party, but Brett and I lingered behind the pack. I don't know if this was intentional or simply because our broken bodies had synced our hobbles to the same speed. I was happy either way.

"You look like shit," Brett said after a moment.

He was both kidding and not. When I looked at myself in the mirror after the game, I saw an entirely new person. My puffy red cheeks had turned white and hollow. Purple bruises and welts were smattered across my body. A partial imprint of someone's face mask was tattooed on my right biceps, and on my neck were five small bruises the shape of fingerprints from a play in which Leopold grabbed my throat, lifted me off the ground, and slammed me into the mud.

"Yeah? Well, you look like a rottweiler's chew toy," I shot back playfully.

I heard Brett sigh, but even through the darkness I could tell he was smiling. I was, too.

You've probably heard all the talking heads on TV and in newspapers complaining about football: the violence, the injuries, the pain. But sometimes I'm like, did anyone ask us—the actual players—how we feel about it? Yeah, the pain doesn't feel *good*, but it sure as hell feels *meaningful*. It's a pretty raw and immediate connection to the guys you line up alongside. And sure, everyone feels pain, but that's like saying everyone on earth knows a language so therefore the whole world should understand each other. *This* pain is a specific language, felt rather than spoken, understood only by football players. If you've ever played, you know what I'm talking about: The random joint, for example, throbbing so intensely you surely screamed in pain when you injured it or at least remember the play vividly, only you didn't, and you don't. The sharp yet somehow unspecified stinging in internal organs so obscure you're only now aware of their existence. I don't know if I'm putting it into words the right way. But I do know that as I limped next to Brett, I was feeling what he was feeling. If pain was the price of admission, I'd pay it every time.

The party was already rocking when Brett and I finally made it over to the plot of grass behind the lighthouse. In the center of the lawn was an old picnic table that bowed under the weight of a dozen cases of beer. Buried somewhere in that tower of cardboard boxes was a portable speaker blaring out tunes. Scattered around the lawn were six or seven small bonfires with clusters of kids sitting in foldout beach chairs, telling stories and jokes. A soggy football fluttered around randomly from person to person, from teammate to teammate, from football player to nonplayer, from guy to girl—it seemed like everyone got their hands on it at some point or other.

I inhaled deeply. The fires smelled crisp and alive and a little like cinnamon. It was nice up on the cliff, where the lighter fog embraced you rather than strangled you. We were also above and upwind from the shore, where the stench of rotting fish assaulted the senses.

Brett scanned the lawn and caught sight of Maddox, Archer, and a few other guys sitting around the bonfire closest to the cliff. We started dragging ourselves in that direction when this dude—I think his name was Jeremy—staggered up to us. I recognized him from my trigonometry class. He always sat next to me in the back and gazed at the ceiling while occasionally stroking his thick, tangled beard, which was kind of disgusting and kind of badass at the same time. He always wore flannel and always reeked of pot.

Jeremy stopped in front of us and held his arms out wide. "Dude!" he said, grinning directly at me.

"Hey, man," I said.

Jeremy's entire right hand was buried in a bag of cheddar Goldfish, which somehow stayed fastened to him like a glove. He looked like Winnie the Pooh with his hand stuck in a jar of honey.

"Dude," he repeated. *"Dude."*

Then he lurched forward with surprising quickness and hugged me. "Dude," he whispered softly into my ear, patting me on the back with his Goldfish hand. "Thank you. For everything."

"Uh, you're welcome?" I could feel Jeremy's wiry beard scraping against my cheek. I caught eyes with Brett and he shook his head, smiling.

Jeremy released me and staggered backward. "That catch, man . . . that fucking *catch*. It was like—it was like a goddam *religious experience,* if religion wasn't a man-made construct used by the top one percent to subordinate the masses. Here, have some Goldfish."

Jeremy yanked his hand from the bag and jiggled the Goldfish package in what I think was supposed to be an enticing manner. I didn't really want Goldfish—they felt weirdly inappropriate in my new social context—but I didn't want to offend Jeremy so I formed a small cup with one hand and held it out. Jeremy tipped the bag at a 90-degree angle, dumping out the entire thing. The waterfall of crackers began spilling out of my hand, so I quickly added my other hand to form a larger vessel. Jeremy tossed the empty bag to the ground.

I wasn't sure what the play was here. I couldn't just smash my face into the pile of crackers like some sort of barbarian, so instead I stood there awkwardly, holding about a hundred Goldfish in my hand bowl.

"Dude," Jeremy now said to Brett, slapping a hand on his

shoulder. It was weird seeing Brett, usually so sturdy, stagger slightly on impact. "D'ya wanna know something about my man Wyatt Parker here? Did ya know that we're in the same geometry class?"

"Trigonometry," I mumbled.

"Oh yeah?" Brett replied politely to Jeremy.

"Yup, same exact goddam class, if you can believe it. So anyway, this is gonna blow your mind into stardust, but . . ."

Suddenly Jeremy stopped midsentence and stared down at my hand bowl of Goldfish. His eyes grew wide. "Holy shit, you've got Goldfish! Mind if I have some?"

Before I could answer he took a small handful and popped them in his mouth.

"So anyway," he said as he noshed the orange crackers. "This whole semester, right, I'm like, *Oh, there's that kid Wyatt who sits next to me.* But then tonight he makes that catch—that *catch,* man—and my brain stands on its head 'cause I now realize that this whole semester *Wyatt* hasn't been sitting next to *me—I've* been sitting next to *Wyatt.*"

Jeremy took another large pinch of Goldfish from my hands and tossed them in his mouth. As he chewed them he looked back and forth between Brett and me with an intense, expectant smile, like the weight of this revelation was supposed to make us collapse and possibly piss ourselves.

"Yeah, that's, uh . . . that's nuts," I said.

"Naw, man, these are Goldfish," he said, taking another

handful from me. "Hey, anyone ever tell you guys you've got, like, the exact same eyeballs? I'm talking *exact same*. Both sets are round, for instance. Both as green as the night sky. Only yours," he said, looking at Brett, "yours are like *two* different sizes. But I'm kind of digging them, if I can be totally honest with you. They're kind of like a 'fuck you' to the establishment, you know?" He took another scoop of Goldfish from me, polishing off the remaining bit. There was a thin layer of Goldfish on my palms, and I dusted it off on my jeans.

"I think I hear Maddox calling us over," Brett said. "Nice meeting you, uh . . ."

"Jeremy. The name's Jeremy. But my friends call me Jeremy."

"Okay. Right. Nice meeting you, Jeremy."

"Anytime," he said. "And Wyatt, thanks again for the catch. And for the Goldfish. For everything, really."

Our short trek across the lawn to the bonfire was the most incredible walk of my life. I could sense every eye on me, and for the first time ever I was proud of the way I looked. Every welt, gash, and lump was like a badge of honor. I felt enormous, but in a powerful way, like my XL chest and stomach were cavernous chambers that could inhale more life than anyone else. It was like my body finally made *sense*, you know? Like it had been placed in its proper context. Not once but twice someone came up to us, knelt before me like I was a king, then chugged a beer in my honor. A moment later, I was surprised by an aggressive butt slap from a random girl who said, "Nice catch, stud." Near the bonfire, a couple of guys were reenacting the last play of the game. The guy running the pass route was rocking one of the replica Brett Parker jerseys that vendors sold outside the stadium. On the back of the jersey below *PARKER* he had used duct tape to stencil a makeshift *6* in front of the *7* to transform Brett's number into mine.

Only one beach chair was open around the bonfire, but Brett quickly settled which of us would take it.

"Hey, I gotta go take care of something real quick," he said to me quietly. "You going to be okay here?"

I nodded and eased myself into the foldout beach chair. It was nothing more than two swatches of coarse fabric stretched over a cheap tin frame, but as I sank my aching body into the seat I thought how I might never get up from this heavenly throne. You might say it felt like a religious experience.

Archer lounged in the chair to my right, and across from me sat Maddox. His girlfriend was sitting on his lap, and her extravagant curtain of blond hair made his shoulder-length flow seem tame in comparison. Her name was Pristine. She was a nice girl—or at least I figured she must've been because she was one of Haley's good friends. I quietly wondered whether Haley was at the party.

On the ground next to both sides of Maddox's beach chair were cases of beer poised like holstered guns ready for lightning-quick access. My butt had barely touched the seat when Maddox shot his hands into the cardboard boxes, grabbing cans and tossing them to each person circled around the bonfire.

My stomach clenched: The only thing I wanted less than a beer was my teammates thinking I was too scared to drink. Even my old daydreams of attending a Grayport victory party included this horrible moment where I'd be forced to choose one side or the other. As Maddox distributed the beers I legit had no idea whether I'd take one or not. All I knew was that either way I'd be disappointed in myself.

Maddox rapidly completed one pass after another—*bang bang bang*—in a clockwise motion. Then it was my turn to catch the toss. He snatched a can from the box and sent it tumbling end over end in my direction, but soon I saw that his intended target was actually the kid to my left, who caught the can easily. I'd been holding my hands up ready for the pass, so I quickly put them down and pretended not to notice or care that he blatantly skipped me. I wasn't sure whether to be relieved or offended. I wriggled uncomfortably in my seat as he finished distributing the beers.

When Maddox had completed the circle, he grabbed a beer for himself and cracked it open. But he didn't take a sip. Instead, he cleared his throat.

"We should probably toast the guest of honor," he said, holding up his can. "I mean, if it wasn't for Wyatt we wouldn't even be out here celebrating tonight. Actually, we'd probably still be out here, but it'd be depressing as hell." Maddox chuckled softly, then fixed his eyes directly on me. "I've got no clue how you're able to run lugging a pair of balls the size of Jupiter between your legs, but you made a hell of a play when the rest of us couldn't get anything going."

"You mean when *you* couldn't get your ass open," Pristine teased.

"Hey, if those bastards weren't double-teaming me all night I would've made the catch," Maddox countered.

"Babe, the only thing you could catch tonight was a cold."

"Well, my throat is feeling a little sore if you want to inspect it . . ."

"Ugh, grow up."

"How about *you* grow *down*?"

"God, you're even dumber than you look."

At that, Maddox and Pristine began aggressively making out. The rest of us glanced around from person to person in an awkward silence.

Archer lifted his beer. "Um, cheers?"

We settled into the evening after that. I mostly listened to the conversations and laughed at everyone's jokes. We recapped the game, exchanged stories about Coach Crooks's batshit ideas, and then somehow got into an argument about whether it would be easier to fight a duck the size of a horse or one hundred horses the size of ducks. We pooled together $35 for Maddox to eat a worm, but after he gulped it down we emptied our pockets and only came up with $8.56 between us. Maddox just shrugged and said the joke was on us because he liked the taste of worms.

Nobody offered me a drink the entire night, despite it flying around liberally. I was both confused and relieved about this, but at some point those feelings evolved into a weird feeling of gratitude. These guys weren't exactly the most sensitive dudes in the world, and they sure as hell weren't above hazing underclassmen, but when it came to my aversion to alcohol, they got it. Like, they knew my family situation. They were there at last night's pep rally. They saw Dad, saw how he acted with a bottle in his hands. They knew why I wouldn't touch the stuff. They decided not to even put me in the awkward position of saying no to them, and for the first time in forever, I felt understood.

But none of my teammates could help me when Haley came over.

She approached our circle with a mix of confidence and apprehension. She was wearing a pair of tight jeans that countered her baggy Grayport Football sweatshirt, the cuff of which was pulled over her hand as a layer of insulation for the cold beer she held.

"Sounds like a good time over here," she said, using her free hand to tuck a stray lock of brown hair behind her ear.

Pristine let out a small excited yelp, no doubt relieved to finally have another girl there to dilute the percentage of the group who ate invertebrates for fun. "Oh my god, Haley, you *have* to hang here awhile," she pleaded.

"Sure, okay," Haley replied as she discreetly scanned the circle of dudes planted in our beach chairs around the fire.

At that moment not one but two ideas hit me. *She's looking for an open seat*, followed by, *Offer her your seat!* This inner voice was definitely a distant echo from my mom, who couldn't stop herself from offering unsolicited love advice whenever I visited her on weekends at Aunt Jackie's house. *Remember to always be a gentleman*, she'd say, totally proving that she had no clue about my world, a place where a guy could eat a worm and kiss a hot girl in a single sitting. *And whatever you do*, Mom would add dramatically, like she was about to drop some magical wisdom, *remember to just be yourself.*

That one always drove me up the freaking wall. I'd been myself for the last sixteen years and it wasn't working. "Being myself" wasn't the solution—it was the *problem.*

But it was all I knew. So as Haley stood uncomfortably on the outside of our circle of chairs, I instinctively went "full gentleman" on her.

"You can have my seat, if you want," I mumbled quietly.

Haley didn't hear me because when I get nervous I've got a real problem with volume control. It's like my voice has a super wide range of volume settings that includes every decibel level except, you know, all the ones used by normal human beings.

"Say that again?" Haley asked.

Rattled, I swung the audio needle to the other extreme. "THERE'S A SEAT FOR YOU RIGHT HERE!"

The entire group erupted in a chorus of amazed laughter and dramatic "Oh shiiiits!" Haley cocked her head at me and narrowed her eyes like she was mildly annoyed, but at the same time the emergence of a sly smile suggested a degree of impressed bemusement. "A little bold," she said. "But I'll allow it."

Then she glided over to me and *sat directly on my lap.*

You know all that bullshit I spewed earlier about finally feeling confident about stuff? That was now gone, *poof,* nothing more than a wisp of smoke disappearing into the fog. I could feel all of my progress—first the catch and now my unintentional pickup line *that had actually worked*—start to feel choked out of me as my nerves brought with them a familiar shortness of breath in my lungs, making my panic even worse because I'm pretty sure it's unsexy to die of an asthma attack at the mere touch of a woman.

I was freaking out hard, so I can't exactly say how many minutes Haley had been sitting on my lap, but I'd guess it was somewhere in the range of three minutes to three hours. Luckily she was chatting with the group and facing forward so she couldn't see the beads of sweat pouring down my face as I concentrated every micro-muscle in my body to avoid any sudden movements that might cause the chair to collapse.

The only minor distraction I faced was the fragrance wafting from Haley's long brunette hair, which fell along the slope of her neck and lightly tickled my shoulder with each turn of her head. I'm not a total creep, so there's really not much else to

say about her hair other than it smelled like a blend of straw-
berries, honey, and happy childhood memories, all mixed with
subtle notes of existential crisis from feeling tragically nostalgic
for this beautiful and fleeting moment right here in the present.
And vanilla—there was definitely some vanilla in there, too.

Anyway, as Haley sat on my lap I realized that there's a small
but critical difference between "smelling" and "sniffing," and
it took a lot of concentration to stay on the right side of that
razor-thin line.

My focus deviated further when Brett, cradling a football
in one hand and holding a folded beach chair in the other,
approached our bonfire. He grimaced in pain as he slowly
unfolded his chair and plunked down directly across from
Haley and me. The flames dancing in the bonfire obscured most
of his body, but I could still see Brett's face flickering in the
orange light. We caught eyes, and he gave a quick raise of his
eyebrows and grinned, like "nice going with the girl."

The group kept chatting but Brett didn't say much to anyone. Once in a while he'd pull out his phone and look at it with
disinterest, but for the most part he stared absently into the fire,
spinning his football slowly between his palms. It made me
feel better seeing him act this way around his friends because it
suggested that maybe all these quiet years between us, though
strained, weren't abnormal.

After a little while Brett finally spoke up, startling nobody
more than me by calling out my name.

"Yo, Wyatt—heads up!"

I glanced up to see Brett cock his elbow by his ear and then snap the football in my direction. The ball cleared Haley's head by a good foot, and I flung one hand blindly into the air in a desperate attempt to snag the pass. The nose of the ball *thwapped* into my palm and miraculously stuck there. I pulled down the one-handed catch casually, even though my internal disbelief was as resounding as the burst of cheers around the bonfire. Haley had swiveled sideways on my thigh and now partially faced me. Her big white smile and excited clapping made me feel like I was floating.

Archer had the loudest reaction. "Dude, why've you been holding out on this crazy skill for so long?" he asked excitedly. Then, to no one in particular he exclaimed, "This kid catches anything!"

Pristine leaned back into Maddox's chest and turned her head toward him. "You taking notes, babe?"

"Come on, I practically invented the one-handed catch," Maddox shot back.

"Well, you do have a lot of experience using one hand . . ."

"Yeah, a lot of experience doing *this*," and Maddox held out one hand and gave Pristine the finger. They started to aggressively make out again. I tossed a wobbly pass back to Brett.

"I dunno, man," Archer said to a seriously preoccupied Maddox. "I think Wyatt has the softest hands in Grayport."

"Really?" Haley chimed in. "I think this needs verification." She placed her beer on the ground and then plucked each of my wrists off our chair's plastic armrests. She guided my hands palms-up onto her lap so my arms were now partially wrapped around her. Then she delicately traced her fingertips across my palms, sending a shiver through my entire being. My heart also skipped a beat as I felt more thread pull apart in the chair underneath us.

"Oh my god, they are *so* soft," she said, still stroking my hands. "And really big, too."

I cleared my throat. This was it: the moment I'd been practicing in my head for like the past three years. "Well, you know what they say about guys with big feet . . ."

Silence.

"You mean hands?" Haley corrected me.

"Oh, right."

"Hey, Haley," Brett suddenly interjected. "Do you trust me?"

"What? Uh, sure, I guess."

"Okay, then hold very still."

Before Haley could ask why, Brett whistled a pass on a sharp line toward the two of us.

Haley's yelp was still hanging in the air as the ball zipped just above the top of her head, cutting so close it skimmed through a tuft of her hair. I pulled my hands from her lap and caught the screaming pass about one centimeter from the top of her head.

The group cheered and Haley laughed with relief and joy. I tossed the ball back to Brett.

"Okay, next question," Brett said to Haley. "Do you trust Wyatt?"

Haley turned toward me, looked me up and down, and giggled at her little mock appraisal. "Yes."

"I mean *really* trust him."

"With my life," she said.

"Okay. Don't move a muscle."

The football shot out of Brett's hands, and within a second it had passed through the flames of the bonfire and missiled directly at Haley's face. She screamed.

THWACK.

When Haley opened her eyes next, she saw my hands wrapped securely around the football, its pointed nose only millimeters from her mouth. I felt her entire body unclench in my lap. Then, without moving her head, she puckered her lips and kissed the ball on the tip of its nose. "Hello, you," she said warmly.

Brett and I kept playing catch like this for minutes that seemed to contain within them entire years, the ball like a spark traveling back and forth on an invisible wire that connected us more than words ever had. Haley kept yelping and giggling; each pass was as thrilling as the last, a real-life magic trick courtesy of the Parker Brothers. Again and again Brett delivered an impossibly precise pass into my hands, and Haley would shudder in a sort of primal excitement, digging her tailbone into my thigh and pressing a deep bone bruise I didn't know I had until just then. The pain was intense, radiating, and amazing, a visceral connection to the game that had changed everything for me.

After a little while I suggested that Haley throw the ball back to Brett.

"Sure," Haley said. "But I suck big-time at throwing spirals. Can you show me the secret?"

"Yeah, totally," I told her. "Is it okay if I, uh, if I put my hand on top of yours?"

"Totally okay," she said.

Haley held the ball and I laid my hand softly on top of hers, adjusting each of her fingers here, here, and here across the laces in a perfect form that I had to learn from a YouTube video since Dad never taught me.

"Okay, now when you throw," I explained, "just let the ball spin a little off your fingers."

Haley cocked her arm and fired an absolute bullet to Brett. A perfect spiral.

"Jesus," I said. "That was a laser."

"Well, I had a good coach."

"You're a liar," I said. "You *totally* have thrown a football before."

Haley flashed a devious grin. "Maybe like one or two thousand times," she said. "I live in Grayport. Isn't learning to throw a football some sort of holy commandment?"

"How could I forget?" I said. "Thou shalt sling inflated pigskins at supreme velocities."

A few hours before I would have never dreamed of being this

comfortable with Haley, but now I felt a surge of . . . I don't know, intangible *certainty* deep within me. It was similar to the rush I felt as I ran to the huddle for the final play with the knowledge that I had half of Brett's DNA in my very foundation. Suddenly, I was certain that I'd catch every pass Brett threw me, certain that I could overcome any awkward moment with Haley, and certain that the threads of my chair wouldn't break because they were woven in double helixes as strong as the DNA in my blood.

The pace of our game of catch eventually slowed, and it ended for good when Brett put the ball down and mumbled about having to take care of something. We watched his shadow grow long in the bonfire's glow as he limped into the darkness, off to do whatever mysterious things Brett did.

When he was gone Haley turned to me. "Selfie time," she announced. "A picture with tonight's hero is going to set a record for likes."

Haley dug her phone from her pocket, but its battery was dead. My phone had a cracked screen and was older than the Stone Age, but it at least had a front-facing camera so I whipped it out and held it at arm's length from the two of us. When I unlocked the screen, there was a text waiting for me from Brett. It was time-stamped from twenty minutes earlier, and Haley and I both read his message:

STOP SNIFFING HER HAIR CREEPO

"Oh, um . . . yeah," I explained. I frantically smashed CLOSE with my sausage fingers. I then quickly opened the camera app. "Ready? One-two-three!"

But the resulting picture was only of the top of our heads, because at that very moment we were plummeting down to a rough landing of wet grass and a heap of mangled chair.

I landed spread-eagle on my back with Haley sprawled on top of me like I was a beanbag chair. She was bursting with the most pure and joyful laugh I'd ever heard.

"You okay?" I asked, laughing myself.

"I'll survive," she said. She flipped over so now she was facing me. Her face was inches from mine, and her hair fell like a blanket around the borders of my face, blocking out the entire world and leaving just the two of us looking at each other in our own private tunnel.

"I promise I wasn't sniffing your hair," I whispered. "I was smelling it."

Haley giggled. "You're cute," she said. Then she leaned forward and softly kissed the tip of my nose.

I felt a lot of things: tingling, numbness, and an oncoming asthma attack, to name a few. The most prominent feeling, though, was from someone's shoe urgently nudging me on the shoulder.

"Um, dude? Can I talk to you a second?"

I knew the voice from outside our secret fortress was real, but I squeezed my eyes shut tightly in an attempt to will it out of existence.

"Dude, Wyatt. For real," the voice came again.

Haley rolled off of me, unveiling a clear view of Jeremy standing above us. He somehow had a new bag of Goldfish.

"I hate to, like, ration your passion and all, but I think you better go check on your bro." He motioned over toward the ocean cliff, where Brett had walked off to. "I'm no doctor," Jeremy continued, "but I was a veterinarian in a previous life, and in my professional opinion Brett is, like, the opposite of okay."

CHAPTER
SEVENTEEN

Brett's body language was usually harder to read than Dad's because his face wasn't very expressive. He almost always wore the same hard-boiled look—didn't matter whether he was stepping over the goal line for a touchdown or stepping over a smashed toaster on his way out the kitchen door. His strides were purposeful, even when he wasn't sure where he was going. He was expressionless but far from emotionless. His dark eyebrows were typically furrowed above emerald eyes that didn't just observe the world but fully absorbed it, allowing it to seep down into a place so private and so deep within him no tremor could ever reach the surface.

Even with so few clues, I could always sense Brett's mood, and it was easy to tell that something was off as I approached him standing near the edge of the cliff. Jeremy had told me that Brett was acting weird about a hundred yards north of our bonfire, and sure enough, when I trekked through the fog in that direction, there was Brett staring out into the ocean.

It felt like a different world out there on the bluff. Even the bass of the party music was drowned out by the heavy *thump* of waves crashing into the jagged rocks fifty feet below. Asking Brett if he was okay seemed like way too personal a question— it felt weird enough going to "check on" my big brother, so I sure as hell couldn't pat him on the back and be like, *Hey, kiddo, why the bad vibes?* So instead I didn't say a word and just stood next to him, watching the sweeping pulse of the lighthouse beam as it revealed and then erased sparkling slices of silver ocean.

"I've got a secret," Brett said after a while. He kept looking ahead, like he was talking to the black horizon.

"Okay . . ." I could feel my entire body scrunching up.

"He's not out there. He didn't make it."

"Who? Dad?"

Brett didn't respond. The lighthouse beam swept across the ocean once, twice, three times.

"No," he said finally. "That little friend of yours—can't remember his name. We told you he made it to the ocean, but he didn't."

Was I imagining things, or was Brett slurring his words? I didn't smell alcohol on him, and it was well known around school that Brett Parker, in his militaristic discipline over nutrition, never drank. But right now something was off. There had also been signs when we were sitting at the bonfire earlier—the way Brett stared into the fire with glossy eyes. I would've been more concerned if I hadn't been so busy concentrating on Haley and resisting the impulse to wrap myself like a burrito in her delicious hair.

I turned to look at Brett now. He was squeezing his eyes shut and rubbing his forehead. "I can't remember his name," he said in a low, quivering voice. "I'm trying, but I can't . . ."

It took me a moment to put together the pieces of Brett's fragmented thoughts, and when I did, I was still confused about why he was bringing this up. He was referring to a time when we were kids.

It all started at my seventh birthday, when my aunt Jackie gifted me a doll. She didn't give it to me until Dad had left my party to "do errands" (aka hit up the bar), because she knew that me having a doll would be *so* not okay with him. I wasn't too psyched about the doll myself. He was one of those talking dolls, squeaking out phrases like *You're my best friend!* and *Hooray for play day!* and, for some reason, *Let's recycle!*

The doll and I didn't recycle much. But we did hang out pretty often when Dad and Brett were out doing football stuff. No tea parties or anything, but I remember watching all the Patriots games with him and teaching him the rules of football. We could afford internet back then, so I also introduced him to the joy of watching YouTube videos of douchey skateboarders eating pavement. I also remember using him as a wrestling dummy, body-slamming him off the top bunk into a fortress of pillows. He took it like a champ. He always had a smile on his face, even when his head popped off and I had to play surgeon by delicately securing it back onto his torso with a sledgehammer. He didn't talk anymore after the operation, so he was like Brett in that way.

Dad eventually found the doll. Who knows what he did with it, but I'm sure it didn't involve recycling. I wasn't too upset since I was getting bored of the doll, anyway. But I'd gotten a small taste of being responsible and caring for something, and honestly I kind of liked it. So I wanted something to replace the doll, something that might even care for me back, something living. I knew Dad would not be down with a girly pet like a gerbil or guinea pig, so for my next birthday I asked for a rat. Mom was horrified by the idea, saying, "No, Wyatt, that's disgusting." But I said, "Ugh, Mom, I'm a boy and I have my needs."

My eighth birthday party was an elaborate affair that featured a hybrid pirates/spacemen theme. I dressed up as a knight with a sword, which I think some people were internally questioning, theme-wise, but I was the birthday boy, so deal with it. When it was time to unwrap gifts, I went straight for the large box with holes poked in it. I carefully cut along the wrapping paper with a pair of scissors, eager to get my hands on that little fur ball with his chompy front teeth and long wormy tail. I tore off the paper, placed the box on the ground, and lifted the lid to feast my eyes on the rugged glory of . . . a tadpole.

I was furious, of course, but what was I supposed to do? I couldn't just *abandon* the thing. So I named him Mr. Giggles and brought his water bowl to our attic room and placed him high up on the bureau.

Mr. Giggles was pretty antisocial. He spent all his time chilling inside his tiny plastic castle. He never left that castle, even when Nate and I smushed our giant doughy faces against the glass and politely screamed at him to come out and play. Sometimes when I was alone Mr. Giggles would emerge from the castle for a quick swim. This made me want to show him off even more. He came out only once when Nate was there, but instead of doing his cool signature move where he swam in super agile figure eights, he just slammed his head repeatedly into the wall of his bowl. Nate laughed at this, so I, as a responsible legal guardian, punched him in the arm. I also expressed my concern that maybe Mr. Giggles had poor vision and needed glasses. But Brett, who'd been lying up in his top bunk, put down the playbook he'd been reading and said no, Mr. Giggles's vision is fine. What he needs, Brett said, is a bigger bowl so he doesn't feel so trapped and hopeless.

Brett had a point, but I knew I was raising Mr. Giggles well because he was growing rapidly. My mom said I was an excellent "daddy," which in my view was an unacceptable term, so she suggested "caretaker," which was a little better, though we ultimately settled that I was an excellent "Tadpole Development Specialist." It was tough to play with Mr. Giggles, but we had some epic staring matches (I always let him win). I read online that tadpoles love fresh water, so I switched his water four times a day.

One afternoon when I came home from school Mr. Giggles was not in his bowl. I frantically ran downstairs and asked my mom if she had seen any thieves enter or exit the apartment because we had a full-blown kidnapping on our hands. She inspected the scene of the crime and noticed a little trail of water droplets leading from the base of our bureau out the door and down the stairs. After following the trail downstairs, Mom returned and gravely told me that Mr. Giggles had grown legs, leapt out of his bowl, and "moved on to a better place."

I was shocked at how readily my tears flowed, and humiliated that Brett was there to see me turn into a puddle. In between sobs I asked if Mr. Giggles had jumped to his death, if his life in the bowl was so terrible that he had grown legs just to climb out and fling himself off the bureau's cliff.

Mom and Brett looked at each other, then told me that Mr. Giggles had grown legs and crawled down to the beach and was now happily swimming with all his frog buddies in the ocean. This made me feel better because, if you haven't been paying attention, the natural sciences aren't exactly a strong subject of mine.

Still, I was heartbroken over the unexpected loss, and as I cried over Mr. Giggles, cried over my failure as a caretaker, and cried about crying, my mom just kept rubbing my back, softly repeating, "You're a good boy, you're a good boy."

* * *

"His name was Mr. Giggles," I said to Brett as we looked out over the cliff.

"Mr. Giggles," Brett repeated to himself. "That's right. I found him dead on the kitchen floor, you know. He escaped that little bowl, but couldn't escape our apartment." Brett's slurred speech sounded distant, like it had arrived by a gust of wind here on the edge of the cliff. "We have to get out of here, Wyatt."

"Okay, sure. Let's go home."

"I mean Grayport. We have to escape. Like Mom did. Like Mr. Giggles tried to."

I had always assumed Brett, like me, desperately wanted to leave town—otherwise, our future would be making minimum wage on a fishing boat. And that's if things went well and red tide didn't reduce our life to a restless waiting game of empty bank accounts, empty fridges, and broken toasters. It would be life like it is now, in other words, only with no football to distract us from the fact that our life was essentially just one giant fourth-and-long. But I was surprised how hearing Brett say this aloud made me profoundly sad. I thought about all those people at tonight's game, thousands of them, little boys and little old women alike, and how they cheered on Brett—*our* Brett from just over there on Pine Street—as he played his ass off not to make the town proud, as they imagined, but to earn a college scholarship so he could leave us forever. This made the town seem pathetically naive, like a fat kid getting excited by a small kiss from a girl who probably had already forgotten his name.

"You're going to escape," I told Brett. "The Boston College recruiter was there tonight, and remember how he said they'd give you a scholarship for—"

"They said the same shit to Dad back when he was a senior," Brett interjected.

This was only the second time I'd ever heard Brett swear. I turned and watched him watching the waves crash into the rocks below. I thought about Dad hurting his hip senior year and losing his college scholarship, and I thought about his old teammates always telling me how Dad could move on the football field as smoothly as a dolphin swims in the ocean.

The rotating beam of the lighthouse slashed light across Brett's profile in intervals, and I was a little startled by the weathered face revealed in the glare: gravelly stubble peppered Brett's sallow cheeks, and his eyes looked vacant and tired. He looked just like the man he hated.

"Are you okay?" I asked.

Brett didn't answer. Instead, he slowly knelt down into a crouch. He placed one hand on the ground to steady himself. With the other he reached up to his forehead. He rubbed it, wincing.

"The bottom of Dad's whiskey bottle."

"What?" I was having such a hard time following Brett's train of thought.

"The bottom of Dad's whiskey bottle," Brett repeated loudly. "That's where I put the dead tadpole when I found it."

My mouth literally fell open. "You serious?" I pictured my

dad taking a big final swig of whiskey, then, feeling that slimy glob of a creature catch in the back of his throat, spewing out his drink in a high arc like one of those European fountain statues. This story was so incredibly unlike Brett, the kid who never cursed, never missed curfew, and who called everyone "sir," including Dad.

"That's pretty amazing," I said, chuckling softly. "Dad must've yelled at you pretty good."

Brett wasn't laughing. "Yeah, sure. If that's what you want to call it."

A heavy silence hit me like a punch to the gut. I tried thinking back to the days following Mr. Giggles's death. Was that the start of it all? Of Brett's unwavering discipline, of him calling Dad "sir," of him silently planning his escape from Grayport?

"You have a gift, you know that?" Brett said, turning to look at me for the first time.

"I do?" This was a weird turn. In a flash my mind went over possibilities: Was he about to tell me I was a good listener? Or had a great sense of humor? I felt a little flutter in my stomach. I can't believe I'm describing it this way, but it was almost like *butterflies*.

"Your gift is that Dad doesn't give a shit about you."

Oh.

The thing is, Brett was right. Sure, I could complain that Dad had never encouraged me before, but he never scolded me either. When he found my doll, for instance, he picked it up by the ankle and left the house without another word. He was a heartless old bastard. But even though I reminded myself of this all the time, it still bothered me. That's what sucked most about this. If you're upset hearing that someone doesn't give a shit about you, then that means you give a shit about *them*. Is that pathetic? I don't know.

"I wish Aunt Jackie had room in her apartment for us," I said. But Brett's attention had switched off again. He stood up and looked east down the shore. When the lighthouse beam swung that direction, you could make out the silhouette of Grayport Stadium, so tiny from this vantage, like a little plastic castle enveloped in a bowl of fog.

"Seriously, what's wrong?" I asked again.

"Headache," Brett said. "It's the lack of nutrition. I can feel it."

He could've been telling the truth. Meals had been tough since the fridge went bare. A couple of neighbors had given us "good luck" treats leading up to the big game, so we had a bit of banana bread and meat loaf in our stomachs. We also got a twelve-pack of Jell-O cups; we had the red ones for dessert and saved the green ones to eat for breakfast. It sucked being hungry—it felt like an indignity reserved for miscreants, shifty ex-cons who chose narcotics over nutrients. But at least this would help me lose weight. Brett, though, was having his regimented diet disrupted.

"We should get home," I said. "It's getting freezing out."

I started walking away from the cliff, and Brett followed.

*   *   *

The two-mile hobble home took over an hour. We didn't talk much, and I was fine with that—our conversation on the cliff, both in length and in content, was such an intense upgrade from our usual exchanges, and I didn't want to topple the progress we made.

When we walked up to the second-floor entrance of our apartment, I'm sure Brett and I were wondering the same thing: whether Dad was home.

The glow of the TV from the living room immediately gave us our answer. We walked through the kitchen and stepped into the TV room. The Blakemore game was already replaying on Grayport Local Access, but Dad had passed out before my winning catch.

We had got there just in time—the last play of the game was coming up. I watched Brett break the huddle, watched myself run up to the line and miss the block on Derek Leopold. My catch looked even more impressive than I imagined. As the camera swung to the right to follow the ball's flight, you could just make out Leopold smashing the crown of his helmet into Brett's forehead. On impact, Brett's body collapsed to the turf with a sickening lack of life, like a puppet cut loose from its strings.

I looked at the real Brett standing next to me. But he wasn't looking at the TV. He was staring at Dad slumped on the floor with his back leaning against our dirty little couch, an empty bottle of Jack Daniel's leaning against his ruined hip. Brett's eyes were wet, a possible first. But that's not what caught my attention most. Most alarming was that Jeremy had been right earlier—the black pupils in each of Brett's irises, those vivid green emeralds usually so full of depth, were two different sizes.

Suddenly, the TV zapped off, leaving the three of us in total darkness. I crouched to the floor and fumbled for the remote lying next to Dad. I hit the POWER button, but the TV didn't respond. In the darkness I groped my way along the couch to the floor lamp that stood in the corner. Its cone-shaped shade was dented and crumpled from various projectiles that Dad had angrily sent flying over the years. I tried switching it on. Nothing.

"Power's out," I said.

"Not out," Brett replied. "Turned off."

I thought about the pile of unopened bills from the electric company scattered throughout the kitchen. I looked down toward Dad. His sprawled-out body was a shade of darkness so deep it stood out against the surrounding shadows. His outline consisted of a total, all-encompassing darkness, the kind that's so rich and pure it doesn't seem real, like an emptiness that is less than nothing, a black hole. I wondered if it had always been there, the darkness, since he was born, or if it first appeared when he tore his hip and the very ligaments that were supposed to carry him forward to football glory—the fabric of his identity—were ripped open. I don't know if the darkness had spread quickly or slowly, but it had definitely bled into his heart by the time I was born.

I looked toward Brett's silhouette. His head was tilted down and he was rubbing his forehead, like he was thinking, or in pain, or both.

This was not the physical pain I felt, not the pain I had stupidly reveled in just hours earlier at the party. The pain I'd felt was tangible, localized, and obedient. Even if it hurt badly, I knew I could carry it. But Dad's pain—and now Brett's pain— seemed unbearably heavy in its emptiness.

"Are you okay?" I asked Brett for the second time that night.

"Grab his feet," he slurred.

We'd done it so many times before, the process had become automatic: Together we dragged Dad to his room and lifted him into bed. I untied and removed his shoes while Brett got the bucket and placed it within puking distance of Dad's head. We turned him on his side, adjusted the pillow under his neck, and laid a blanket over him.

When we were done, we brushed our teeth, trudged up to our attic room, and went to sleep without saying good night, all three Parkers in their own beds, each in his own unique state of consciousness.

CHAPTER
EIGHTEEN

The stench of rotting fish jolted me awake. I didn't know what time it was, but the room glowed with a hazy morning light that seeped in through the open window next to my bottom bunk.

I wondered if Brett was still in his bunk, but that was soon answered when a disembodied groan from above made it seem like the top mattress had come alive.

"Ugggggh."

"Brett?"

"Yeah?"

"You okay?"

"Yeah. Actually, I don't know. I feel like crap."

"How so?"

"My head is pounding. And it's way too bright in here. Opening my eyes hurts."

"Oh."

"Do you think this is how Dad feels every morning with his hangovers?"

"Dunno," I said. "I think his entire body hurts him all the time."

"It feels like an elephant sat on my head."

"I know the feeling. An elephant sat on my head last week when Trunk pounded me in the shower."

My bitter response caught me by surprise. I guess deep down I was bothered by how long it took Brett to defend me from Trunk. We may not have been that close, but we were brothers. Where was Brett's loyalty? His protective instincts? Why did it take so long for them to kick in?

My welts from the fight had nearly faded away, but it was the first time either of us had ever mentioned the brawl. Still, I instantly regretted talking to Brett that way. I don't know what felt more unnatural: standing up to Brett, or standing up for myself.

There was a long pause before he responded.

"That was my bad," Brett finally admitted. "I wanted to give you a chance to defend yourself, you know? You gotta learn that you can rely on yourself."

That logic teetered annoyingly along the line between astute wisdom and complete bullshit, so I didn't respond.

"I should've stepped in sooner," Brett went on. "I'm sorry. Really."

I lay there and thought for a while. I should've been relieved, but I wasn't. The phrase *I should've stepped in sooner* echoed in my head. Not for what it meant, but for how much Brett slurred each *s*.

"You were pretty out of it last night at the party," I said.

"Was I?"

"Do you remember any of it?"

Brett didn't answer immediately. I suddenly felt very hot under my sheet, so I kicked it off onto the floor. "Well," he said after a moment. "I have a vague memory of you sniffing Haley's hair."

"I was *smelling* it."

"Same difference." The *s* in *same* was slurred, but Brett's voice had at least become lighter, more playful. Whatever tension we just had seemed to have dissolved.

"No," I sparred back through a widening smile. "There's a big difference. *Sniffing* is active, like a choice to be creepy. *Smelling* is totally passive and innocent. I just happened to be in the waft zone of her hair's aroma."

"Waft zone?"

"You know, the area where you can, like, luxuriate in occasional whiffs of someone's essence."

"And this is your argument for how you're *not* a creep?"

"Shut up."

Brett chuckled. I smiled. We lay in silence. Through the window I listened to the waves crash against rocks on the shore.

"So?" Brett said after a minute.

"So what?"

"So what did her hair smell like?"

"Who's being the creep now?"

"Come on, Wyatt. The tide out there smells like a rotten egg's asshole. Either close the window or give me a good smell to at least imagine."

"Since when are you a guy who swears?"

"Well, it's the first time I've had a splitting headache while being directly in the waft zone of a rotten egg's asshole. Come on, what did her hair smell like?"

"Sorry, but I don't sniff and tell."

"So you admit you were sniffing!"

"No! I meant smell. I don't smell and tell."

"Okay, okay. I respect the loyalty to her."

We kept lying there. I don't think we'd ever had such a long inter-bunk conversation. It was everything I'd ever wanted. It was almost perfect. Except for one thing.

"What do you remember about the final play?" I asked softly.

"I remember calling the play in the huddle. Then the next thing . . ." Brett trailed off. "I guess the next thing I kind of remember is being in the end zone, celebrating with you."

"I missed the block on Leopold," I blurted.

"But you made the catch."

"And now your head is all messed up."

"But you made the catch."

"Are you mad at me?"

"You made the catch."

"Do you think Dad will be mad at me?"

"We won. Why would he be mad?"

"Because he's always mad."

"Good point," Brett said.

We lay there some more, thinking to ourselves. Through the window, I heard an extra-loud wave smash against the rocks. Whenever I feel stressed, I close my eyes and sync my breath to the sound of the waves, inhaling slowly on the rolling crescendo, exhaling quickly on the sudden crash. I tried it now, but any sense of calm was suffocated by wafts of rancid fish—our food, our income, our sustenance, our lifeblood—decaying on the shore.

"Hey, Brett, remember when we were little and red tide came and you convinced me it was the blood of our enemies?"

Brett laughed. "Yeah, I do."

"What if, like, *we* are the enemies?"

"What do you mean?"

"I dunno. Everyone here is always, like, so sure that the Grayport way of life is the right way, and we're a bunch of virtuous badasses for enduring all the hard stuff. But maybe crappy things have happened here because we *deserve* it a little. Karma-wise, I mean. There are a bunch of really toxic people here, you know? Maybe this isn't a case of the innocent being cursed. Maybe it's punishment."

Brett was quiet for long enough that I started to worry I offended him by throwing shade at the town. In some ways, or at least in the football way, Brett embodied Grayport. But he answered calmly. "Well, maybe those people are only toxic because bad stuff keeps happening to them."

I thought about it. "Could be," I said. "I guess it's like the chicken and the egg."

"How do you mean?"

"Like, what came first? What started the cycle? Do the disasters only happen because karma or God or whatever is punishing us for being bad, or are we only bad because the disasters come first and push us to that point?"

"You're making my head hurt more."

"Sorry."

"All I know is that people and towns aren't just good or bad. Life is way more complicated than that. Everything has shades of gray."

"Dad doesn't have shades of gray," I countered.

"We only know one version of Dad."

"I don't follow."

"I mean, he couldn't have always been this way."

I thought about the old picture of Dad hanging in our locker room's Wall of Fame. Even as a teenager he looked like a fiery son of a bitch. But at least he had some fire in his eyes, as opposed to the cold nothingness in them now. I wondered if that picture was taken before or after he mangled up his hip.

"Brett?"

"Yeah?"

"Can I ask you something?"

"Sure."

"Do you have a concussion?"

"Wyatt, come on."

"Do you?"

"No."

"How can you be sure?"

"Because."

"Because why?"

"Because it's not allowed."

"By who?"

Three waves swelled and crashed before he answered. "By everyone. Everything."

Everyone. Everything.

I can't tell you how many times I've thought about these words since Brett said them. And I still don't really know why he thought a concussion wasn't "allowed" by everyone and everything. Sometimes I think Brett meant it literally, that if this injury really was a concussion, people like Dad or Coach Crooks would pressure him to hide it and keep playing.

Other times I think Brett meant the concussion wasn't "allowed" by Grayport as a whole. Not by the individuals of Grayport, necessarily, but by the very spirit of the old town itself, its stubborn ideology born from centuries of endurance, its hard-ass attitude that forces its residents—and especially its football players—to keep going, keep playing, no matter the pain, no matter the cost.

Or Brett could've been talking about himself: how his personal code of toughness and loyalty to the town would never allow him to admit having an invisible injury that, unlike his broken arm last season, he could theoretically play through.

Mostly, though, I got the feeling that by "everyone and

everything," Brett meant—or hoped—a severe concussion wasn't allowed by whatever higher power controlled such things, that even in a world as rainy and dark as ours there wasn't enough karmic injustice to do him like that. Not to a guy who just finished a grueling year rehabbing a broken arm, not to a guy who desperately needed a healthy senior season so he could finally escape this place.

From my pillow I stared up at the slab of plywood that supported Brett's mattress. I thought about the body fat–measuring caliper that he was hiding there, and how a guy so dependent on measurable numbers was now reduced to hoping that the whims of fate wouldn't end his season, and his dreams, prematurely. I thought about the watercolors I once found under his mattress, and wondered if Brett still occasionally painted the ocean's horizon, dreaming of his escape to a distant and undefined place where he wouldn't have to hide his art. Brett said everything had shades of gray, even Grayport. But I knew the town would *never* have shades of pastel, and I so badly wanted Brett to have them in his life.

I heard a rustling of sheets above me, and suddenly Brett's upside-down face hung over the edge of his mattress. His crisp green eyes locked onto me.

"Wyatt, you can't tell anyone about my head."

I diverted my eyes from his, stalling. I could tell the blood was rushing to Brett's reddening face, and soon he pulled his head back up to his bunk.

"Promise me, Wyatt," came the voice from above.

I *wanted* to promise Brett. I wanted to seal our secret and our newly formed bond. I wanted another chance to protect his blind side. But I was scared. I'd heard enough about concussions to know that playing through one can be incredibly dangerous. I'd seen what permanent hip damage could do to a man. I didn't want to see what permanent brain damage was like.

"Wyatt? Do you hear me?"

"Lavender."

"What?"

"Her hair smelled like lavender," I said. "And honey."

"That's bull. You don't even know what lavender is."

"Do too."

"Then what is it?"

"It's a spice," I guessed.

"Wrong," Brett said. "It's a flower."

"Yeah. A spicy flower."

"Flowers can't be spicy."

"The flower Super Mario eats lets him shoot fireballs. That's spicy as hell."

Brett laughed. I closed my eyes and imagined Haley, her smile and her gentle confidence and the fragrance of her hair, delicate lavender swirling in the cool salt air. The memory of the smell was almost strong enough to snuff out the putrid rot drifting through the window. Almost.

"Promise me, Wyatt. Promise me you won't tell."

I kept my eyes shut and listened to the waves hurl

themselves against the rocks. I listened to the wind lightly rattle the shutters outside our attic window. I listened to a pair of seagulls call out to each other through the fog, cutting through the shroud of mist in their own intimate and secret language, and then I listened to myself say, *Yes, Brett, I promise.*

CHAPTER
NINETEEN

I've got serious beef with Facebook. Or more specifically, with the people who designed their phone app. Not only did a poor design choice put me in an incredibly awkward situation with Haley, it *almost* reduced the science wing of Grayport High into a smoldering crater of ash.

Let me explain.

The morning after the Blakemore game and bonfire party, I casually sent Haley a Facebook friend request. It really was no big deal and I would've forgotten about it entirely if not for the 489 times I refreshed the app to see if she'd accepted my request. She *finally* accepted it before school on Monday morning. This was pretty clutch because I was going to see her first period in physics.

Haley was already seated when I got to class, and as I walked to my desk, which was behind hers, I had a mini freak-out trying to think of something to say. For some reason my dumb brain kept urging me to address our burgeoning Facebook relationship with a line like, *Hey, thanks for hitting me back on The*

'Book, or something equally as stupid and life-ruining. Miraculously, I was able to fight off my instincts and bailed on the idea at the last second. But since I had no backup plan, I didn't say anything at all to Haley. I didn't even acknowledge her—just sauntered on by and sat down at the desk behind her.

It turns out this was a brilliant move because it played into the brash persona I'd adopted accidentally a few nights before when I unintentionally invited Haley to sit on my lap. My bold "flirting" at the bonfire, followed by this morning's sudden aloofness, was a magic combination that made Haley more interested in me than I ever imagined possible. Sure, it was a dick move, this unpredictable push-pull, but it worked. It also made me realize how a brazen guy like Trunk always managed to get girlfriends despite the fact that he looked like the offspring of a hippo who'd mated with a blood relative.

When I plunked down in my seat, Haley instantly turned around.

"Aren't you going to say hi?" Her tone was inviting, so I knew she wasn't too annoyed with me.

"Oh, yeah. Of course. Hey."

"Hey," she said, smiling. "How was the rest of your weekend?"

Well, let's see: My brother's head is scrambled because I missed a block; we licked Jell-O cups clean like we were stray dogs at a dumpster; our landlord cut off the power because we're behind on payments; and I had to sit on the sticky floor of a 7-Eleven as I charged my phone in case you accepted my friend request and sent me a message.

"It was really good. Just chilled and did some stuff and things."

Most of the class had filed in by this point, and from my right I heard someone singing out to me: "Brooooo. Broo-OOO-ooo."

I ignored it, and kept my attention locked on Haley.

"Stuff and things, huh? You must be exhausted," she teased.

"Brooooo," the call came again. Frustrated, I turned and looked at Jeremy, who still had his hands cupped around his mouth to project whatever this weird stoner mating call was.

"Hey, Jeremy," I said, trying to sound annoyed.

"Bro! Bro-seph. Frosty the Bro-man. Edgar Allan Bro."

"Yes?"

"Just wanted to say 'what up.'"

"Okay, hi." I turned back to Haley. "Sorry about that."

"That's okay. A lot of people must want to talk to you now that you're—" Haley cut herself short. "Not that you weren't before, I mean. I'm sure you had, er, *have*, lots of frie—I just mean that since the game and all, you've become—"

"Like Bro-seidon, God of the Bro-cean."

"Thanks, Jeremy," Haley said, glancing at our third wheel before turning back to me. "Anyway, I was wondering if you wanted to be lab partners today? Not because of the game— because of afterward. I had fun at the party, I mean."

I said yes just as the classroom door swung open and our teacher, Mrs. Crooks, stomped in. Yup, you read that right: My physics teacher was Coach Crooks's wife. She was about two decades younger than Crooks, making her roughly ninety-seven years old. But she was still sharp as a fishhook. According to my barber, Jack, who knows all the town gossip, back in the day Mrs. Crooks lived in Houston and worked for NASA doing quantum astrophysics. Supposedly she was fired for hazing too many of her coworkers. Like, we're talking wedgies and stuff. After getting canned, she researched towns that matched her gruffness and found Grayport. She met Coach Crooks in the early sixties at a town hall meeting where he was proposing a law that made wearing bow ties a misdemeanor.

Mrs. Crooks slammed the door, took off her raincoat, and hung it on the doorknob. Like always, the jacket immediately slipped off and fell to the floor. She didn't bother picking it up.

"Alright, you turd goblins, quiet down. My hangover has a hangover so we're gonna be real quiet today." She really was the personification of a rusty nail.

Suddenly the door swung back open and Nate scampered in. The kid was so good at physics he once made his own functional sundial, but even with his genius he could *never* get anywhere on time. He stumbled over Mrs. Crooks's rain jacket, like always, and mumbled an apology.

"Tardy again," Mrs. Crooks squawked. "Come on now, you know the penalty."

Nate sighed, slipped off his anvil of a backpack, crouched down to the floor, and performed fifteen push-ups. When he was done he dragged his backpack to his desk, which was to the left of mine.

"Today's lab is on friction," Mrs. Crooks explained to the

class. "We'll do it in pairs, so find a partner you won't want to strangle after working together for forty-five minutes."

Chairs scraped loudly against the linoleum floor as everyone got up and slowly meandered to the lab stations that were set up on the counters along the back and sides of the classroom.

As I made my way over I felt a tap on my shoulder, and I turned around to see Nate.

"Alright, partner," he said. "Let's do this."

Grinning, he hit me with one of his sarcastic butt slaps and headed over to the lab station where we always worked together.

"Wyatt! Over here!" Haley waved cheerfully from a lab station on the opposite side of the classroom. She had already set up our beakers.

Shit. Every ounce of me wanted to partner up with Haley. But I'd been thinking a lot about the promise I made to Nate in the cafeteria: that I wouldn't become somebody different. In retrospect, it was a pretty dumb promise, because part of me *did* want to become somebody different. I owed Nate, though. I really did.

I froze in the middle of the two lab stations, racking my brain for a way out of this dilemma.

I looked at Haley, who was pulling a latex glove over her hand. She gave me a sly grin and let the glove's elastic cuff snap against her skin, which was, for some reason, the hottest thing I'd ever seen. I turned back toward Nate, who picked a piece of food out of his braces.

"Our test tubes have a strange growth in them!" he called over excitedly. "You coming or what?"

I'd normally ask Nate for advice on this type of conundrum, but I had to work it out myself. Part of me figured that since my friendship with Nate went all the way back to elementary school, it was strong enough to endure one more hit. But lately I'd been thinking a lot about the dangers of assuming something will always be there for you, even (*especially*) if it's a staple of your life.

But all that is really an illusion, a veil as thick as the Grayport fog. *Nothing* is permanent. One minute football is there and the next it's gone, severed like a ligament in your hip. So when you *are* lucky enough to have something that important in your life, something so vital and reliable that you can be fooled into believing in its permanence, then you gotta pour all of yourself into it. Can't turn your back on it, even once.

But then again, can't the same argument be made *against* devoting all of yourself to a staple, a constant, your football, your Nate? My dad may be a Grayport football legend, but when I saw him passed out on the floor the other night like a monument that had crumbled into a pile of rubble, I started to think about the importance of never getting to a point where the loss of one thing means the loss of everything.

"Parker!" Mrs. Crooks snapped. "You lost or something? Stop lollygagging and partner up."

I still hadn't made up my mind, but Mrs. Crooks forced my hand. I sighed and walked over to Haley. She handed me a pair of rubber gloves.

"Remember to always wear protection," she said.

"I'm really sorry about this," I mumbled down into my shoe-laces. I couldn't believe what I was doing. "I know I said I'd be your partner, but Nate and I sort of have this unspoken agreement that we're a couple. Not a couple in *that* way—not that there's anything wrong with that—but a couple, you know . . . scientifically. Like a dream team, but in physics." I really needed to shut up. "Anyway, I can't ditch him."

"That's very noble of you." Haley's tone was so soft and kind it was either dripping in sarcasm or sincerity. "It's fine," she went on. "I'll just work with Jeremy. He should be pretty good, right? Since it's like the third time he's repeated the class . . ."

I laughed and thanked Haley again. Feeling slightly better about the situation, I walked over to Nate. He looked at me dumbfounded.

"I know you're the hero of Grayport right now, but since when do you talk to girls? And to *Haley Waters*. You can barely talk to my *mom* without puking on your shoes."

"You and I have *a lot* to catch up on," I said.

"Everyone paired up?" Mrs. Crooks shouted as she picked up a stack of photocopied lab instructions from her desk. Like all our lab directions, these were written out in longhand because Mrs. Crooks didn't "believe" in computers. She marched up and down the aisles of desks passing out the lab instructions, licking her index and middle fingers before grabbing each sheet from the top of the stack. Not the best way to start your week, seeing that much of Mrs. Crooks's lumpy purple tongue before nine A.M. on a Monday morning. It's a sight you can't unsee, and

I needed to recover emotionally from it, so instead of listening to Mrs. Crooks recite all five hundred steps of the lab, I discreetly pulled out my busted old phone, positioned it between two pages of my physics textbook, and opened up Facebook.

This was a high-risk move—if Mrs. Crooks caught you on your phone, you had to go outside and run a lap down to Grayport Stadium, a journey that involved crossing a two-lane highway. So with extreme caution and minimal movement I slowly typed out Haley's name in the app's search bar. I was also careful to make sure I was typing in the correct spot. In the first of several major design flaws in the app, Facebook placed their search bar and status update bar *directly* next to each other, and the other day when I tried to search for Haley's profile, I accidentally typed her name *as my status* and hit ENTER. It took me a while to realize my mistake, so for about two hours my profile had a published status update that read simply "Haley Waters," leaving my entire network of friends with no mystery about the answer to the question, *Which hot girl is Wyatt creeping on tonight?*

Anyway, physics class was my first opportunity to peruse Haley's profile since she had accepted my request. I have to admit it felt kind of weird doing this with Haley a few yards away from me, totally unaware that I was rapidly thumbing through every picture on her profile. I wondered if girls have a sixth sense, like a little shiver out of nowhere that makes them think, *I feel like I'm being perused right now.* Since Mrs. Crooks was yapping on and on about friction and velocity, I managed to scroll through several hundred photos of Haley. I mean, I was in *deep*.

And that's when I made an absolutely ginormous mistake. Because flicking through photos on Facebook requires you to swipe right to left, it's possible, if your thumb has the general size and dexterity of a Polish sausage, to accidentally (and catastrophically) hit the LIKE button in the lower left-hand corner of a photo. And that's exactly what happened to me as I wiped my greasy paws all over Haley's photos.

I unliked the photo of Haley during the millisecond it took for my heart to drop into the pit of my stomach. But it was too late. In another infuriating Facebook design flaw, a notification of the initial like was *immediately* sent to the owner's phone. So at that very moment an official Facebook notification was traveling faster than the speed of light through the air of our stuffy classroom and dropping like a bomb onto Haley's phone. When she next looked at her phone, she would see that Wyatt Parker had just liked a photo of her . . .

. . . in a bikini . . .

. . . from two and a half years ago . . .

. . . licking an ice cream cone.

Suddenly a sprint across the freeway didn't sound so bad.

Ding.

I looked up and traced the undeniable sound of a mobile Facebook notification to where Haley was sitting. She didn't reach for her phone yet. But she would soon.

While Mrs. Crooks continued her lecture, I urgently tugged on Nate's sleeve.

"Look," I hissed, and discreetly angled my phone so he could see the photo of Haley.

"I can't tell if you're more turned on by her tongue or the ice cream," he whispered back.

"I liked it by mistake! She got a notification about it!"

Nate looked up from the phone to me. His eyes widened. "Yeah, that's bad. Real bad."

"I know!"

"How do you know she got a notification?"

"I heard her phone ding."

"You're going to look extremely pervy."

"What should I do?"

"Well, the notification is on her phone now so you're kind of screwed. The only way to delete it is from her actual phone."

Together we looked over at Haley. She was leaning forward slightly on the counter of her lab station. Stuffed in the back right pocket of her skintight jeans, projecting halfway out like a column of toothpaste being squeezed out of an overfilled tube, was her phone. Nate and I looked at each other simultaneously.

"No," I said.

"You can totally do it."

"*No.*"

"It's either that or she gets notified of how creepy you are, and the closest you'll ever get to her will be the distance declared by the judge in the restraining order."

"*Way* too risky to swipe it. My clumsy fingers are what got

me into this in the first place! I'll, like, accidentally grope her . . .
well, you know . . ."

"Her butt?"

"Yeah."

"She'd probably punch you in the face."

"Probably."

"You should totally try."

"No."

"You just have to be stealthy. Or wait for her to be distracted."
Suddenly Nate's eyes lit up. "Wait, I have an idea."

My body language senses were activating again. Sometimes
when Nate had a good idea, like a *really* good idea, the type of
idea you and I are lucky to come up with once a decade, he
would radiate a barely perceptible energy in his posture. It's
hard to describe. Actually, it was a similar positive aura to what
Brett wafted in the huddle whenever we needed a first down
and he called a QB keeper.

Still, one always had to be a little wary when Nate got amped
liked this. Sometimes his ideas blew up in his face—literally.

"Alright," I said cautiously. "Let's hear it."

"We can distract her with the 'Methane Mamba.'"

"No."

"You don't even know what it is."

"Don't care. It sounds ridiculous."

"It *is* ridiculous. And that's the beauty of it. Just follow my
lead. You'll know when Haley is distracted enough for you to
snag the phone from her pocket."

By this point Mrs. Crooks had finished explaining the lab, but neither Nate nor I had any clue what it was about. It didn't matter, though, because we were engaged in a totally different mission. Nate ordered me to look in the cabinets for a large beaker the size of a two-liter bottle of soda and fill it with water. By the time I placed the beaker of water on our counter, Nate had lugged over a large canister of gas from the lab's equipment area. The canister was labeled METHANE, and smattered across its surface was an aggressive number of warning stickers, including one that was a skull and crossbones.

I anxiously scratched the back of my neck. "This seems like a bad idea."

"Well, methane is the same gas that's in farts, so frankly I think you're a bigger threat to the safety of the class than this canister."

That shut me up good and allowed Nate to proceed with his plan. A thin rubber tube was attached to the nozzle of the canister, and he took the open end of the tube and plunked it into the large beaker of water. Then he turned the canister's valve to release the gas.

Immediately a steady stream of small bubbles flowed out of the tube and floated to the top of the beaker. The bubbles clung to each other at the top, creating a layer of thick, sudsy foam.

"It's begun," Nate whispered to himself in a tone that was a little more mad scientist–y than I was comfortable with. He reached for the gas valve and turned it further right. The bubbles built up faster now, and soon the mass of suds extended past the lip of the beaker. But instead of toppling over the sides, the bubbles clung together like magic, the mass growing taller and taller, like a tower of foam building up toward the ceiling. Science, man. It's wild. I watched the column rise and sway eerily like a mamba being summoned from a basket by a snake charmer.

"*Methane Mamba*," I whispered in dorky awe.

Nate kept his hand on the gas valve. The tower of bubbles was two feet . . . now three feet . . . now four feet tall. I glanced nervously over at Mrs. Crooks, but as usual she was using this Monday morning lab time to chuckle over the obituary section of the newspaper.

By the time the tower of suds was six feet tall, a semicircle of classmates had gathered around our lab station. Haley was one of them.

"Get in position," Nate whispered to me.

I casually moseyed over to the crowd and stood a little behind Haley. A few feet from my hand was her phone poking out from her back pocket, taunting me.

"Hey, Jeremy," Nate said from the other side of the counter. "Pass me your lighter."

"Whoa, how'd you know I had a lighter on me?" Jeremy said, passing it to Nate and unleashing a waft of marijuana odor that could kill a small cat.

The lighter had me seriously nervous. HIGHLY FLAMMABLE was plastered all over the methane tank, and all of those hundreds and hundreds of bubbles were filled with the gas.

Nate held the lighter in one hand. He held the palm of his other hand flat and then carefully slid it into the base of the tower of bubbles. He lifted his hand slowly, separating the column of bubbles from the beaker so he now held the entire Methane Mamba in his palm. The top of the column teetered, and Nate darted back to keep it centrally balanced on the palm of his hand. It steadied, and Nate slowly walked the Mamba to the center of the room. The bubbles were practically scraping the ceiling.

"Ready?" he said to the crowd. Then he ignited the lighter and slowly moved the quavering orange flame to the bubbles.

The Methane Mamba instantly *whooshed* into a column of fire that shot toward the ceiling in a dazzling inferno. It was such a mind-blowing sight to see my best friend, if only for an instant, morph into a fireball-wielding wizard that I almost forgot about the reason he was doing it.

I set my sights on Haley's butt—er, phone. With the painstaking focus of a SWAT team officer disarming an active bomb, I slowly reached my trembling hand toward the phone. I pinched the top of it between my index finger and thumb, and gave it a small tug. It wiggled out of her pocket a little bit, so I pulled it again, harder this time. The phone slid out of the pocket entirely.

By this point the flame in Nate's hand had burned out, but now everyone was staring at a patch of ceiling above him. Grayport classrooms were so old and decrepit that pink and spongy tufts of insulation sprouted forth from sections of the ceiling, and Nate's flame had ignited one of these exposed swaths of insulation. I don't think that was part of his plan.

People were yelling and cheering and laughing as Mrs. Crooks grabbed a fire extinguisher, stood on a chair, and sprayed white foam at the smoldering ceiling. Haley, meanwhile, had brought her hands to her mouth as she watched the chaos unfold. I looked at her phone's screen, and to my horror I was confronted with a prompt for a password. I hadn't considered this obstacle.

Damn Nate and his stupid Methane Mamba plan! Okay, focus, Wyatt—focus. Haley's password . . . what could it possibly be? Think. Think!

Think harder!

Suddenly an idea came to me and I frantically tapped it out on the keyboard: "*Wyatt.*"

Incorrect.

I know, I know: Totally wishful thinking to imagine her password would be less than six characters and with no numbers in it. I tried a new one:

WyattWyatt69

Incorrect.

Haley+Wyatt4ever

Incorrect.

Time was running out. She was going to turn around any second; I could feel it. This was going to be my last attempt before I aborted the whole operation: *Haley123.*

IN! I couldn't believe it. And even better than getting in, here was some concrete evidence that Haley and I were most definitely soul mates: We used the *exact* same password!

I looked down at the unlocked phone, and sure enough, there was a pop-up notification from Facebook waiting for her: *WYATT PARKER HAS LIKED ONE OF YOUR PHOTOS.*

Underneath the message were two buttons: There was VIEW, which would open up the photo of her and that incredibly lucky scoop of mint-chocolate chip, and there was DISMISS, which I smashed repeatedly with my sausage finger. The notification vanished.

My relief was short-lived, though, as I watched Haley, who'd clearly noticed that unsettling sensation when your pocket suddenly feels less than whole, like it's missing its soul—its constant—pat the backside of her jeans.

She spun around, her eyes darting from my flustered face to her phone in my hands. Here was another fatal flaw of Nate's dumb, half-baked plan.

"Your phone fell out of your pocket," I said, handing it to her.

I still can't believe I thought of this fix on the spot. I guess Nate is correct when he says that even a broken clock is right twice a day.

"Oh jeez, thanks," she said, inspecting the phone for any cracks before sticking it back into her pocket. "You and Nate are insane, by the way," she said, shaking her head partly in concern, partly in impressed bemusement.

"Well, we're always trying to make advancements in the scientific community," I said. "I don't know how much Mrs. Crooks appreciates it, though."

We looked at Mrs. Crooks, who fired a few final puffs of extinguisher foam at the ceiling. The remaining embers of the fire fizzled out with a low hiss, and white foam mixed with ash plopped down from the ceiling in heavy glops. The small cloud of smoke hovering above Mrs. Crooks's head looked like the product of her smoldering anger.

My stomach churned thinking about the wrath she was about to unleash on us. But just as she opened her mouth to torch us with an inferno of her own, a cacophony of yells and stampeding feet rumbled in the hallway outside our classroom. Mrs. Crooks scurried over to the door and poked her head out. Then, seeing whatever the source of the commotion was, she followed the horde of students and teachers bustling down the hallway. The rest of my class funneled out the door to see what was up.

A noisy crowd had surrounded the announcements bulletin board at the end of the hall. Nate and I were too far back in the crowd to read the message, so I tapped on the shoulder of a kid in front of me.

"Hey, what's going on?"

"It's an announcement from the mayor," the kid said ominously. "She's declared a state of emergency because of red tide."

"So what does that mean?" Nate asked.

"It means that all our government funding will be redirected to help the families who've been screwed out of their income. It means any nonessential town programs have been postponed, including . . ."

He trailed off, but I didn't need him to finish anyway. I knew the answer just from looking at the postures of the students and teachers gathered around the bulletin board. Their slumped shoulders, their tiny fidgets, and their twisted faces of disbelief told me everything. I knew this look. It was the look people get when they lose the one thing they always assumed would be there for them.

"Football," the kid choked out. "It's been canceled indefinitely."

Nate and I looked at each other, each of us processing the news in our own horrible silence.

Then I saw it—or rather, felt it: the spark of energy radiating from Nate. This occurrence twice in one day was truly a marvel.

"You've got another idea," I said.

"I do," he replied quietly. "If we pull it off, we could save the football team *and* the town at the same time."

"And will it blow up in our faces again?"

"Probably," he said. "It's a long shot. A Hail Mary."

"I thought you weren't religious."

Nate sighed. "Not usually. But it's all we have left."

CHAPTER
TWENTY

The next afternoon, Nate and I stood among a small enclave of adults at the fifty-yard line of Grayport Field. It was one of those raw days where the cold seems to rise from the core of the earth itself, bypassing all your warm layers by shooting up through the soles of your feet and clanging a hidden nerve in your chest that makes your entire body feel frail. Everyone stood silently, hands stuffed in pockets, impatiently shifting their weight from one foot to the other. All five of us were looking at the sky.

"You know, we'll probably hear it before we see it," Nate said.

No one responded. We kept our necks craned upward.

"Remind me again how you contacted these people?" Coach Stetson asked.

"Blind emails. Yesterday we combed the internet for the addresses of anyone in the company, and then we sent personal emails to nearly each one we found. Probably sent out how many, Wyatt? Twenty? Thirty? Didn't get a single response, but

I guess it makes sense they'd contact you guys first instead of us."

I appreciated that Nate was taking the lead here, but I also kind of wished he would shut up. It felt inappropriate being so chatty with adults as serious as Coach Stetson, Principal Hobbs, and Mayor Pickney. I myself was still recovering from what happened earlier that day. The two of us had been sitting in physics, Nate frantically scribbling notes, me casually staring up at the burnt hole in the ceiling, when Principal Hobbs knocked on our classroom door and asked us to join him in the hall. I was convinced he'd heard about the Methane Mamba and had come to rip us each a new one the approximate circumference of said hole. But instead he showed us a printed email that Coach Stetson had forwarded him. He told us we had to go to the football field immediately.

Nate turned out to be right: The low, rolling purr of helicopter wings preceded the vehicles' arrival by a good five minutes. Even when the helicopter finally came into view, it circled around the stadium four or five times, bobbing and weaving between the wooden light towers before settling over midfield. It wobbled down to us in a deafening whirlwind of sound and wind.

The pilot cut the engine, and the passenger in the back stepped out onto the field. She was wearing a sleek black coat with a white-and-brown fox fur that rimmed the top of the coat's hood. Her glossy, golden hair may have been the brightest thing I'd ever seen in Grayport, and her skin was so smooth and tan she practically looked photoshopped. Draped over her shoulder was a large leather handbag that looked more valuable than my entire life.

The woman took a step toward us and stopped suddenly. The long, pointy heels of her black stilettos had sunk into Grayport's soggy field.

Nate turned to me. "Is that . . . ?"

"Yup," I said with a contrasting mix of certainty and disbelief. "That's Natalie Hyde."

I was convinced that Nate and I were now in a different reality, as though the Methane Mamba explosion was so powerful it tore a hole in the space-time continuum and we had fallen into a parallel universe. I'd been watching Natalie Hyde on TV since elementary school; she started her career as a sideline reporter for *Monday Night Football*, but soon left to produce and host a popular series of shows about youth football in America. When Nate and I contacted every ESPN executive, assistant, and intern whose email we could find, we *never* imagined it would actually make its way up the chain, and that Natalie herself would consider our proposal to slot a Grayport-Blakemore game in the network's *Small-Town America* high school football showcase.

The five of us started walking toward her.

"She's shorter in real life," Nate said to me softly.

"You think so?"

"Naw, I just always wanted to say that."

Mayor Pickney, a tall woman in her fifties who was very

warm and friendly (in periods free of red tide, at least), shook Natalie's hand and welcomed her to Grayport. She introduced Coach Stetson and Principal Hobbs, then gestured to Nate and me. "And this is Mr. Parker and Mr. McConnell."

When Natalie looked at me, her perfectly manicured eyebrows shot up in surprise.

"Oh," she said with some discomfort. Then, after a short pause, "I-I'm sorry, you just look . . ." She shook her head. "Never mind, let's get started."

We had very little time; earlier Mrs. Pickney had told us that a secretary at ESPN had called her saying that Natalie could "squeeze in" a twelve-minute meeting this afternoon to assess whether Grayport would be a good fit for the show.

"Nice to meet you," I said nervously, extending my hand for a shake. Natalie presented her hand, which was dainty and limp as a dead fish, and I clasped it awkwardly, wiggling it up and down.

"The two of you really saved our butts," she said to Nate and me. Her voice was as rich and silky in person as it was on TV. "We were all ready to air a game this Saturday between two powerhouse high schools in Arkansas, but the home team canceled the game after three players were killed in a car accident." Natalie shook her head. "We were just about to refund our advertisers when my intern Johnny or Jimmy or whatever told me about this email he got from a little fishing town with an all-American quarterback. Honestly, we never even considered the possibility that New England would have two teams good enough to showcase for a national game. But we started doing some research, and the whole thing is just made for TV. I can picture the program description: *A blue-collar town with a red tide problem: The story of a gritty community that unites and rolls up its sleeves to survive the trenches of football and life."*

Natalie spoke that last part with the dramatic flair of a commercial announcer, then returned to her regular tone. "Seriously, when I first saw your beach from the helicopter, I was like, *OMG, this is perfect.* I couldn't believe our luck. The water in your bay is *literally* red as blood. I can already imagine the opening segment before the game. Do you want to hear it?"

The five of us looked at each other dubiously. It seemed as though Natalie would keep going regardless of our response, so Mayor Pickney nodded. "Please," she said. "Go on."

"Okay, so the camera starts zoomed in on a mysterious black circle, right? And then we slowly pull back and see that it's actually the eye of a dead fish lying on the shore. We pull back more, revealing ten, then a hundred, then a thousand dead fish all rotting on your disgusting beach. Everything is just oozing with despair. Then we pan over to that majestic wooden wall that protects the stadium from the ocean, and we pan up the wall to the row of old ship masts planted along the top. We continue up and up, and when the camera gets to the top of the masts, just before the fog is too dense to see through, we finally see all the state championship flags that, like the citizens of this humble village, are tattered, run-down, and still flying high. Then we switch the camera's depth of field to focus on the green below, where preparing for battle is the Grayport football team, the last bastion of hope in this withering town."

Natalie beamed with pride. It was startling how white and flawless her teeth were. Nothing about her seemed real.

"Trust me," she added. "Audiences are going to eat this up. Our market research indicates that stories about poverty are *very* 'in' with the key demographics these days."

Mayor Pickney and Principal Hobbs had been politely nodding along to Natalie's speech, but Coach Stetson just stood there chewing his gum with his arms crossed. I could tell what he was thinking: *This New York lady has no freaking clue.*

And I mostly agreed. People here in Grayport know there's nothing noble about being poor, no romance about going to bed hungry. Here the substance of your character is diluted—not strengthened—when prices force your family to switch from regular milk to cheap and chalky powdered milk. Despair doesn't unite a community; it tears it apart and makes its people afraid and angry and suspicious because that knock on your door is more likely to be a bill collector than a neighbor bringing leftovers for your hungry kids. Here "rolling up your sleeves" is what you do at the blood plasma center, where you sit for two hours with a needle in a forearm vein as a loud machine slowly sucks out the custard-yellow fluid that contains the proteins and electrolytes you can sell to a hospital for a little cash. And when you're done, when you're drained of all that substance inside you, you take your money to the grocery store to buy your powdered milk, avoiding the judgmental glares of customers who wonder whether all those scars on your inner arm are from plasma donation or heroin use—and they might be right either way.

"Of course," Natalie went on, "the linchpin of the entire event is Brett. Contemporary sports entertainment isn't about teams or even the outcome of the game—it's about the *characters*. It's about star appeal, and Brett is a budding star, an all-American quarterback who, inspired and mentored by his heroic single father, overcomes a gruesome broken arm *and* poverty to be one of the nation's elite players." She turned to me. "What kind of house do you live in?"

I really didn't want to answer. I looked down at my feet and mumbled, "I wouldn't really call it a house."

"Perfect," Natalie said. "We'll shoot some good B-roll footage of your living conditions to include in the program's cold open. The poverty is the main focus, but we also love the redemption and revenge angle with Derek Leopold."

"Hold on," Coach Stetson interrupted. "You realize we just played Blakemore last week, right? We won't be playing them again until the playoffs."

"Already taken care of," Natalie assured him. "We spoke to the league commissioner and he agreed to bump the schedule back a week. This will be an exhibition game. Won't count toward the standings."

Coach Stetson frowned. "Don't love the idea of Leopold getting an extra shot at Brett, but I suppose we don't really have a choice here. It's either this or no football at all."

"Oh, and that reminds me," Natalie added. "During the game we'll have to give the cameras plenty of chances to zoom in on your scar, so you can't wear long sleeves."

There was a confused silence as the Grayport contingent looked among each other.

"Uh, you know this isn't Brett Parker, right?" Nate finally said. "This is Wyatt, Brett's brother."

Natalie brought her hand to her chest. "Oh, right. Of course. This is all making *much* more sense now."

Natalie glanced at her watch, and then rummaged around in her oversized handbag. She pulled out a thick folder.

"I've seen enough here to know a Grayport game will draw big numbers," she said, opening the folder and handing each of us a heavy stack of papers. "Here's a copy of the contract for each of you—look it over today and fax back a single, signed copy. I've spoken to Blakemore reps and they've already agreed. I think you'll find the number on page seventeen to be more than fair."

With frozen fingers, each of us awkwardly thumbed to page seventeen. We found the number under Section 12: COMPENSATION & REMITTANCE, in Paragraph 2, Clause D. I don't know which one of us—it could have even been me—let slip a soft, audible *"Oh"* in awe at how many zeros followed the dollar symbol.

"I'll read it over," Mayor Pickney said. "But at first blush I can say that this is looking good. The compensation for the game will be an enormous boost to our economy and families in need. Maybe even lifesaving." She then turned to Coach Stetson. "Coach, I'll draft a press release and notify the town later this afternoon that we have a football game this Friday after all."

Coach Stetson nodded, and his mouth twitched faintly, the closest he ever got to a genuine smile.

I felt a surge of adrenaline, too. Nate and I had *done it*. With this deal, we had helped Grayport get the two things it needed most: money and pride. But this conversation with Natalie also made me realize how naive I was. When Nate and I wrote our pitch email to ESPN, we didn't consider all the things that Natalie had actually cared about. There wasn't a single mention of "market trends" or "demographics" or "ad revenue." We genuinely thought that Grayport was a good fit for ESPN solely because we were really, really good at football, and we foolishly assumed that this alone would be enough. I of all people should've known that most of the time, being really good at football isn't enough to fix everything.

Natalie Hyde snapped closed her leather-bound folder and stashed it in her handbag. "Well, I'd love to stay and chat, but the big city calls. Thank you for sharing your little town with me. Stay dry."

With that Natalie shook our hands and high-heeled herself back into her helicopter. The engine roared to life and the helicopter lifted into the sky, orienting itself due south toward New York City before hurtling off with desperate velocity. The five of us stood in our huddle and awkwardly waved as Natalie

Hyde, *the* Natalie Hyde, escaped our little town and turned into a black speck on the horizon.

Principal Hobbs made Nate and me return to class, but it was impossible to concentrate the rest of the day. There still hadn't been an official announcement from Mayor Pickney when afternoon classes ended, so I speed-walked home. I figured that if the ESPN game was a go, Brett would be one of the first to find out.

Brett was hunched over at the kitchen table when I got home. The power to our apartment was still off, and it was cold. The only light came from a thin ray of sun that sliced through the kitchen window and skipped off the glossy pages of a history textbook that Brett had positioned on the table for readability.

"Hey," I said.

Silence.

Brett kept staring at his textbook, eyes open but unmoving. The sight of it made me sick in the pit of my stomach. I'd been monitoring him the past couple of days to see if he acted out of sorts. But Brett was almost always quiet and aloof, so it was tough to tell whether his recent behavior was unusual. He'd been spending a lot of time lying in the top bunk, going to bed around nine P.M. From how much he tossed and turned, I don't think he was sleeping much.

This wasn't exactly unexpected behavior for a guy who

thought his football season, and by association his chances of getting recruited, had just gone up in smoke. Whenever the canceled season came up in our short conversations over the last day, he just mumbled, "It is what it is."

"Hey," I said again, loudly.

Brett flickered back on and turned toward me. "Hey."

"You okay?"

"The Jell-O keeps melting during the day and then congealing at night." Brett grabbed the cup next to his textbook and poured down the remaining green juice like a dose of NyQuil.

"Has Coach Stetson or anyone called you?"

Brett looked at his phone.

"Yeah, he called, but I didn't pick up."

"Did he leave a voicemail?"

Brett tapped his screen, and seeing a voicemail notification, lifted the phone to his ear. I leaned against the hollow fridge to watch his reaction. As Brett listened to the message, he squinted his eyes shut and held two fingers to his forehead. I could hear Coach Stetson's deep timbre on the other end. Brett didn't react one way or the other.

When the message ended, Brett kept his eyes squeezed shut, phone to ear. When he opened them again, they were wet.

He stood up and walked over to me. "Thank you." He was standing so close to me, like he was about to hug me for the second time ever. I was super uncomfortable at the thought of it, but I also didn't want him to turn around and leave.

Suddenly the kitchen door crashed open, and Brett and I

looked up to see the outline of Dad's figure stumble across the threshold of outdoor light into the darkness of our kitchen. Once inside, he took an instinctive first step toward the fridge, but then, remembering that it was empty of everything, even of beer, he stopped.

"Was downtown with the boys and saw the mayor on TV," he said. "Game Friday night."

I waited for Brett to say something, and when he didn't I spoke up. "Yup."

"This is because of you?"

"Yeah, kind of. And Nate."

Dad slid over to the kitchen table and let out a pained grunt as he sat down across from Brett. His hobble was there, but I'd noticed a little spring to it.

"Now listen, and listen good," he said, looking at Brett. "They're going to come at us with a lot of pressure, especially on edge contain, trying to funnel your scrambling back toward the center of the field. That'll open the C-gaps for QB option. The pitch man will be contained by the outside backers so you'll have to lower your helmet and grind through some hits in the muck. But the yardage will be there between the tackles—four, five yards a pop. I've also been thinking about those quick slants from shotgun—"

Dad stopped short. "You listening to me, son?"

I looked at Brett, who was staring blankly into his textbook.

"Brett . . . ," I said.

"Brett!" Dad snapped.

Brett tilted his head up from his textbook excruciatingly slowly, like he was trying to balance an invisible plate on his head. "Huh?"

"You okay?" I asked.

"Have you noticed the Jell-O keeps melting during the day and then congealing at night?" he asked.

"You just told me that a few minutes ago . . ."

Brett looked at me, confused. He rubbed his forehead and squeezed his eyes so tightly it was as though he were wringing out dirty suds from the sponge of his brain. "I need some aspirin," he said, getting up. He walked slowly to the stairwell to our bedroom, placed one palm flat against the wall, and guided himself up the stairs.

Left alone with Dad, I started to pull out my phone. But from the corner of my eye I could still see the sharp outline of his figure, a deep and endless black cut against the gray light, nothing showing except the pinks of his bloodshot eyes. I could feel him seething.

"You did this to him," he spat, cutting into me quietly like a dagger in the night.

I kept staring down at my cracked phone screen, tears welling in my eyes. I wanted to leave, but I didn't have anywhere else to go.

"Christ, what's taking him so long?" Dad muttered to himself. "Brett, hurry your ass up! And bring down the playbook when you're done!"

CHAPTER
TWENTY-ONE

Dinner at Nate's house was always a good time, but it used to be even better before the McConnells got their family cat. It's not that I disliked Bonkers, necessarily, it's just that he creeped me out big-time. First off, he had his own seat at the table, and he sat very upright as he delicately lapped up warm milk out of a little ceramic saucer on the table. He was dignified as hell, and you could tell he thought he was a big shot with his good manners and all. The most disturbing part, though, was how Bonkers *always* stared at me while he was licking up his milk. He wouldn't blink his big yellow eyes, or glance around, or even look down at the milk he was drinking. He'd just *lick lick lick* his milk while staring straight into my eyes, straight into my *soul*. I'd make a menacing face at him, like "stop sipping milk and staring into my soul, you dumb cat," but he was freaking relentless. Nate says I imagined all this and that, in general, it was a bad look to have a cat as your rival. But each of the McConnells had a soft spot for Bonkers, who they adopted a couple months ago after finding him scrounging for food in the dumpster behind the pharmacy Mr. McConnell owned. Basically, they were under his spell. They'd fallen for his shenanigans. But not me. I kept my distance from the shenanigans.

"Bonkers sure loves his milk," I said, avoiding his glare across the table as I slopped a heap of mashed potatoes onto my plate. Mr. and Mrs. McConnell were both great cooks—Mr. McConnell handled all the side dishes while Mrs. McConnell took care of the main course, which tonight was lemon roast chicken. They made a perfect team and the whole McConnell household made me jealous of Nate, who had stable parents and his own room in a decent-sized house that always seemed filled with the aromas of banana bread in the oven or garlic sizzling in a skillet or pinewood logs burning in the fireplace.

"I just can't believe how fast Bonkers is developing cognitively," Mrs. McConnell said. She beamed proudly at Bonkers, who lapped up the last bit of milk in his saucer and excused himself from the table with a soft *meow*. "This afternoon while I was dressing the chicken, he discovered Mozart. I put Symphony no. 41 on the stereo and Bonkers sat in front of the speaker and just bathed in the melody."

That's the other thing that annoyed me about Bonkers. He didn't experience new things, he "discovered" them. Nate's family was always going on about their precocious cat and his "discoveries." *Today Bonkers discovered Mozart. Today Bonkers discovered hummus. Today Bonkers discovered the scent of lavender. Today Bonkers discovered existentialism.* And on and on.

"Uh, I think Bonkers may be discovering that plant over

there." I motioned to the corner of the dining room, where Bonkers was fertilizing the soil of a potted fern. As he squatted and did his business, he stared right at me. I swear it.

Mr. McConnell went into the kitchen and came back with a pooper scooper and baggie. "Bonkers has discovered how to mark his territory," he declared proudly.

I wanted to change the subject, so I asked Nate's older brother, Owen, how he liked his new job. Owen had just graduated from a two-year junior college and moved back in with his family to help his dad with the pharmacy. A good dude, Owen. Super smart like Nate. Looked just like Nate, too, with his lanky frame, bony shoulders, and thin face. Main difference was that he had clear skin. When they were together, the brothers looked so much alike that their one difference, Nate's acne, stood out even more. It seemed unfair.

"Job at the pharmacy is good," Owen said. "So far my boss seems decent enough." He grinned over at Mr. McConnell, who was scooping Bonkers's butt nugget out of the plant pot.

"Things slowed down at all with red tide?" I asked, one eye politely on Owen and the other ravenously on the chicken platter, which was making its way around the table.

"Yeah, for sure. People aren't buying as many inessential items—you know, magazines and chocolate and—hey!"

Owen popped up an inch in response to an under-the-table kick from his mom. "Oh, that's not to say that you and your mom—I mean, like, that fudge is inessential or whatever." Flustered, Owen attempted to regroup with a big gulp of water.

"Anyway, prescription medication sales haven't dipped much. You'd think antidepressants would go up, but god forbid if anyone in this town abandoned their 'grin and bear it' mentality."

"Are you helping the pharmacist or something?" I asked.

"No," Owen said, grinning proudly. "I've actually been appointed the pharmacy's chief financial officer."

"You work the cash register," Nate interjected.

"Yeah, well, it's a big responsibility."

"You literally count pennies for your job." Nate admired his brother, he really did, but I wasn't surprised by his edge here. I'm pretty sure Nate's worst nightmare was that he'd work his ass off in school, get a scholarship to college like Owen did, sharpen his already brilliant intellect, and *still* end up back where he started, in Grayport, working at a counter in the pharmacy. I don't think Nate blamed Owen, but he blamed the town, which he claimed sucked people back in like a black hole.

Still, just getting to college was more than I could ever imagine, at least until the Boston College scout mentioned that he could get me accepted in two years as part of a package deal with Brett. It seemed unbelievable, but then again, some pretty unbelievable promises have been kept for top end college recruits. The thought of going to BC excited me so much that I tried to squeeze it out of my mind altogether. If it fell through, I knew I'd be crushed.

Mr. McConnell returned to his seat, took some chicken from the platter, and passed it to me. "Help yourself."

I served myself two slices from the breast and an entire

thigh. The delicious brown drippings from the chicken spread across my plate and were absorbed by the mashed potatoes and my hot dinner roll, which had been split agape, a slice of butter melting at the hinge of its mouth. I could feel myself salivating, but I was careful not to tear into the food like a crazy person. I was nervous that in my hunger I'd forgotten how to eat at a normal, civilized pace, and I didn't want to give away just how bare the fridge was at the Parker residence. I decided to mirror Nate, taking a bite of food whenever he did.

"Owen, did you hear about Wyatt's big catch against Blakemore?" Mrs. McConnell asked. "It was spectacular."

Owen nodded. "Of course I heard about it! There was even a little blurb in the *Boston Globe* about the game. Nice going, man. That must've felt incredible. What went through your head when you got to the end zone?"

The honest answer was that I wanted to find Brett to celebrate, but that sounded too mushy. I knew I was bad at answering these types of questions, so I panicked a little and relied on my strategy of copying what I'd heard NFL players say.

"I don't know, I guess I just thought of how God is good."

An awkward silence fell over the table. I took a sip of water. From another room, we heard a small *thud* as Bonkers discovered a perfectly clear glass door.

"Oh, nice," Owen finally said. "I'm so impressed by all you guys, to be honest. Takes some serious guts to strap the helmet on these days. I'm not sure I'd have played football if science knew everything it knows now."

A knot formed in my stomach. "What do you mean?" I asked. But I knew what he meant.

"Just with all the research on concussions," Owen answered. "Last spring I took a neuroscience course and we did a unit on concussions." He tore a piece off his dinner roll and stuffed it into his mouth. "People used to think that concussions were just bad headaches—'getting your bell rung' or whatever. But the lasting cognitive effects are wild. Atrophy of the primary motor cortex and horizontal diplopia, to name just a couple."

"Your elbow is planted in the butter dish," Nate said. "Stop it with the fancy words."

Owen extracted his elbow and wiped it with a napkin. "I'm talking about reduced memory recall. Trouble with balance. Double vision. Clinical anxiety and depression. The loss of reasoning capabilities. And maybe worst of all, reduced sex drive."

"Owen!"

"Sorry, Mom, but they need to know. Stuff is serious. And I haven't even started on CTE."

"Sorry—what's CTE?" Mr. McConnell asked.

"Chronic progressive encephalopathy," Owen replied.

"We get it, Owen, you know big words," Nate said.

"I was just answering Dad's question."

"What are the effects of CTE?" I asked, trying to seem interested but not *too* interested. "The symptoms?"

"It's easier if I just show you. Mom, can I use my phone at the table?"

"I suppose."

Owen pulled out his phone and typed something. He handed it first to Nate, who then passed it to me. "The left half of the image shows a healthy brain," he explained as I looked at the image. It was pink and spongy and robust. To its right was a brain labeled CTE. It was festered with large patches of black tissue and looked like it was rotting with decay. It was dried and withered, like a decomposing lump of cauliflower that not even mealworms would want to eat. I quickly handed the phone back to Owen. Looking at the image any more would make me sick.

"I know, right?" Owen said in response to the look on my face. "You read about patients with CTE, and it's just so tragic. Their brain deteriorates and they're consumed by paranoia, hopelessness, and rage. Suicide isn't uncommon."

"Can we change the subject?" Nate said. "Not exactly an uplifting dinner conversation here." Earlier that day I'd told Nate about Brett's head and made him swear to secrecy. I appreciated that Nate was trying to protect my feelings now, but I needed a more complete picture of Brett's current situation, and the risks if he kept playing.

"So how can you tell if someone's had a bad concussion?" I asked softly. "Besides, you know, them having headaches and stuff."

"Mismatched or foggy eye pupils, slurred speech, moodiness, nausea," Owen recited. "Concussions can mess with more than your brain—they can screw with other internal organs, too. It's crazy to think how your stomach can puke because of a hit all the way up at your head. It's like crapping your pants from stubbing your toe."

I hadn't seen or heard Brett puke yet. But some of that other stuff—the moodiness, the foggy eyes—I'd definitely noticed. Earlier that afternoon at practice Brett threw the ball well, which I hoped was a sign that his head wasn't bothering him as much. But the practice was noncontact, so fairly low stakes, and I noticed that in between drills he kept taking off his helmet, which he never used to do. Relief would wash over his face for a moment, then the whistle would blow and he'd plunk the helmet back on, wincing like he'd just put his head in a vise.

God, what was I going to do with all this? *I* was the one who put Brett into this mess, first by missing the block on Leopold, next by setting up the rematch on Friday. On our league's website I learned that you could report someone to the league's concussion hotline, and an independent neurologist would give him a test to determine if he could play. Brett would fail that test for sure, and his brain would be safe. But I remembered there being talk around town last year that the reporting system was no longer anonymous since a mysterious person (who everyone knew was Coach Crooks) called the hotline about seventy times in a row to report every single player on the Blakemore team. They had no choice but to spend an entire day of practice meeting with the independent neurologist. Obviously the system was flawed. So after that the hotline remained, but the reporting process was fully transparent. If I called about

Brett, the entire town would know about it. Brett would never speak to me again. Dad would kill me. Bonkers would dance on my grave.

"And is it true that the second concussion is always worse than the first?" I asked.

"Well, I think it depends on the severity of the original concussion and the impact of the next blow," Owen started. "See, after the first concussion, the brain diverts all of its resources—especially the sugar energy in glucose—to try to repair the initial damage. This makes it extremely vulnerable to another blow. A bad enough hit could cause internal bleeding, leading to a coma or even death." Owen forked a piece of asparagus and bit off the tip of its head. "Or the damage could severely limit your brain function, reducing you to a vegetable-like state."

"Wyatt, are you okay?" Mrs. McConnell asked. "You're flushed."

I nodded.

"Owen, you're being so dramatic." She put a reassuring hand on my shoulder. "Don't worry, hon, all that stuff won't happen to you."

CHAPTER
TWENTY-TWO

"What do you mean, you're not getting the soup?" Nate asked. "We're at a *soup kitchen*. It's the house specialty!"

"Stop talking like we're at a freaking five-star restaurant," I snapped back. "See this? It's a spork." I jammed the plastic prongs of the spoon/fork hybrid into my tray. "It's a culinary mutant."

"It's an engineering marvel, but whatever," Nate said. "I can't wait for you to eat something so you'll stop being so cranky."

Of course I was cranky: My hunger had finally surpassed my pride, so here I was at a charity meal center trying to decide what color of mush to have for dinner. I don't think Nate's family would ever *not* let me eat at their house, but I was conscious of wearing out my welcome there, so I limited my dinners to once or twice a week. The rest of the time I was on my own with food. It was nice of Nate to tag along, but he couldn't understand what I was feeling. Money was tight for his family, too, but his dad's pharmacy was doing well enough to keep food in their fridge. So he got to experience the soup kitchen as a sort of field trip, an anthropological expedition. While a single mother of three tried to spork-feed a bowl of split pea soup to a scream-ing toddler, Nate could sip "the house specialty" and swish it around his mouth like he was analyzing its flavor profile for a goddam Yelp review.

I hadn't been to the soup kitchen since red tide hit when I was a kid. It seemed darker inside than I remembered—a few overhead lights were out—but otherwise everything looked the same. About a dozen volunteers were lined up behind a long row of tables, slopping out single scoops of soup, creamed corn, wilted salad, refried beans, and chicken casserole. The drink station was in the same corner with two ten-gallon dispensers of water and pink lemonade. The Jell-O was even the same color. Mom, Brett, and I used to call it Frog Belly Green. I can't remem-ber why, but we got a real kick out of it.

Waiting in line now, I was surprised by a little pulse of nos-talgia. It used to be a fun adventure coming here. The food wasn't great or even decent, but the soup was warm and so were the people. I remember one time sitting next to an old fisher-man who was missing an eye, and he slowly rolled his remain-ing eye toward me and said, "I bet you're wondering how I lost my eye." Ummm, yes times infinity squared. The fisherman entertained Brett and me for an hour with stories of his voyages out at sea. There was just a feeling of community here, you know? People actually sat down together and ate, talked, told jokes. But really my good memories weren't defined by the people who were there, but the person who *wasn't*: Dad. He refused to accept charity of any kind. We were relaxed without Dad there. Brett would actually talk sometimes. He'd take risks, try jokes, think creatively. He'd look at the lime Jell-O and say Frog Belly Green.

"Screw it. I'll try the soup," I said to Nate when we finally reached the front of the serving line. A man with a white goatee and yellow sweater vest ladled me some soup, then poured some for Nate. Nate said thanks and grabbed the lip of the flimsy paper bowl, causing it to bend and spill a bit over the opposite edge.

"Ah, you must be new here," the volunteer said, dabbing the blotch of soup on the table with a paper towel. "Hold the bowl from the bottom. Also, welcome. I'm Stewart."

He extended his hand for a shake, but at that moment a woman with a clipboard tapped Stewart's shoulder. Next volunteer group was here, she said. Thanks for your help—dirty aprons go in the bin by the door.

The swinging doors from the kitchen flung open, and a stream of beefy dudes lumbered to the serving tables. They were all wearing white aprons over shirts that looked suspiciously like the navy-and-white uniforms of—

"Blakemore," Nate hissed. "You gotta be kidding me."

There were about fifteen Blakemore football players total, and they strode to their positions at the servery with shit-eating grins stretched across their tanned faces. Some of them were wearing their stupid Under Armour headbands, you know, just in case their frosted tips got sweaty from all that scooping and plopping.

The previous volunteer group must have also been from Blakemore, because Stewart, when he saw the football team roll in, practically began hyperventilating, reacting as though he were Nate meeting the inventor of the spork. He shook each player's hand, thanking them for all they did for the town and, presumably, the universe. I gave him a dirty look. Stew, I thought I knew you.

It's crazy how quickly a room can go from feeling warm and supportive to cold and belittling. Sure, we beat them in the game Friday, but now as they stood behind the pots of food and enforced the one-scoop limit, it felt like they were beating us at life. And they knew it. The guy serving the refried beans flung down a scoop onto my plate with a *thwack* that was just hard enough for me to bobble my paper plate, just hard enough to show me who had the power here. He then turned to a team-mate next to him, and in a voice just loud enough for me to hear, said, "I thought starving people were supposed to be skinny." I wanted to shrivel up like one of the petrified bugs stuck in the fluorescent lights above us.

The player working the creamed corn station was worse. Way worse. I slid my tray in front of the serving bowl and looked up—*way* up—into the barren black eyes of Derek Leopold. He somehow looked even more enormous without pads on. His neck was like a tree stump, sloping straight from his ears into his shoulders. The serving ladle looked like a teaspoon in his hand.

Nate tapped me on the shoulder. "Let's get out of here."

But something weird was going on inside of me. Even though I desperately wanted to leave, an even larger part of me wanted that creamed corn. I was hungry, dammit, and I deserved to eat. What did these assholes do to deserve food? They were born in Blakemore; that's it. Total chance. A few degrees of latitude north and they'd be standing on this side of the table, clutching their sporks. And in that case they'd deserve food just as much as anyone else. Maybe that's what was getting me so fired up: the injustice of fate. Random chance is blind, but it gives birth to privilege, whose narrowed eyes home in on the weak and vulnerable.

I picked up my plate from my tray and held it out toward him. "Creamed corn, please."

Leopold didn't react. His cold stare tunneled straight into my brain. But I'd had plenty of practice deflecting evil glares. Leopold had nothing on Bonkers.

I cleared my throat. "I said I'd like some damn creamed corn, please."

Without taking his eyes off me, the giant dipped his ladle into the pot and scooped up a wad of yellow mush. He plopped it down so hard my paper plate fell out of my hands and onto my tray.

"Thanks," I said, picking up my tray. "I heard it's good."

I picked an empty table in the corner farthest from the serving area. Nate sat across from me. "Well, that was a lot of things," he said. "But I think it was mostly awesome. What's gotten into you?"

"I dunno exactly," I said. "I guess the unfairness of it all."

"Jeez, so specific."

"I think I'm just starting to realize the difference between deserving and undeserving people. Myself included. Take a look around. Almost all of these people are hungry because of serious issues. Mental health problems and addiction and stuff. Single moms with three kids."

"I'm not following."

"They all have real life problems that actually deserve sympathy. But I'm just here because my selfish dad spends our grocery money on liquor."

A thick film of opaque green skin had congealed across the surface of my lukewarm soup. I punctured it with the prongs of the spork and then scooped some soup into my mouth.

"First off, I told you the spork was clutch. You were wrong about it, just like you're wrong about this."

"How so?"

"Like, I don't think your dad wakes up in the morning—"

"Afternoon, lately."

"In the afternoon and thinks, 'Hmm, I think I'll be a massive prick again today. Where's my drink?' He's an alcoholic, Wyatt, and any doctor or scientist would tell you it's not a choice, it's a disease."

I rolled my eyes. "Science doesn't automatically excuse everyone's flaws, Nate."

"I'm just saying that major brain chemistry is at play. At the very least, shouldn't his depression count as a form of mental illness?"

"You're dangerously close to sounding like you're on my dad's side."

"I mean, don't get me wrong: He's an asshole. We're on the same page there. But, like, maybe we should think about *how* he became an asshole. That story is probably deserving of some sympathy, don't you think?"

I slurped down the rest of my soup and started in on the refried beans. "Nope. I'm convinced he came out of the womb as a fifty-year-old prick."

"Come on, there must be something you can pinpoint."

"I mean, yeah. I think his busted hip hurts him all the time. That must suck."

"And my guess is the fall hurt him even more than the injury."

"Fall?" I was confused.

"From the top of the mountain. Think about it, dude. Back in high school your dad was a *god* in Grayport. You've seen the way people talk about his football days. The guy's picture is on the wall of practically every store in town. Like, the mental image of your dad playing quarterback is probably what Coach Crooks uses instead of Viagra."

"And now look at him," I added. "A hungry drunk whose wife left him."

"Exactly. Imagine going from the highest high to the lowest low. I don't think that's something you or I can really relate to."

"Yeah, I guess when he was seventeen he had a lot to lose. And he lost it all."

"I feel a little sorry for him, to tell you the truth."

I'd never thought of it like that, so I tried it out, dipped my toe in that pool of sympathy. It still didn't feel right, giving sympathy to someone completely devoid of it himself, so I pulled back. But part of me thought Nate was onto something, so I told myself I'd try it again someday when I was less hangry.

"Hey, Wyatt," Nate said softly. "Look who it is."

I followed the direction of Nate's subtle nod and saw an elderly woman waddling straight for us. She was draped in layers and layers of shawls that were as ragged as her stringy gray hair. Her lower jaw protruded out so her two canine teeth stuck out of her lips, kind of like a bulldog. In one hand she held a cane, in the other a takeout box of leftovers. I immediately recognized her as Ms. Moss, the older lady who sold hand-knitted winter hats at Grayport football games. Nate's mom once bought a purple hat from her out of pity. She said the hat was very pretty and delicately crafted, but the material just wasn't warm enough for Grayport winters. Hardly anyone bought Ms. Moss's hats.

"Sorry to bother you," she said as she approached us. "But aren't you one of Henry Parker's boys?"

I was surprised by how melodic her voice was, soft but with the clarity of a bell. I realized in that moment that I'd never spoken to her, despite seeing her every week of every fall for the last three years.

"Yes, ma'am. I'm Wyatt Parker. And this is my friend Nate."

"Well, I saw you fellas from across the room and thought I'd say hello before I departed. What a catch you made the other night! My word, it was something."

"Thank you," I said, still not exactly sure how to respond to praise like this. "It was an honor." From the corner of my eye, I could see Nate wince. *An honor?!*

"And how's your father doing, if I might ask? I used to watch him play football when he was your age, you know."

I looked at Nate, then back to Ms. Moss. For some reason, I didn't feel the need to gloss over my dad's flaws with some canned response. That was a nice thing about the soup kitchen: You didn't have to fake anything. You were already stripped raw for everyone to see.

"He's not doing great, to be honest."

"Ah, well isn't that a shame," Ms. Moss said in her sweet voice. "He was dealt a tough hand, that one. I still remember clearly how he played through all those games with that terrible hip. It was inspiring and heartbreaking all at once."

"He actually injured his hip in the final game," I corrected her. "The state championship."

"Oh no, dear. I remember it very well. He was injured in the first game of the season, a bootleg left in the second quarter. But he played through it the whole season. It was all anyone could talk about. Every week you could almost see how each stride tore a little bit away from him. He could barely move by the state championship game, but by golly he went out there." Ms. Moss sighed.

"Oh" was all I could manage.

"It was a magical season, but he certainly paid the price, didn't he? And we as a town pushed that young man to do it. He kept giving and giving and we kept taking and taking. People say it was his choice to keep playing. But what choice does a boy really have, when the whole town is counting on him?" Ms. Moss shook her head. "I feel bad about that. Very bad." She handed me her carton of leftover food. "Here, please give this to him."

"Oh no, he's fine," I said, pushing it back toward her. "Really."

"I insist. He sacrificed a lot for our little town. Please give this to him. I'll be insulted if you don't."

I took back the carton of food. Holding it, I thought of all those times growing up when the baker would slip Dad an extra loaf of bread, free of charge. How when cops found him passed out at the beach, instead of booking him for a night of lockup in the drunk tank, they always delivered him home, even carrying him to his bed until Brett and I became big enough to do it ourselves. I'd always assumed he got this treatment simply because he used to be so good at football. I thought he was still drawing from a savings account of goodwill that he accrued from being an all-American. But maybe the favors from Grayport residents actually came from a deeper source, one of guilt and appreciation.

"Thank you," I said. "I'll be sure he gets this."

"Wonderful. Now I must be pushing along. Enjoy your meal, boys."

"We will," Nate said. "As long as we don't have to look too long at those Blakemore jerks!"

"Oh, don't call them that," said Ms. Moss, her mild voice suddenly stern. "They are far, far worse. Stuck-up dickbags, every last one of them." Then she winked at us and hobbled to the exit.

I looked at Nate. "A lot to process there."

"That's for sure," he replied.

We stared at our trays for a moment, thinking. Nate looked worried. "Hey, Wyatt? Are we going to talk about Brett or not? You can't avoid it forever."

But, man, did I *want* to avoid it forever. I picked up my spork and poked at my creamed corn. I'd completely lost my appetite. "I mean, Brett can't play on Friday," I said after a minute. "He just can't. You heard all that stuff Owen said about head injuries."

"So you're going to report the concussion?"

"Yes," I said, hoping that hearing the decision aloud would strengthen my resolve in it. It didn't. "Actually, no. Ugh. I don't know. So much is on the line. Like, he's got to play this season if he wants to get a scholarship and escape all this. The hunger. The constant stink of fish. Dad."

What I didn't mention, since I knew it revealed me as a selfish son of a bitch, was that *my* college chances were on the line, too. For the past couple of weeks I'd been thinking a lot about the Boston College scout's promise to include me as an admissions "package deal" if Brett committed to playing there. I'd get to meet really interesting and smart people, people from Brazil and Ireland and Nigeria and even Idaho. I'd have the ability to head down to Fenway Park with a bunch of friends and catch a Sox game in the cheap seats. I'd have the opportunity to finally take classes with teachers who didn't incorporate cigarette breaks into their lesson plans.

"Then there's the ESPN deal," Nate added. "I really wish they didn't include that clause in the contract about Brett having to play as a requirement for payment. What if he played just one snap, then told Coach he was hurt, took himself out of the game?"

I shook my head. "C'mon, you know Brett would never do that. He wanted to play through a broken arm last year, remember?" I picked up my lemonade and started anxiously scraping off flecks of foam from the cup. "It's so much money, Nate."

"*So* much," he agreed.

"Mayor Pickney said it would all go to the food crisis and stabilizing the economy. I mean, look around. Everyone here deserves better than this. The money from this game would literally change our lives."

We slouched in chairs quietly for a few minutes, each processing the various options and their consequences.

"I keep thinking back to what Ms. Moss just said about your dad," Nate finally said. "How he thought playing through the hip injury was his choice when it really wasn't. Can't that apply to Brett, too? He thinks he wants to play, that it's his choice, but maybe he's just blind to the reality that he's really a puppet performing for the town?"

"Maybe. But what right do I have to just swoop in and report him, like I know better? Who am I to prevent him from playing for the town? For his college future?"

"Um, someone who cares that he actually *has* a future?"

"But what if he doesn't get hurt? What if he plays and is alright and he gets his BC scholarship and the town gets its money from ESPN? There's a chance of that happening. There's a chance everything works out in the end. But if I turn him in, there are guaranteed bad outcomes. No money for the town, no college for Brett."

I paused. There was another guarantee, too, one that scared me the most. "Brett would never speak to me again if I call that concussion hotline."

Nate sighed. "You're probably right. But then again, he also would never speak to you again if he were a vegetable."

"'If,'" I said.

"Right. 'If.'"

CHAPTER
TWENTY-THREE

It was pitch-black in our apartment when I got home from the soup kitchen, and I tripped over Dad's body sprawled out on the floor by the oven. I held my hand in front of his nose, and when I felt his soft exhale against my palm, I walked carefully to his bedroom and returned with a pillow. I knelt down and, cradling Dad's head in one hand, gently slid the cushion underneath with the other. I stayed kneeling and looked at him.

"I feel sorry for you," I whispered. The words sounded like they were coming from a stranger, but they made me feel slightly better. I got up and turned the oven's temperature up a few degrees.

The grunt of the oven's internal gas flame igniting was echoed by a low cough from the bathroom on the other side of the kitchen.

"Brett?" I whispered. "You good in there?"

"Yeah, I'm good."

He didn't sound it. I walked across the kitchen to the bathroom door, then crouched down and peeked through the keyhole. It was hard to make anything out in the darkness, but I could tell Brett was on his hands and knees, scrubbing the floor around the toilet. Next to him was a pile of used paper towels. A stench of vomit wafted out from under the door crack.

I stood up slowly. I went over to the kitchen table, pulled out a chair, and sat down. I looked at my hands. They were trembling.

After a few minutes, the door creaked open. Holding a small trash bag, Brett moved quickly toward the sink and, stepping over Dad, stashed the bag in the garbage. The smell filled every corner of our dark kitchen.

"Brett?"

"Yeah? What's up?" His casual tone was clearly forced.

I hadn't rehearsed what to say, so I just came out with it in a single breath. "I need you to tell me what I should do about you and your head and the game."

Brett leaned against the kitchen counter and crossed his arms. He breathed in deeply. "I'm playing in that game, Wyatt."

"Your head is totally messed up."

Brett laughed bitterly. "You think I don't know that?"

"Do you even know the effects of playing through a concussion? They're bad, Brett. It's not like a broken arm that you can just put a cast on and expect to heal. We're talking permanent brain damage. Maybe even death."

"I know what the risks are," Brett stated firmly. "I've thought about it carefully, and I'm playing. That's the end of it."

"Yeah, but how can you say you've thought about it carefully when your concussion makes it so you can't even *think* clearly? You're slurring your words even now!"

Brett was silent. Through the darkness I could see his chest heaving. I could practically feel his pulse pounding. I know mine was.

"If you play and something really bad happens," I went on, "and I'd done nothing, how am I supposed to forgi—"

"Jesus Christ, Wyatt," Brett suddenly snapped. He smacked the counter with his fist, causing me to flinch in my seat. "Stop acting like the fucking victim here. This has nothing to do with you, and you have *no* right to decide my future."

"I'm sorry," I said, my voice shaking. "It's just hard seeing you like this. This decision is eating me alive."

"Oh, I'm so *sorry*, Wyatt. It must be so *hard* being you. So sensitive. So emo."

I'd never heard Brett talk like this. I averted my eyes to the floor.

"Give me a break with that stuff," he went on. "*You're* not the one with the headaches that feel like an ice pick to the brain. *You're* not the one who can't even watch TV without feeling like puking. *You're* not the one who has the town's future on his back."

"But I *do* have the town's future in my hands. Don't you get it?" I waved my phone at him. "One call to the concussion hotline. That's all it takes for me to stop the game, to save your head, and screw over the town and our college chances. I have to make a decision here."

I waited for Brett to respond, but he didn't. It was so quiet in the kitchen you could hear Dad's rhythmic breath punctuate the air.

"I have only two choices," I continued. "Make the call or not. But either way I know I'll be destroying someone's life. You don't think that's hard for me? You don't think I already hate myself for whatever decision I end up making? You could at least make this a tiny bit easier for me."

"I *am* making it easier for you," he snapped back. "I'm telling you that I know the risks, and that this decision isn't on you. It's on me. There: Your precious conscience is clean."

"You know it's not that simple," I mumbled.

The argument once again slipped into a stillness. My eyes were starting to adjust to the darkness, and I could see Brett shaking his head slowly. "I always defend you to Dad," he said, pronouncing his slurred words more deliberately now, like he was chewing each one. "Did you know that? Whenever he's ripping you behind your back, calling you soft, calling you a wuss, I stand up for you. I tell him that I know what you're made of, and that you're loyal. Strong. Well, here's your chance to prove it, Wyatt. Because making the call wouldn't just be betraying me, it would be betraying the entire town. All that money, gone. They'll despise you for it. All of them, including that girl you've been obsessing over."

"But this *is* loyalty," I shouted. "You're my brother, whether you like it or not. And I'm doing what's best for *you*, even knowing the town will tear me to shreds for it. *That's* what loyalty is."

Suddenly, we were interrupted by a muffled chortle coming from the floor by the oven. The chortle grew louder and clearer, evolving into a throaty laugh. Brett and I looked down at Dad, who had propped himself up so his back was leaning against the cabinet.

"That's a good one, Wyatt," he said, heavily slurring his words. He cackled some more. "It's funny because they tell me you're the smart one."

I shouldn't have engaged with him, but I was so adrenalized. The cover had finally blown off this stifled family, and I was ready to throw everything on the table. "What are you talking about?" I asked.

"Help me up and I'll show you," he said.

I got up from the chair and stepped toward him.

"Don't," Brett ordered. I stopped.

Dad cackled some more, and then rolled over onto his stomach. He lifted himself up to his hands and knees and, grabbing the kitchen counter, pulled his brittle body up until he got the foot of his good leg flat on the floor. In a final heft, he pulled his bad leg up so both feet were steady, and then he straightened himself upright.

"You know how many times people ask me if you and Brett are actually brothers?"

"Dad . . . ," Brett said cautiously. "Does this have to—"

"Come on now, Brett. Wyatt suddenly thinks he's a big man with all the answers, so let's talk some truth with him, man to man."

"You're just a rambling drunk," I said.

"Maybe I am. But some smart-seeming people have asked about you two actually being brothers. Hard to blame them. I mean, look at Brett, then look at all of you." Dad spread his arms out, like he was outlining my XXL silhouette. "But those people are smart, like I said. And you know what I think? I think they aren't just wondering about your size difference. They're wondering about your heart. They've seen you play ball, Wyatt. They've seen how you play scared. How you play to protect yourself—*selfish*. They've seen you stutter and look at your shoelaces whenever you talk to a girl." Dad took a small step toward me. I was close enough to smell the whiskey on his breath. "They think you can't really be a Parker. They're wrong, sadly. You're somehow our flesh and blood. But that doesn't mean your brother and I are happy about it."

"Just go to bed, Dad." I tried to sound in control, but I wasn't. My heart was beating through my chest. My fists were clenched.

"You think you know what loyalty is," he went on. "You don't know the first damn thing. You don't have our family's back. You definitely don't have Brett's back. Never have. And he knows that."

"Jesus, Dad," Brett said firmly. "Just get out of here. You're not making sense. Sleep this off."

"Suddenly defending Wyatt, eh? That's not how you were

before the Blakemore game when you asked the coaches not to put Wyatt in the game for any reason. You needed a left tackle you could trust. What was it you said to me? That you'd rather have anyone else protecting your blind side? Even that pencil-necked kid Nate?"

I closed my eyes and drew in a deep breath. *Keep it together, Wyatt.* "I'm not going to get lectured on loyalty from a man who can't even keep his family together."

"Your mom *left* us, Wyatt," he sneered. "Abandoned us when things got tough. She doesn't know the first thing about loyalty, just like you." Dad paused, and I watched his eyes dart down to my clenched fists. A deranged smirk spread across his withered face. "Look at you," he said softly. "You're not even loyal to yourself. You want to hit me, don't you? You want to rip right through me. But you won't because you're a scared little boy."

"Stop," I said softly. "Please."

"Go ahead, do it." He took a step closer to me. "Be a man for once and stand up for your sorry ass. Do it. Pop your drunk old man right in the mouth. Be loyal to yourself. Show us you can at least do that."

I stood there, seething. Deep within my fists I could feel my nails sharply digging into my palms. The pain felt good.

Suddenly, Dad grabbed the middle of my shirt and yanked me toward him. He was inches from my face. His bloodshot eyes burned with something hotter than anger. "DO IT!" he shouted, bits of spit flecking my cheeks. "Hit me, goddammit! DO IT!"

A surge of power radiated from my clenched fists throughout my entire body. I looked at this injured, pathetic old man and knew I could obliterate him. That's one thing I gained this football season—the knowledge that, in the right circumstance, I could really hurt someone. I'd even done it to Nate, my best friend. I could easily do it to this bastard in front of me now. I breathed my anger in and out, in and out, let it boil into rage.

I leaned in toward him so our foreheads were almost touching. I stared at him hard—really looked at him.

"I'm not you," I finally said. "And I never will be."

I released my fists and stepped back.

Then I glared at Brett, still over by the sink. "Tell me it's not true," I demanded.

"Tell you what's not true?"

"That you didn't want me playing on your line. That you told the coaches." I bored my glare right into his uneven pupils. They were eerily gray in the moonlight that filtered through the kitchen window. "Brett," I stated firmly. "Tell me."

Finally, after a moment, he opened his mouth, spun toward the sink, and puked into it.

CHAPTER
TWENTY-FOUR

"Wyatt, wake up."

"Leave me alone."

"Seriously, you need to get up."

"No, Nate, I don't."

"But Brett is in the kitchen."

"Fine then."

I peeled myself off the lumpy couch in Nate's basement. I'd been crashing there since shit got real in my kitchen two nights before. I'd skipped school on Thursday, and ditched practice, too, which was probably enough to lose my starting spot in the game, which was later tonight. I didn't give a shit, obviously. I'd basically been existing these past days in a dreamlike state, drifting in and out of sleep.

When I met Brett upstairs, he tossed me a certified Poncho Pete poncho and told me we were going on a walk. He looked like shit—ashen skin, eyes puffy and red. I'm sure I looked much the same.

He said there was something he wanted to show me on the beach, so we walked down toward an entry point about a quarter mile from Nate's house. We hopped over the yellow DO NOT CROSS tape and weaved around the small forest of red tide warning signs pounded into the ground.

"It reeks," I said, pulling my poncho up over my nose to deflect the stench of the thousands of fish rotting on the shore.

"It's not far," Brett said. "Come on."

He led me westward along the beach in the direction of Grayport Stadium. The sun was supposedly rising behind us, but you wouldn't have known it from the canopy of darkness brooding overhead. A whopper of a storm was in the forecast for tonight, and already the first rain clouds were pelting us with light drops, like an approaching army that was calibrating its distance with arrows before unleashing the heavy catapults of destruction. Natalie Hyde must've been weeping tears of joy—the game tonight would be a monsoon and feature a nice big helping of gritty, blue-collar grit with a side of gritty and muddy trenches.

I really had no clue how I was feeling about Brett at this point, but I was relieved that walking with him didn't feel nearly as awkward as I'd imagined. I still felt betrayed by him telling the coaches he didn't have faith in me. But at the same time, after everything we had gone through the past few days, I felt like I knew him better now than ever before. It was oddly comforting walking with him, carving a path together through the maze of dead fish.

"Okay, there," Brett finally said, pointing to the far distance. "On the sand just in front of the stadium wall. You see it?"

Squinting, I could make out an enormous, dark mass. I was still unsure what it was, though. We walked faster.

"Holy shit," I blurted when I finally realized what it was.

I slowed down and approached the whale carcass cautiously. I don't mean to insult you by stating the obvious, but it was *massive*. It lay at the foot of the huge wooden wall that protects Grayport Stadium from the ocean, and at its thickest point the whale reached almost halfway up the towering barricade. It was low tide now, and there was something deeply sad about the way the foamy water again and again stretched up the beach toward the whale, but stopped just short every time. It was like the ocean was desperately reaching out in vain for its old friend.

"Humpback?" I asked.

"Yeah."

It was on its back. Long grooves ran like pleats along its massive throat and crusty white barnacles the size of my fist were latched under its lip. Its white fins were the size of a surfboard and scalloped along the inner edges like a bread knife. What struck me most, though, was the whale's skin: Its surface was a deep slate gray and profoundly smooth, like a glossy stone that had been polished to perfection over thousands of years. It was mesmerizing to look at.

"Natalie Hyde was real fired up when this washed ashore yesterday," Brett explained. "She said it was symbolic of Grayport and perfect for filming the little bio piece of me they were putting together. They made me stare at the whale for like twenty minutes with my hands in my pockets while making a face like this—" Brett softened his face into a dramatic look of sullen contemplation. "It was ridiculous. Then for twenty minutes they made me skip stones in the ocean, all pensive and moody."

"Doesn't sound like you at all," I said sarcastically.

"Fair point," Brett said. "They also had me crouch down and run the sand through my fingers like I was a Viking about to sail away from my homeland. They even had me skip stones in the ocean while looking pensive."

"You already told me that," I said.

"Oh," Brett said. "Sorry." He closed his eyes and took a deep breath, like that would refocus his brain. "But it does make you think, though. The whale, I mean."

I wasn't sure what he was getting at, so I stayed quiet and kept circling the animal, checking it out.

"It's sad seeing it here," Brett went on. "But it puts things into perspective, you know? Look at the *size* of it. We're like a pebble standing next to it. But then you look out into the ocean, and you realize that the whale is infinitely small in comparison. And realizing that somehow makes its death feel less sad. It makes you feel more at peace with it. The world doesn't feel as heavy when you realize how many things are holding it up."

"You're still super concussed. Either that or you've been eating some of Jeremy's special mushrooms."

Brett smirked briefly, but then his expression turned somber again. "I'm sorry about the other night," he said.

I shrugged for some reason. "I mean, I'm not going to stand here and say it was no big deal. Like, I get it. People think I'm soft. Hell, *I* think I'm soft. But for a while there when we were preparing for the Blakemore game together, it really seemed like you maybe had some faith in me. It made me feel really good, you know? Now I feel like a complete tool knowing it was all in my head."

Brett shoved his hands in his pockets and looked out toward the ocean. "I didn't think you were soft, necessarily. I just wasn't sure you had the right mentality for the football field. I know it sounds real dickish of me, but I honestly think of it as a compliment. Like it's one of your good qualities."

"Weird way of complimenting, then," I scoffed.

"I know. I messed that up. Probably should've been up front with you."

I tried to envision how that conversation would've gone, but it was impossible to imagine Brett and me having an intense, intimate conversation like that. Then again, we were doing that at this very moment, so who knows.

"A couple of years ago I read this poem," Brett said. "Can't remember the whole thing, but the opening line was, 'It takes strength to be firm, but it takes courage to be gentle.' It made me think of you. You're brave as hell because somehow you manage to be gentle in this goddam town, in our messed-up family. I probably would've popped Dad right in his stupid mouth the other night. But you held back, and not because you were scared. Imagine if you *did* fight him. That would've really broken us."

"I guess," I said. "But I'm starting to think none of this matters as much as I thought. Our family is broken, probably beyond repair. The sooner I accept that, the sooner I can move on."

"You're wrong about that," Brett shot back. "Like yeah, we're a weird, totally messed-up, dysfunctional family. Things have *not* gone how we've drawn it up in the playbook. We're the definition of a broken play. But we're going to improvise. We'll figure it out. Trust me on that."

I pulled the hood of my poncho over my head. It was raining harder now. "Can I ask you something?"

"Sure."

"How much do you really like football?"

Brett sighed. "It's complicated. Sometimes I think I don't love it as much as I used to, which is pretty scary, you know? I see Dad, I see myself . . ."

He trailed off before continuing again. "The game costs a lot. It takes from you. But it gives a lot, too. And you can't easily find its good parts anywhere else. Its rewards are really meaningful, really personal. Or at least they used to be." Brett ran his hand along the slick gray skin of the whale. "Lately I've been wondering who I'm really playing football for."

"You talking about Dad?"

"Sometimes it feels like I'm only playing for Dad, or the college scouts, or the hardcore fans who call in to the shows on Grayport Sports Radio. It's a weird feeling. Kind of makes me feel empty, or like a robot. An empty robot."

Brett patted the whale twice, like a kind of goodbye, then turned and faced the ocean. Rain pelted his poncho, which billowed in and out with each gust of wind. "Every now and then, when we're in a tough battle and we have to really grind out every yard, I have this moment of incredible clarity, and I remember who I'm playing for."

"Yourself?"

"Yeah, but also my teammates. I know you know the feeling. You look around the huddle, then around at the fans and the championship flags along the wall, and you feel like you're a part of something that's bigger than yourself. But at the same time you're part of a group that's so close-knit. Those guys are like my brothers, and for a while I thought there was nothing in the world more rewarding than lining up alongside them. But then I got to play with my actual brother."

I was glad that Brett and I were facing the ocean and not each other. My eyes were getting moist and I didn't want him to see.

"I haven't reported your concussion yet," I said.

"I know. And I'm sorry it's turned out this way," he said. "But I don't have a choice. It's become bigger than me. Do you know what I mean?"

"Sometimes I do. But mostly I don't."

"I know I rip on Grayport, but there are good people here. They deserve better than they've gotten. You deserve better. This game will change things for everyone."

"I want there to be another way." My voice was shaking. I could barely hold it together.

"There's not," he said, now looking at the ground. "And that's okay. I've made my peace with it. It's what I'm supposed to do."

"Are you afraid?"

Brett was quiet a very long time. "Yes."

We stood looking at the ocean awhile, its bubbling red foam continuously stretching up the beach, reaching for our muddy boots before retreating back to where it came. "I have to go," Brett finally said.

"I'm going to stay here awhile."

"Okay, sure." Brett patted me once on the shoulder. "I want to tell you something now. In case tonight . . ."

His voice faded. I forced myself to look him in the eyes, but his darted away.

"For the longest time," he started, looking into the horizon now, "I could barely remember the day Mom and Dad brought you home to live with us. But somehow the image of you being carried into the kitchen has gotten clearer as I've gotten older." He paused, thinking through his next words. "Even with my head like this, the image still gets sharper. And so does my feeling that that day was the best thing ever to happen to me. I want you to know that."

I bit my lip to fight off the moisture swelling in my eyes.

"Tell me you know that, Wyatt."

"I do."

With that, Brett turned and started walking back down the beach.

"Brett!" I called out suddenly. "Don't do it. Don't play. Please!"

He spun around and looked at me fiercely. "Jesus, Wyatt!" he shouted back, his voice wobbling over the low rumble of rain and waves. "Can you just be a man? Stop crying." Tears were streaming down his cheeks. "I'm serious—stop!"

But I couldn't, and neither could he. He turned around again and kept walking. Behind him, each wave erased his boot prints from the sand.

CHAPTER
TWENTY-FIVE

Natalie Hyde's bright white fur coat glowed like a lighthouse in the raging storm. But she was in game mode and, microphone in hand, she stomped up and down the sideline as an intern held an umbrella over her head. A second intern held another umbrella at an angle to block the sideways rain from pelting her.

The same torrential rain pattered on my helmet so loudly I could barely hear Brett as he counted out calisthenics to our team. I sat in a puddle on the ten-yard line and hoped the ESPN cameras wouldn't zoom in on me giving the ol' groin a good stretch. Somewhere through the monsoon on the other half of the field Derek Leopold was warming up and, probably, performing his pregame blood sacrifice to his demon lord in the underworld. I could hear waves smash relentlessly against the stadium wall behind me, thumping the old wood over and over. I could even feel the vibrations in the ground, like a giant was stomping his feet somewhere just out of sight.

If I hadn't been so distracted with everything going on, I would have noticed that something fishy was going down and that a particular sound was conspicuously absent: the satisfy-ing rip and pop of the championship flags streaming in the wind above the wall.

But it didn't cross my mind. I was too busy watching the people of Grayport file into the stadium. The ponchos they were all wearing seemed almost quaint; with the rain coming down in sheets, wearing a poncho was the equivalent of putting on a bulletproof vest to take a bazooka to the chest. *They really are crazy sons of bitches.*

As I stretched, I thought about that poem Brett mentioned: *It takes strength to be firm, but it takes courage to be gentle.* I real-ized that Brett was right: I didn't have the right mentality to be a great football player. Being gentle was so counter to what Grayport seemed to stand for, yet after years of being immersed in its tough-guy culture, I turned out this way. After Mom left, the town raised me more than anyone else, so clearly there were gentle elements of the town that I absorbed. I was a part of Gray-port, and Grayport was a part of me.

That's when it hit me: Maybe I was basing my decision not to report Brett's concussion because of a false assumption about the town. Like, maybe I was majorly underestimating Gray-port's level of empathy. Yes, there'd be people who would resent me for turning in Brett, and yes, they'd probably open a Wyatt dart-throwing booth in the stadium concourse. But maybe some people would agree with my decision, or at least under-stand my inner conflict. For every Coach Crooks, there were good people like Nate and Haley and Murray Miller. There were people who read *Charlotte's Web* to their child before bed. There were football players who kept watercolors under their mattress. Dudes who eagerly shared their Goldfish. People who bought winter hats from Ms. Moss even though they knew the hats weren't warm. Cats who loved Mozart.

The wind intensified, and the thunderous crashing of waves against the end zone wall grew louder. But the crowd kept filing in as they always had and they always would.

And that's when it clicked. Brett and I were *both* underestimating Grayport's best, most invincible quality: its endurance. The ESPN money from this game would go a long way, but what would happen if we didn't have it? Would red tide beat us? Would we just give up? Would we crumble into the sea? Of course not. We were going to survive, because that's what Grayport does.

The town couldn't die.

But Brett could.

I shot up from my spot on the ten-yard line and ran toward our bench.

"Wyatt!" I heard Brett scream from midfield. I kept going, and he broke into a sprint after me. He knew what I was about to do.

I got to the doctor first, almost slipping on the mud and straight onto my ass when I braked my momentum.

"You're the independent medic, right?"

"That's right," the doctor said from under his umbrella. "You okay? You seem upset."

"I'd like to report a possible—no, a definite—concussion on our team."

Someone grabbed my shoulder and pulled me violently backward. "Wyatt! What the hell are you doing?"

"I'm doing it, Brett," I said fiercely. "Get out of my way."

Brett shouldered himself in between me and the doctor.

"My name is Brett Parker and I'd like to be evaluated for a concussion."

The doctor looked at Brett gravely. "Okay, son. Come with me."

It took me a second to realize that the powerful blast in my ears was not the sound of my mind exploding, but the sound of a *literal* explosion. I didn't see the source, but the crowd in the stands was scrambling frantically, some pointing to the sky, others ducking under their seat for cover. Suddenly, an object the size of a snowball smacked into the top of concussion doctor's umbrella and bounced to the muddy turf. He crouched down and picked it up, turning it over in his hands. It was a chunk of something shiny and a little rubbery. Its surface was dark slate gray and immaculately polished, as though it were an ancient stone.

"What in god's name?" the doctor exclaimed.

"I think that's a chunk of a whale," I said, just as another piece of debris walloped down next to us. It was spongy, pink, and slimy.

271

"Is that—is that a piece of *tongue*?" the doctor asked in disbelief.

I swiveled around and looked toward the end zone wall. Hanging in the air above it, like a remnant cloud of smoke of an exploded firework, was a fine red mist of pulverized whale guts. Chunks of the demolished sea beast continued to rain down onto the field—a piece of blubber here, a sliver of organ there, a gooey mass of unidentifiable nastiness over there.

The explosion had been so powerful it blew open a hole in the side of the end zone wall. It was the size of a cannonball, and red ocean water spurted through it with the force of a fire truck's hose. The waves from the storm continued to ravage the now weakened wall, which was sprouting new leaks by the second.

Then it broke open entirely.

My entire team sprinted away as a tsunami of ocean gushed onto the field. As the red sea cascaded down, all the other players, coaches, and officials scrambled up into the stands, desperately seeking higher ground. The doctor, Brett, and I did the same.

By the time the water leveled out, the field was covered in a foot of foamy red water. Dead fish were floating everywhere. Thunder cracked down from the sky.

Then the stadium speaker system hummed on:

"Ladies and gentlemen, we regret to inform you that this evening's game between Grayport High and Blakemore High has been canceled due to . . . whatever this is."

The crowd didn't need to be told twice—they evacuated the stadium in a hurry. The flood continued to get higher and higher. I joined the throng of people running up the aisle toward the exits.

"Hey, Wyatt!" someone hissed.

I peered down a tunnel to the concourse and saw Nate's head poking out behind the abandoned Poncho Pete booth. He waved me over.

"Holy *shit*, Nate," I exclaimed when I got to him. He was absolutely *dripping* in red, syrupy whale gloop.

"Everyone okay out there?" he asked.

"Yeah, seems so. Just pretty wet."

"Phew. My calculations were a little off. The explosion was bigger than expected."

"Wait—*you* had something to do with this?"

Nate grinned. *"Methane whale."*

"What?"

"You never heard of the exploding whale phenomenon?" he asked. "Wikipedia it sometime. It's pretty cool—except the dead whale part, of course. That's just sad. But basically, it works like this: As soon as a whale dies, it starts decomposing at a super-fast rate. As a byproduct of the decomposition process, there's an enormous buildup of gases. Including methane. A lot of times it seeps out harmlessly into the atmosphere. Other times it stays trapped in the carcass, making it a powder keg of pressure."

"You're legitimately insane, you know that?"

"Insane, or *insanely* awesome?"

"Insane."

"Well, let me finish. Everyone was talking about the beached whale at school, right? So, being the morbidly inclined individual that I am, I went down to check it out during lunch. And there it was, just decomposing next to the wall. The idea hit me right away. But there was a problem: The incoming storm was going to wash away the carcass from the beach."

"I'm guessing you had an idea for that, too."

"The championship flags," Nate stated proudly. "I lowered each one and threw their ropes down to the beach. I had to dig a little bit of sand out from under the whale to loop the ropes underneath its corpse. I threw the ropes back up to the top of the wall and tied them to the flagpoles, so when I was done, that bad boy was fastened securely to the wall. It was *really* secure to the bases of the flagpoles. So many championships, so many ropes and flagpoles. The whale was essentially pinned against the wall. The rest was easy. I just waited at the top with my fire spear for the right moment to puncture the organic bomb."

"Fire spear?"

"Just a piece of driftwood whittled down to a point, lighter fluid, and a match."

"You scare me a little bit," I said, smiling. "But I am really glad you're you."

"You haven't even heard the best part." Nate grabbed the backpack at his feet. He was *wired* with energy, and might've been the next thing to explode if he didn't slow down. The backpack was covered with whale goo, but the papers and books inside were clean when he unzipped it. Nate wiped his goopy hands on my wet jersey, and then pulled out a large stack of papers.

"The ESPN contract," I said.

"The ESPN contract," Nate repeated, grinning. "Take a look, if you'd be so kind, at Section Three, Paragraph Eight, Clause B."

He handed the contract to me, and I read aloud: "*In the event that GRAYPORT VS. BLAKEMORE must be canceled due to an accident or catastrophic event resulting from natural causes, then the network shall file an 'act of God' insurance claim and distribute to each town the complete sum of payment originally agreed upon.*"

I looked up at Nate, stunned. "Did anyone see you trigger the explosion?"

"Nope. As far as anyone knows, this was an unfortunate, disgusting, and fairly awesome natural phenomenon that occasionally occurs when natural gases accumulate in a decaying sea mammal."

"So we still get the money?"

"We still get the money."

I beamed down at the contract. "Unbelievable. An 'act of God.'"

"No, my friend. An act of *Nate.*"

CHAPTER
TWENTY-SIX

The thought of the body fat forceps made me queasy, but on this visit they remained in the scout's duffel bag. All he pulled out was a fountain pen and a letter that was printed on official Boston College stationery. He placed them both on our kitchen table. They gleamed brightly in the glare of the overhead light, which flickered back to life earlier that morning following Dad's payment to the electric company. Mayor Pickney had wasted no time distributing the ESPN funds to Grayport's fishing families. Brett seemed a little agitated when the lights had switched back on—he winced at the glare that penetrated his foggy head—but I myself found the surge of energy uplifting. Finally, it was beginning to feel like we were emerging from the darkness.

"Shame what happened last night," the scout said to Brett. "I was excited to see what you could do on such a big stage. But to be honest, with all the national attention and promotions this game got, we feel that we need to step up to the plate and make you an offer now before others start knocking on your door.

Hell, some are probably booking flights right now to come watch your next game. But we hope you remember that we've been interested in you from the beginning, and we hope you view this commitment letter as a powerful show of faith in you and your ability."

Brett stared at the pen a moment, and then picked it up. "And this includes admissions assurances for Wyatt?"

"Oh yes, Waldo will be taken care of."

"It's Wyatt," I said. "W-Y-A-T-T."

"Wyatt, of course," the scout replied.

"Alright then," Brett said. "Let's do this."

He signed the letter of intent and pushed it back across the table to the scout. I looked at Dad—or Henry—or whatever he was to me now. He was leaning against the fridge, arms crossed, with a weird, crooked smirk tugging against the skin of his face. I wondered how he felt watching Brett reach the very milestone that he himself had just missed back when he was in high school. Was he proud? Jealous? Relieved? At this moment, was he thinking about Brett's life, or his own? I decided that for fathers, maybe there is no difference between the two.

I hadn't really spoken to him since that night I almost punched him. There was little chance he even remembered the conversation. I didn't know yet whether I was ever going to bring it up with him, but honestly, I didn't feel a rush to make a decision on that. In a little over two years I'd have an escape from him and this apartment, which was all I needed right now. Sure, it wouldn't be fun living at home during that interval. I'd never respect Dad. I'd always dislike him. At times I'd feel like I hated him. But now I was able to look at him differently, able to see him as a third-party observer would see him. And what I saw was a tired, defeated old man. I saw a guy who'd faced Life and wasn't up to the challenge. Not unlike me versus Derek Leopold, Henry versus the world was a mismatch, and it was hard to know how much of that was his fault. So I was able to feel sorry for him, and that glint of light in my black hatred for him would at least be enough for me to navigate the next two years of living alone with him.

CHAPTER
TWENTY-SEVEN

Some lazy bastard had stuck a spatula covered in chocolate icing into the serving bowl of vanilla frosting, but the mismatch didn't faze me because honestly I wanted each flavor equally, and this unexpected commingling of frostings could work out for me very well indeed.

I was sitting next to Brett at an empty table in the soup kitchen. News of the ESPN insurance money had spread, and as they always do to celebrate (usually for football wins) the soup kitchen set up a make-your-own-cupcake station. I'd been quietly keeping surveillance on it, and let me tell you, it'd been a long eight minutes waiting for the crowd around the station to clear out. See, when it comes to crafting my ideal cupcake, I need physical, emotional, and spiritual space. What I don't need is a mob of people elbowing me out of the way just so they can assemble their cupcakes all haphazardly with no respect for even the most fundamental principles of art like uniform sprinkle distribution.

But I have to confess, when the crowd dispersed and I finally approached the cupcake station, the magnitude of the moment got to me. I mean, I *completely* froze up when I looked at all those rows of cupcake bases—chocolate and vanilla and red velvet—just waiting to be frosted, dozens of empty canvases that contained within them the burden of all possibilities. I stood there for a long, long time.

"You know the soup kitchen closes at nine, right?" The voice came from behind me. I was in such a dreamlike trance it almost sounded like Haley's. Then I turned and saw that it actually *was* Haley. Never good bumping into your crush during a cupcake crisis of existential proportions.

"Hey," I said tentatively, trying to regain my bearing on reality. "I didn't know you came here."

Haley shrugged. "Sometimes. Tonight I brought my little sister." She turned around and motioned toward a girl, about ten years old, sitting alone at a table. The girl's peppy ponytail countered her slumped posture as she prodded a slab of rubbery chicken with a spork.

Haley turned back to me. "So are you going to get one?"

"A little sister?"

"No, silly. A cupcake."

I surveyed the jubilee of confection that lay before me. "I'm carefully weighing my options," I said. "You can't just dive in without a strategy. That's how cupcakes get hurt. That's how dreams get broken."

"A real cupcake tactician. I like it."

"It's a high-stakes process. For the base of the cupcake there's chocolate, vanilla, or red velvet—an impossibly tough call that's humbled far greater men than me. Then I have to choose between vanilla and chocolate frostings, *then* choose again between chocolate and rainbow sprinkles. A lot of pressure, even for an experienced cupcake tactician. The potential combinations are endless."

"Twelve. There are twelve potential combinations."

"Get out of here with your nonsense of numbers and logic," I said, grinning. "This is a mystical space and you're harshing the vibe."

Haley squeezed her eyes shut and pursed her lips.

"What are you doing?"

"What does it look like I'm doing? I'm sending you vibes."

"Good vibes?"

"Ehh, they're mostly just decent vibes. You have to really earn my good vibes."

I could tell Haley was fighting back a small smile from the corners of her pursed lips.

"And how does one do that?" I asked.

"By making my sister a cupcake so delicious it will blow her mind."

"Blow her mind?"

Haley opened her eyes and turned to face me.

"Yup," she said, taking a step closer to me. "Into a hundred million pieces. I want it to be so good she takes one bite and then afterward sees the entire world differently. She needs some, I don't know, *buoyancy* in her life. Like, I want her to see the world the way an oil painter looks at a sunset, the way an astronaut looks up at the stars, the way . . ." Haley hesitated a second. "Well, the way *you* look at m . . ."

She trailed off and we stood there silently and I looked into her eyes, which, now that I really saw them, reminded me of those rare, cloudless skies over Grayport Harbor at dusk, vast and glowing in a swirl of the deepest, most calming navy blues you could ever dream of.

Haley reached up and tucked a stray twist of hair behind her ear. Her lips momentarily parted like she was going to say something. Then, in what seemed like a nervous jolt, she quickly spun herself from me and faced the table of cupcakes.

"My sister likes red velvet," she said.

"Then she has a very refined palate. Red velvet is the flavor of the gods."

"So, can you make her one?"

I stroked my chin in demonstrative contemplation. "No," I finally said.

Haley frowned. "Why not?"

"Because one does not simply 'make' a red velvet cupcake. It exists already on a spiritual plane. To bring it into this world you must discover it and, in the process, also discover yourself."

Haley burst out laughing, a sound infinitely sweeter than the entire table of cupcakes in front of us. "Well then," she said between giggles. "Can you discover two cupcakes for me and my sister?"

I selected two red velvet bases and began my work, meticulously spreading vanilla frosting on each one in a conical swirl. But as I crafted my masterpieces and explained my creative process to Haley, I was suddenly hit by a familiar sensation. I don't know if you've ever had this happen to you, but sometimes I can, like, *see* myself, in the third person, from a short distance away, like my mind is a security camera on the ceiling observing Wyatt go about his business. Only I don't have control over when this special view happens—it's not some kind of superpower. It's the opposite. It's self-consciousness. And what I see from this zoomed-out perspective is never good. Like right then, all I could see was a fat kid next to a pretty girl as he hovered over a table of cupcakes, pontificating on the finer details of icing-to-cake ratios.

I watched myself hand Haley two finished cupcakes. Then I saw her ask me a question that I couldn't hear, and I zoomed back into my body.

"Sorry, say that again?"

"What cupcake are you going to make for yourself?"

I hesitated. I noticed my hands had somehow ended up in my pockets, their typical refuge during onslaughts of self-consciousness. I reached one hand out and grabbed a vanilla cupcake base. "I think I'm just going to have a vanilla muffin. No frosting."

"Okay, Wyatt? Two things here. And they're both really important." Haley plucked the vanilla cupcake base from my hand and put it back on the table. She then grasped my free hand, and with her other hand she reached out toward my pocket and gently tugged my wrist, freeing my other hand from its hiding spot. She looked at me intently as we faced each other, our hands lightly clasped in front of our waists. We must've looked like a couple about to be married at an altar of cupcakes. "First," she said. "Please, *please* tell me you don't think a cupcake without frosting is a muffin."

I grinned. "But it is. I mean, look at those cupcake bases. They are indistinguishable from muffins."

Haley shook her head slowly and spoke in mock disappointment. "Wyatt, Wyatt, Wyatt. Those are *so* not muffins." She let go of my hands as she motioned to the trays of cupcake bases. "Those are just cupcakes without frosting."

"Yes, which is the same as a muffin," I explained. "They look exactly like muffins and they're made from the exact same core ingredients: flour, sugar, and eggs."

"But muffins have such a different consistency," Haley countered. "A different texture. And cupcakes are always sweeter. They're dessert."

"Try a double chocolate muffin from Dunkin' Donuts and tell me muffins can't be dessert."

Haley frowned. "So you're telling me you could take a bran muffin, slap frosting on it, and suddenly it's a cupcake?"

"No, a muffin with frosting is not always a cupcake. But a cupcake *without* frosting is always a muffin. It's like rectangles and squares: Not all rectangles are squares, but all squares are rectangles."

Haley looked at me with a bemused smile. "Getting a glimpse inside your brain is like visiting one of those funhouse mazes full of mirrors. I'm never sure where I'll end up, and I'm kind of weirded out the entire time, but I also can't stop laughing."

"And at the end of the maze is a delicious red velvet muffin."

"Okay, that brings me to the second thing we need to talk about," Haley said in a less playful tone. "Even if that *is* a muffin—which it isn't—why would you choose a muffin over a cupcake?"

I could tell from the focus on Haley's face that she was fully aware of the sensitive territory she was treading on.

"I dunno," I muttered. "Muffins are just healthier, you know? More lean and more reliable. Cupcakes are good for the right occasion, but sometimes when I look at frosting I just see sugary, fatty excess."

"Well, when *I* see frosting," Haley said, "I see extra sweetness. I see warmth and coziness and charm."

I felt my cheeks getting warm, and I looked down at my shoelaces. "I think people generally prefer muffins. Ever heard of the term 'stud muffin'?"

"Muffins can be good, but I prefer cupcakes," Haley stated plainly. "Does that count for anything?"

Yes, it counted for everything.

I lifted my gaze from my shoelaces and looked back into Haley's deep blue eyes. They were soft and steady under her gently arched eyebrows, and I suddenly realized they were inviting me to see myself through them: without judgment.

It was the last step in a process that I now knew was mostly complete. For almost my entire conversation with Haley, I'd felt free and easy. I felt nimble and witty. I even felt light. Yes, the self-consciousness hit me at one point, but it was brief. For a while, I didn't even feel the typical tug-of-war between desire and guilt about the dessert. A few months ago, if you were to tell me that the one and only *Haley Waters* would see me ogling a tray of free cupcakes at a soup kitchen, I'd be completely and utterly mortified. But that scenario was exactly what had just happened, and I was fine. Better than fine. *I made her laugh.*

The third-person camera watching from above had seen a fat kid next to a bunch of cupcakes. But who was really behind that camera? Was it the *only* view of the scene? Another angle might see a varsity offensive lineman fueling himself up for the season. Another might see a cupcake tactician channeling his best possible vibes toward his work. And another might see Wyatt Parker, warm and cozy and charming.

"Pass me that spatula, please," I asked Haley, pointing to the bowl of vanilla frosting. Smiling, she handed it to me.

"Now," I said. "Watch carefully as I magically transform this pathetic muffin into a godlike cupcake."

With the spatula I scooped up a giant glob of frosting and carefully slathered it on the red velvet muffin.

"Hold on," Haley said when I was finished. "That icing-to-cake ratio is totally off." She grabbed the spatula and slapped on an extra glob of vanilla icing. "There," she said proudly. "Now that is one cozy and charming cupcake."

The move was so heartwarming I didn't even tell Haley her frosting form was freaking terrible.

CHAPTER
TWENTY-EIGHT

"Wyatt?"

"Yeah, Brett?"

"Can I ask you a favor?"

"Sure."

"Please stop saying 'aye, aye.'"

"Aye—er, okay. Sure."

"You're not a pirate."

"I know."

"And I'm not your captain."

"I just get caught up in the moment."

"I can tell."

"I haven't been on the water in a while," I explained. "I'm pretty fired up." The boat we borrowed was a small sixteen-footer, but the engine was still loud enough that I had to shout over it.

The afternoon sun had started to break through the clouds as we barreled south from Grayport Harbor. Brett put on his sunglasses and checked the compass above the helm. "If you're going to make me drive the boat, I wish you'd tell me exactly where we're going."

I grinned. "You really can't handle surprises, can you? Just trust me."

"I know you suck at driving, but why can't *he* drive?"

"Dude, look at him."

We glanced over our shoulders at Jeremy, who was sprawled out on the full length of the deck. He lay prone on his stomach and rested his chin on a cushion made partly of his crossed arms, partly of his springy, disheveled beard.

"He's so high he could probably make this boat levitate," I joked.

"I still don't get why we had to bring him," Brett said.

"That was the deal. We borrow his boat, he gets to join."

Jeremy popped his head up from his folded arms. "I wasn't going to miss this trip for the *world*," he said. "It's going to be so worth it just to see how surprised Brett is when we get to the Museum of Fine Arts."

"Jeremy, come on!" I shouted.

"Wait, we're going to the MFA?" Brett asked.

"Well, yeah," I said.

"In Boston?"

"The one and only. We'll dock in Boston Harbor and take the subway from there."

Brett is *not* one to show excitement, but I could tell this was really getting him going. He reached his hand up to scratch an "itch" around his mouth, but there was no denying the smile he tried to hide underneath. He then anxiously crossed his arms, uncrossed them, and then crossed them again. He started chewing his gum so rapidly it hurt my jaw to watch.

Suddenly, Brett turned to me, a grave look on his face. "Wyatt," he said. "I don't know how to act at a museum. I've never been."

"I think it's pretty easy," I said. "You just look at paintings with a slightly tilted head and whisper things like 'brilliant' in a British accent."

"Bro, you can just follow my lead," Jeremy chimed in. "I'm super into art. Like the other day, I saw a mind-blowing painting of a really bright penny at the bottom of a lake. I stared at this painting for legit twenty minutes, and then I was like, oh shit, that's not a penny in a lake, that's supposed to be the sun in the sky! *And then* I realized, oh shit, that's not a painting at all, but the *actual sun*."

Brett and I looked at each other.

"You stared at the sun for twenty minutes?" I asked. "Is that why you're wearing an eye patch now?"

Jeremy reached to his face and felt around for the eye patch, like its presence was news to him. "Bro, I think you might be right."

Brett tugged on the sleeve of my jacket. "Wyatt, does the MFA have a dress code? I think there's a dress code. I'm not dressed for any dress code. I'm in violation of the dress code!" He plucked the gum from his mouth and fired it into the ocean.

"It's okay," I assured him. "First, I'm almost sure there's no dress code. Second, if there is, then we're both in trouble together."

I unzipped my jacket and showed my T-shirt underneath. In big black letters, the front of the shirt read: I DON'T SWEAT. I GLISTEN.

"When did you get that?" Brett asked.

"Thrift shop the other day. There's not going to be a dress code," I reassured Brett. "And if there is, maybe we'll be lucky and it's only against eye patches. It'll be a chill afternoon, I promise. We'll just go check things out, hang around Boston some, then head back to the boat."

"Right, right," Brett agreed. "Plus it's good for you to practice this route for the times you visit me at college next year."

"For sure," I said, reaching up to scratch an "itch" around my mouth.

"Yo. Dudes. Bros. Bro-yos. Vincent van Bros. Pablo Picass-bros."

"Yeah, Jeremy?"

"I just had a thought."

"Uh-oh."

"I call you guys 'bro,' right? But we're not, like, *real* brothers. At least I don't think. But you two are real live actual brothers. So do you say 'bro' to each other all the time? Things like, 'Bro, pass me the salt' and 'Bro, check out that penny in the lake'? Stuff like that? Or when you talk to each other, is the 'bro' subconscious?"

I looked at Brett, who was either ignoring Jeremy's question or thinking deeply about it. The reflection of the ocean flickered on his sunglasses as he charged the boat ahead into the horizon. We'd been on tons of fishing trips with Dad, but this was the first time we'd ever dock somewhere other than Grayport and not simply loop back to where we started. Knowing this, the little town growing smaller behind us felt different. It no longer seemed like a black hole that always swallowed you back in. Instead, it felt like a hub with two-way spokes projecting out to the world.

I suddenly thought about Brett leaving for college next fall and was hit with a wave of nostalgia for a shared childhood and a brotherhood that wasn't nonexistent, like I once thought, but there all along, just under the surface. The brotherhood was and is constant, and when things are going well or shitty or both, we could always return to it, the way we'd be able to return to Grayport tonight despite it being completely blotted out by fog, inaccessible even to those looking for it. We'd know the way. We'd carve through the mist and the darkness, then dock in the harbor where the water was red and thick as blood.

"Dudes. Bros. Bro-seidons, Gods of the Bro-cean. You haven't answered my question. Do you call each other 'bro' nonstop, or is there no need because it's, like, always implied?"

Brett and I grinned at each other.

"Implied," we said in unison.

Acknowledgments

Thank you . . .

. . . to my wife, Leigh. Night after night you held a draft of this novel in one arm and our infant son in the other, nurturing each from your infinite well of patience, humor, and wisdom. You're a superhuman, and your qualities lie at the center of every good-hearted character I write.

. . . to my son, Alden. This book was my baby until you arrived. If you're reading this, it means that you (and the book) are now much older, so let me briefly explain what you were like at the beginning: Your first word was *banana* and your second word was *cheese,* and you always requested both, immediately, after waking from a nap. You filled buckets with dirt, rooms with laughter, and me with wonder. Whenever I became stuck on a stubborn chapter, your giggles would open up my heart and my eyes and the story within these pages. Thanks for being such an awesomely perfect little dude.

. . . to Mom and Dad. There's a lot of bad parenting on display in this book; thank you for raising me with the exact opposite approach. You have always been incredibly supportive of my writing, even when my first "novel," crayoned at age seven with the ominous title of *Big Bird's Bad Day*, had way too little plot and way too much carnage.

. . . to my family: Grammie, Kelsey, Ian, Fiona, Graham, Kirsten, Evan, Laurie, Doug, Catie, Jason, Ben, Michael, Michela, and the Spielers. Your love and support throughout this project provided the scaffolding I needed to see it through. I love you all so much.

. . . to my agent, Helen Zimmermann. I always dreamed of becoming an author and never dreamed that the business side of it could be so complex. Thank you for making the former come true and the latter feel painless. I am so deeply grateful for your knowledge, support, intuition, and friendship.

. . . to my editor, Grace Kendall. You were the backbone of this project even before a single word hit the page, and I still can't believe how lucky I've been to work with you. Thank you for sharing your remarkable imagination, steadiness, empathy, and humor with not only me but also all the characters in this story. An enormous thank-you, as well, to the entire team at FSG for your diligence and care.

. . . to my students at Middlesex School. My favorite parts of Wyatt—his sensitivity, humor, and intelligence—are modeled entirely after you all. Thank you for teaching me how to properly use cool teenager terms like *lit* and *turnt*, and thank you for telling me, a few weeks later, that these terms were no longer cool. And to my faculty colleagues at Middlesex: Your care and compassion for teenagers inspired me every day as I wrote this story. I can't thank you enough.

. . . to my dear friends, the Burkes (especially Matthew, EJ, and Brendan for teaching me about teenage brotherhood), Alex and Brian, the Lauers, DeLamarters, Petersons, Swifts, Plumlees, McLaughlins, Hahns, and Colgans: Thank you for years of support and love.